Second Chances

*Book One
in the
Second Chances Series*

D. A. Lawson

Second Chances

ISBN-13:978-1516910724
ISBN-10:1516910729
1. Fiction: Romance: General
2. Fiction: Christian: Romance
3. Fiction: Families

Dedication

To friends, the real kind, those who are there for others rain or shine, thick or thin, day or night, the people who love when they don't have to, the kind who give second chances. I have a feeling you'll know who you are.

Chapter 1

Josh Peters stared at the smooth tabletop in his real estate agent's office. When Tammy slid documents into his line of vision, his ex-wife's neat, elegant *Monica Simpson-Peters* caught his eye. It was strange that she had no problem keeping his name when she didn't want anything else from their years together.

He studied the familiar loops and curves of her signature and ran his fingers over the indentations made by the firm pressure of her pen. Sensing a hint of Monica's perfume that was probably only in his mind, he closed his eyes and took a deep, silent breath. He'd thought selling a place full of such bitter memories would be a positive thing, but this final step was more difficult than he'd imagined.

"Josh, you should be smiling, not frowning. You're making a very tidy profit here."

Josh attempted a smile. With one hand, he covered Monica's name and with his other hand, signed in the place indicated by Tammy's Post-it tab. She was right. The money from this would more than cover what was left on his building loan. If he had to start life over at forty, at least he should be thankful his finances were in good shape.

But the sale of this house represented the last step in the demise of a relationship that spanned most of his life. He would have no more conversations with Monica, no discussions, no planning, no hearing her voice on the other end of the line. Once this link was severed, there would be nothing between them. Nothing she would acknowledge anyway. He didn't expect Tammy to understand his sense of loss. He didn't understand it himself.

He forced his smile wider and slid the contract back to Tammy. "You're right. I should be glad this business is over. I appreciate all the work you've done, all the overnight shipping you had to do to get the documents to Monica and back. Thanks for everything."

Tammy's expression warmed. "I should have a check for you sometime this evening. I could call you when I have it. Maybe we could meet for drinks? Or dinner?"

"Dinner could work. I was planning on the pizza place on Mulberry—"

"Not the one with the game room! That's funny. I don't even go there with my kids. I leave that unpleasant task to my ex." She stopped and focused on his face. "You're serious?"

Josh cleared his throat. "Yes, but don't worry about it. I can come by Monday and pick it up."

"I could meet you for pizza." Her tone sounded unsure at best.

"I don't expect you to do that."

Tammy stood when he did. "Well, I hoped we could . . . What about tomorrow or Saturday? Would you be available to get together one of those days?"

"No, I can't, but it's no problem. I don't mind coming by on Monday." He offered his hand and she shook it. "Thanks again for everything. Have a nice weekend."

Tammy maintained her grasp on his hand and stepped closer. "What about Sunday? Name a time and I'll be available."

"That's not necessary, Tammy. Thank you, but Monday will be fine."

"Oh." She let go of his hand and adjusted her expression, offering him her usual warm smile. "Thank you, Josh. It's been a pleasure working with you. I look forward to seeing you Monday."

Josh left Tammy's office and drove out of town to take one more look at the house he'd sold. He pulled into the circular drive and remained in his truck. It was the first week of March, and tulips and daffodils were already bright against the perfectly trimmed evergreen shrubbery. Soon, white blooms would cover the Bradford pear trees that lined the drive.

The house was well over 5,000 square feet. Inside, every room had the perfect furniture, wall color, floor coverings, and accessories. It looked like something from a magazine. The house was his—his design, the place he'd lived for four years—but it had never been a home.

Thursday morning the school secretary, carrying a large box of books, met Dana at the library door. Between checking books in and out and helping students find books, Dana entered information on the new volumes into the library computer. The work demanded her constant attention. She was glad, glad to keep her mind off other things—like what day it was.

A library full of children made her focus on the here and now, but in the afternoon, she found herself alone and her mind wandered to the past. She wouldn't allow herself to cry where someone might see her. Instead, she blocked out the thoughts of what she'd lost two years ago and focused on the information she logged into the database.

When she finished with the final entry, she felt someone watching her. She looked toward the door to see one of her son's classmates. Relieved that she was no longer by herself, she smiled. The little girl smiled in return and came to stand close to Dana's chair. The girl leaned into her, and Dana got the feeling she would love to crawl into her lap. Dana put her arm around the girl's shoulders.

"Hello, Victoria. What are you up to?"

"I finished my spelling exercises. Ms. Anders told me it was okay if I came up here. I wanted to see if you were done with the new books yet."

"The information's in the computer, but I still need to print the labels and put them on the books. Would you like to help me?"

"Could I?"

"Absolutely, if Ms. Anders is done with you for the day."

"We're done. After spelling, we can do computer games or have free time. I'd rather be here with you."

Dana smiled again and pulled a chair up to the desk for Victoria. While they worked together to stick labels on the books, Dana answered Victoria's questions about what the numbers and letters meant.

Victoria studied one of the labels. "That's a lot of numbers. How do you know what numbers to put on there?"

"The library has a book that I use to look it up," Dana confided. "Otherwise, I wouldn't have any idea."

Victoria glanced at her and back at the label. "I still think you must be smart to know to put all that on there."

Dana laughed. She placed books on the shelves while Victoria looked through a dog book that had just arrived. When Dana finished, she asked Victoria if she'd like to take the book home.

"Yeah, I'm gonna read it to my dad. I think he'll let me have a dog since Monica's gone."

Dana felt her eyebrows shoot up and was glad Victoria was looking through the book. She'd heard that Victoria's parents divorced, but she didn't know any details.

She checked out the book for Victoria and looked at her watch. "It's about time to go home. How would you like to walk with me back to your class?"

Victoria nodded and hopped from her chair.

Dana shut down the computer and then grabbed her purse, jacket, and lunch cooler. After she turned out the lights and shut the library door, she felt Victoria's hand slip into hers. Dana looked down at the girl and smiled. While they walked hand in hand down the hall, Dana listened to Victoria talk about the rainbow her dad had painted on her wall.

When Josh's turn came in the school's pickup line, he watched his daughter come out holding the hand of a woman who wasn't her teacher. He recognized her as the mother of one of Victoria's friends. The woman murmured a hello in his direction before helping Victoria into the backseat of the truck.

"Thanks for letting me help with the books today," Victoria said. "And for the dog book."

"You're welcome, honey. Thank you for helping me."

"Bye, Tori," her friend Patrick said from behind his mother.

"See ya tomorrow," Tori answered.

The woman gave Josh a smile and a wave, which he returned. She shut the door and gave Victoria a bigger smile and a wave. Then she and Patrick walked toward the parking area. Josh watched the little boy slip his hand into his mother's. Their arms swung between them as they walked.

Josh glanced at his daughter in his review mirror. Her gaze followed the mother and son.

"Why did Patrick's mom help you into the truck instead of one of the teachers?"

She continued to look out the window. "Patrick and her were leaving when you pulled up and I asked them to walk with me. Ms. Anders said it was okay."

He didn't bother to correct her grammar. "Was Ms. Bradley at school all day today? Was there something special going on?" He stopped at a light and turned to look at his daughter, who now faced him.

"It's Thursday."

He turned to watch the road and drove through the intersection when the light changed. "What's special about Thursday?"

She sighed. "Daddy, Ms. Bradley works in the library every Thursday. I think she's done it since I was in kindergarten. She does it for free, too. Nobody pays her nothin' for it. She does it 'cause she wants to. I always go to the library on Thursdays, even if I don't need a book. I like Ms. Bradley. She helps me find the books on animals I haven't read yet. She's really nice. If she's not too busy, she'll come eat lunch with Patrick. I make sure I sit at Patrick's table on Thursdays so I can sit with Ms. Bradley, too."

Tori attended a small Christian school that depended a great deal on parent volunteers and involvement. Josh had driven for field trips and helped with morning drop-off from time to time, but he didn't volunteer every week. He felt bad that he didn't already know about his daughter's admiration of Ms. Bradley. He ran a hand through his hair. He'd had too much on his mind during the last few months.

"Honey," Josh said, "you should say, 'nobody pays her anything.'"

"That's what I did say."

"What you said was . . . Oh, never mind." He shook his head and gave up the argument.

"She never eats much. Why do you think she doesn't eat much?"

"Who, sweetheart?"

"Ms. Bradley."

He didn't have any idea why his daughter had an interest in what the library volunteer ate for lunch.

"Yogurt is all she eats. Yogurt and a bottle of water. Don't you think that's weird? I try to give her my dessert every Thursday, but she won't take it."

"Maybe she's on a special diet," Josh said.

"Are skinny people supposed to be on diets? I thought diets were for people like Nana Simpson."

Monica's mother, who often spoke of being on a diet, was on the plump side. He shrugged to avoid commenting on his mother-in-law's obsession with her weight.

"Maybe Ms. Bradley has diabetes and has to watch what she eats. Not all diets are for . . ." He met Tori's gaze in the rearview mirror. ". . . for people like Nana."

"Nah. I know about diabetes. Becky Snider in my class has that. She has a little machine, and Ms. Anders helps her check her blood. One time she had trouble. Becky, I mean. She got all weird acting. Ms. Bradley was there that day and she remembered that Becky has diabetes and she knew what to do to make her better.

Ms. Bradley's smart. She doesn't have diabetes. Patrick would've told me if she did. He says she won't eat because she's sad. Have you ever heard of not eating 'cause you're sad? Patrick said she's been sad ever since his daddy went away. He said she didn't eat nothin' at all for a long, long time."

"She didn't eat anything," he said automatically.

"That's what I said."

He didn't argue, and they were quiet for the rest of the ride. Josh didn't know the Bradley family well, only from school, but he remembered Patrick's father.

"I'll fix your snack while you change clothes," Josh said after they reached his parents' house.

Tori took off to the basement. She liked to shed her school uniform the minute she got home. Josh washed and sliced an apple, then scooped some peanut butter into a small dish. He heard Tori on the stairs and poured her a glass of milk. She thanked him and took a generous bite.

"Do you have much homework?" Josh asked.

He caught words that resembled *spelling*, *test*, and *read* when she tried to talk around a mouthful of apple and peanut butter.

He laughed. "Don't talk with your mouth full. It's rude. Besides you could choke."

She grinned up at him with chipmunk cheeks.

He waited for her to finish chewing, swallow, and take a drink of milk. "How would you like to go out for pizza after I help you with your spelling and you read to me?"

"Yes! Games, too?"

Josh nodded and smiled at her. It wasn't a difficult thing to make his daughter happy.

While Tori continued eating, he unpacked her lunchbox and cleaned the inside. When he finished with it and put her snack dishes in the dishwasher, he sat next to her and looked through her graded papers. She was busy copying her spelling words into her notebook.

"Your papers are all very good, sweetheart."

She continued writing and didn't look up. "I know."

Josh grinned. When she finished copying the words, she handed him her spelling book. He called off words and listened to her spell them.

"You know what would be neat?" she asked between words.

He lowered the book. "What, honey?"

"If I could have a mommy exactly like Patrick's."

Chapter 2

When Dana reached her driveway, she had to pull around a minivan to drive into her garage. She hadn't expected to see the familiar vehicle, but she wasn't surprised either.

Patrick's best friend, Alex, jumped from the back of his family's van as soon as Dana stopped in her garage. Patrick did the same, leaving his door open.

"Pat-trick!" Dana called from the driver's seat.

Without a word, Patrick ran back to the car and shut his door.

"I wanted you to get your—" Dana stopped when she realized he wasn't listening.

Patrick, Alex, and Alex's older brother, Wesley, scurried into the house, talking and laughing. When the boys went in, Patrick's little beagle came out. Dana shook her head and scooped up her and Patrick's things. She turned to face her friend Jennifer. Without a word, Jennifer's husband took everything out of Dana's arms.

"You've got him well trained," Dana said.

"It has taken years, but he's beginning to come around," Jennifer said.

Mark made a point of ignoring them both and carried his load into the house.

"How'd you rate a day off?" Dana knew she wouldn't get an honest answer, but she forced herself to maintain her smile.

"My last three appointments cancelled, and everything else was slow. They had it all covered, so I left early. We've come to take you and Patrick out for pizza. We'll celebrate your being in your new house for almost a month. What do you say?"

Dana would much rather they take Patrick and leave her alone to cry, but she knew none of them would go for that. "Sounds good to me," Dana said, hoping her voice didn't give her away. She looked toward Jennifer's van to avoid her steady, searching gaze.

"Where's Paige?" Dana asked after clearing her throat.

"She's babysitting for a neighbor."

When Dana got inside, her purse and Patrick's backpack were hanging on their designated hooks in the laundry room and the lunch coolers were by the sink. With an open Diet Pepsi in one hand, Mark flipped through TV channels in the living room.

Dana and Jennifer sat at the kitchen table and continued to talk. Just when Dana thought she could no longer pretend everything was fine, she heard noise on the stairs. Both women turned toward the basement door. The three boys burst through it into the kitchen.

"Mom, when's Steven gonna hook up the XBox and the Wii?"

"I'm sure he'll do it as soon as he gets around to it. He's busy working and going to college. Be patient. If

Steven says he'll do something, he will. It's been nice outside anyway. You don't need video games when you can play outside."

"But I haven't played since we packed up and moved. It's been over three weeks. Why can't Mark do it for me?"

"No can do, sport. I'm not at all electronically in-clined. Anything like that at our house has to be done by the Geek Squad since your da—"

The room fell silent. Every face turned toward the living room when Mark stopped talking. He was leaning over the arm of his chair, looking into the kitchen. Dana felt the familiar rush of nausea. She knew what Mark was doing, but the fact that he wanted to talk about Brandon and didn't made it worse. Neither Jennifer nor Mark had spoken of Brandon in her presence for nearly a year. She wanted to talk about him, needed to talk about him, but with her closest friends it had become uncomfortable, if not impossible, to do.

Mark cleared his throat and started to speak, but Jennifer shot him down with her eyes. Mark took a long drink of Diet Pepsi.

"Boys," Jennifer said, her voice too cheerful, "we're taking you to your favorite pizza place for dinner and games. Go outside and play for a while. When you come inside, you can do your homework and then we'll go."

It worked. Even Patrick whooped before the three of them made for the door. A barking Zoe chased them across the yard. From the window, Dana could see the boys kicking a soccer ball.

Dana opened her mouth to say something, to attempt to let them know that acting weird about Brandon made it worse than talking about him possibly could.

"Who's Steven?" Jennifer asked.

Dana took a deep breath, deciding it wasn't worth the battle. "You remember meeting Tom Farris, the man who built my house?"

"I think so. His mom's the one who thinks so much of you."

Dana nodded. "Steven is Tom's son. He works for his dad and goes to Western to school. He's getting a master's degree in computer programming. He's great with all that electrical computer stuff that drives me batty. I'm sure you met him when I moved in. He set up the computer for me and hooked up the surround sound system in the living room."

"Ah," Jennifer said. "Tall, dark hair? Good-looking guy, right?"

Dana nodded and felt a smile creep across her lips because of the look on Mark's face. He walked into the kitchen and moved behind his wife. Then he rubbed her shoulders. "You know you find men with freckles and a hint of red in their hair much more appealing."

Jennifer patted Mark's hand. "You know it, baby. You're the only man for me."

"How about you, Dana? Do you still hold that special place in your heart for me?"

Dana laughed, stood, and kissed Mark's cheek. "Always, but be sure your wife doesn't find out about us."

The three of them laughed. At least some things hadn't changed. Smiling, Dana went to the sink and cleaned out Patrick's lunch box and her cooler.

"How much does the Farris guy charge to hook up game systems?" Jennifer asked.

"He won't let me pay him," Dana said over her shoulder.

Jennifer gave her a look of disbelief.

Dana waved a hand. "I've known Steven since he was a kid, a teenager anyway. He probably thinks of me as the older sister he never had. His whole family's like that—doing nice things for people."

Once Dana was done with her cleaning, she sat back down at the table. The three of them talked about how the kids were doing in school and about fourteen-year-old Paige wanting to date. The nausea disappeared, and when the boys crashed back inside, she felt almost normal—at least as normal as she ever felt now.

"Is it time to go?"

"We're hungry!"

"When are we leaving?"

Three voices spoke at once, making it impossible to tell who said what.

"What about your homework?" Dana asked, trying to sound stern.

The three of them grumbled about doing it later because they were starving.

"I don't think so," Dana said.

"I'll do it before we go," Patrick said, sounding like a condemned prisoner. "Do you have homework?" he asked the other boys.

"I'm sure they do," Jennifer said. "You two run out and get your stuff. By the time the three of you are done, it should be time to go eat."

The Morgan boys went out the door while Patrick retrieved his own things from his backpack in the laundry room. He pushed a heap of graded school papers toward Dana, sat at the table, and began to copy his spelling words. The other two came back and joined him. Dana was amazed by how quietly they studied after the grumbling they'd been doing. The lure of pizza and a game room must be strong. By the time she ran through Patrick's spelling words with him until he could spell each one correctly and listened to him read the assigned pages in his reading book, the other boys were done with their work.

The boys climbed to the back of the van. Mark offered Dana the front passenger seat, but she refused so that he could sit with Jennifer. Once they were on their way, she made the mistake of looking at the empty middle seat next to her. Images that she'd blocked all day rushed into her mind. Another jolt of nausea hit her full force, and she wished she'd remembered to grab the new bottle of Zofran she had in the kitchen cabinet. She'd taken the last one from the bottle in her purse at school earlier in the day.

Josh returned his wallet to his pocket and heard someone across the dining room call out his daughter's name. He turned to see Patrick Bradley wave. The boy said something to his mother before making his way over to them. Two other boys followed him.

"Hey, Tori," Patrick said when he reached them. "These are my friends Alex and Wesley. You wanna sit with us?"

Tori looked up at Josh. "Can we, Daddy? Please."

"It's okay with me if it's okay with their parents."

Josh and Victoria followed the boys back across the restaurant. Ms. Bradley and the man moved a small table next to a larger one while the other woman moved chairs into position for two more people. Introductions were made and Josh shook hands with Mark and Jennifer Morgan.

Because he was in the buffet line after Ms. Bradley, Josh watched what she put on her plate. Tori had more food on hers. When the group returned to the table, the friend and her husband exchanged glances. For the first time, Josh noticed how thin Patrick's mother was.

Once the kids settled in at their end of the table, the adults turned to their own food and conversation. Ms. Bradley sat beside him, and Josh watched her pick at the contents of her plate. She took drinks of her Sprite, but he saw her put only two or maybe three bites of food in her mouth.

While he and the Morgans talked and ate, Josh was distracted by how they watched her. He couldn't keep from watching her either. She sat silently, her mind obviously somewhere else. Josh got the feeling he made her uncomfortable. Partway through the meal, she murmured something and hurried toward the restrooms. Mark, Jennifer, and Patrick watched her go.

"Is she sick?" Josh asked.

The husband and wife looked at each other as if asking whether they should say anything. "Today's . . ." Jennifer looked toward the other end of the table where the children sat. "She's been like this since she lost her husband," Jennifer said in a low voice after clearing her throat.

"I knew Brandon," Josh said.

Jennifer studied his face.

"We weren't close or anything, but I did know him. We talked at school functions and birthday parties. I know what happened. Well, at least part of it. My wife and I were at the funeral."

"You know about the accident?" Jennifer asked.

"I know he was killed in a car wreck. I know the casket was closed. That's all I know."

She studied his face again. She took a deep breath and let it out slowly. "Something sparks a memory for her. I've tried for two years, and I still haven't picked up on the pattern. I don't know what triggers the vomiting. Sometimes she's fine. Other times, like today—of course, today." She sounded close to tears, and she stared at her lap for a moment. Her husband rubbed her back.

The woman took a few deep breaths before raising her head. She looked weary and careworn. "We thought talking about Brandon made her sick, but we don't talk about him anymore." She looked at her husband. "At least we try not to."

"The four of you spent a lot of time together?" Josh asked.

Both of them nodded. Mark glanced toward the restrooms and cleared his throat.

Josh turned to see Dana's slow approach. He stood with the intention of aiding her, but something in her expression froze him in place.

"Is that right?" Jennifer said in a tone that belied the conversation they'd been having. "So your daughter and Patrick are in the same class?"

"Yes, same class since first grade," he answered absently. He held Dana's chair while she sat down.

All color had drained from her face, and Josh worried that she'd pass out at any second. She murmured an apology and made a pitiful attempt at a smile.

"You all right, Mom?" Patrick asked.

"Absolutely," she said with a firmness that surprised Josh. "The salad dressing didn't agree with me."

Doubt and concern shone in Patrick's expression. The woman wasn't fooling even her seven-year-old. Trying to pretend everything was normal, Josh watched Dana out of the corner of his eye. She finished her Sprite, and he offered to get her a refill. When he returned and she thanked him, their eyes locked for a moment. She had green eyes—pretty but sad. He felt bad for her, but he had his own problems that he couldn't fix.

When the kids finished eating, they begged to go to the game room. The group made their way down the hall to an area filled with loud sounds and flashing lights. The kids took off to use up their tokens, while the adults sat on benches at the perimeter of the room. Some of the color came back to Dana's face, and she was smiling.

The four adults took turns checking on the children while they played. Several times Josh caught Patrick watching his mother. The boy had worry etched on his face that far exceeded his years.

Despite his concern for Tori's friend and his mother, Josh was enjoying himself. Usually, he and Tori were alone or with his parents when they went anywhere. He hadn't socialized at all since Monica left. Her kind of socializing never included children anyway. It was nice to be out with Tori and other adults. He needed to do this more often; it would be good for both of them.

Josh learned that Dana and Jennifer had grown up together. Jennifer worked as a nurse practitioner in the pediatric clinic at Fort Knox, and Mark operated his own lawn care business. Dana was a pharmacist at Food Mart and had been for several years.

It turned out that she worked with Craig Reynolds, one of Josh's high school buddies who was also a pharmacist. Craig filled all of Josh and Tori's prescriptions. They didn't take any routine medications, but Josh didn't understand why he'd never run into Dana at the pharmacy. When he asked her about it, she explained that she'd been working part-time since Patrick was born.

Dana somehow already knew he was an architect. He wanted to ask her how she knew, but was sidetracked when Mark questioned him about what types of buildings he designed.

Twenty minutes later, the kids were going strong at the games, Dana and Jennifer were talking about medical stuff, and Josh and Mark were discussing the good and bad of owning their own businesses. Their conversation turned to University of Kentucky sports, and Josh told Mark that he had played college baseball at UK.

"You know," Mark said, "I coach my boys' baseball team. The guy who helped me for the past three years is military. He and his family moved away a couple of months ago. I don't suppose you'd be interested in coaching?"

"I don't know. I'll think about it."

"I've tried to talk Patrick into playing. Alex would love it if he would."

Josh could see Patrick at a basketball shoot-out game. Tickets poured out of the machine as he made shot after shot. "Why do you think he doesn't want to play baseball?"

"He used to be busy with soccer." Mark glanced in the direction of Dana and his wife. "He doesn't play soccer anymore, but he still won't play baseball."

He pulled a business card from his wallet and extended it toward Josh. "If you decide you'd like to help out with the baseball thing, give me a call. Practice won't start until after the kids have spring break. I know it's a big time commitment. No pressure. I understand if you aren't interested."

Josh took the card and tucked it in his wallet, still wondering why Patrick wouldn't play ball. He remembered his dad coaching him when he was a kid. It was great. It'd given him a love for the game. He'd been good enough to get a full scholarship. He'd been far from professional caliber, but baseball paid for four of his five years of college.

Josh smiled at Mark. "I'll think about it and let you know."

At that point, the four adults were bombarded. All the children talked at once, displaying the prizes they received for the tickets they had won on the games.

"Daddy," Josh heard Tori say through the other voices, "look at my bouncy ball. I didn't have enough tickets to get a bouncy ball, but I wanted one. Wesley got this bouncy ball for me. I didn't even ask him to. Isn't he nice?"

"That was nice of him, sweetheart. Did you tell him thank you?"

Her eyes widened. "I forgot."

She rushed to Wesley and grabbed him in a hug. "Thank you, Wesley. You're the best!" Before she released him, she pressed a kiss to his face.

The whole exchange happened in a matter of seconds. She was back at Josh's side in a flash. Only this time she squeezed herself against him. Josh guessed that she'd shocked herself. She'd certainly shocked him. Tori was usually reserved with people she didn't know well. From the look on Wesley's face, he was a bit shocked himself, but not unhappy. The little boy reached up and touched the spot on his cheek where Tori's lips had been. Josh couldn't help smiling. He looked at the other three adults. They all wore grins even though they looked as if they were trying to stay straight-faced. Patrick and Alex had their tongues out, silently gagging.

"We better get you kids home," Jennifer said. "It'll be bedtime soon, and we still have to pick up your sister."

The kids moaned and complained, but all of them made their way without much resistance toward the exit. Outside the building, the group said their goodbyes. Josh and Tori walked toward his truck while the other six people loaded into a minivan.

Chapter 3

Later that night, Josh knelt with his daughter beside her bed at his parents' home and listened to her say her prayers. He peeked at her. Her eyes were squeezed shut, her eyebrows were scrunched down, and her small hands were clutched together under her chin.

"Dear, God. This is Tori Peters. I know you already know that. Thanks for my new friends I met today named Wesley and Alex. Thank you for my friend Patrick, too. Thank you for pizza. Thanks for my daddy and for Jesus. God, please bless Daddy, Ms. Bradley, Ms. Anders, Grammy and Gramps, Nana and Grandpa, and all my friends. Amen."

"How about your mom?" Josh prompted.

Tori took a deep breath. "God bless Monica, too," she murmured.

Josh raised his head. Tori held the same position but was quiet. He waited, watching the subtle changes in his daughter's expression. She seemed to be working out something in her mind.

"Dear God," she said after a minute, "please let me have a mommy who loves me."

A lump formed in Josh's throat. Unable to speak, he pulled the comforter over her polka-dotted pajamas and tucked it under her chin. He kissed her forehead and brushed his fingers over her cheek.

He swallowed hard. "You know I love you. Don't you, Victoria?"

She reached up with her slender arms, wrapped them around his neck, and pulled his face down so their cheeks touched. "I know you do, Daddy. You're the best dad in the world. It's just that all my friends have a dad *and* a mom. Except Patrick."

Josh pulled back enough to look at her face. Her eyes were wide and sparkling, and Josh could see the wheels in her head turn.

"You and Ms. Bradley can get married. Patrick would be my brother. I'd have a mom, and Patrick would have a dad. It would be—"

"Now, honey, that isn't going to happen."

"Why not?"

Josh looked at the ceiling and then back at his daughter. "It's complicated, sweetheart."

"Because you still love Monica."

He stared at her, not knowing how to respond.

"Is it my fault she never liked me? Is it my fault she left?"

Josh continued to look down at Victoria. She dropped her gaze to her fingers that were plucking at her comforter. When what she said registered, he sat beside her, gathered her in his arms, and pulled her against his chest.

For a few moments, he held her and ran his fingers through her soft hair. "You're a wonderful person, Tori. You're beautiful and funny and smart. You share better than any other kid I've ever seen. Your mom didn't leave because of you. Please believe me. I'm not saying that because I'm your dad." He took a deep breath and let it out. "Your mother left because she doesn't want to be a wife or a mother. She wants to focus on her career and herself. That has nothing to do with you, or me either for that matter."

After holding her for a few minutes, he laid her back on her pillow and gave her another kiss. He talked with her for a while about school and their time at the restaurant.

"Do you think you can go to sleep now?"

She yawned. "Yeah. Love you."

"I love you, too, honey." He turned out the light and left the room.

Josh stood outside his daughter's door, listening for any sounds of restlessness. After a few moments, he heard her say another prayer asking God to please let Patrick's mom be her mom too. He ran a hand through his hair and waited a while longer, but all was quiet.

Upstairs, Josh slumped down on the sofa in the living room. He let his head hang down and rested his forearms on his legs. His life wasn't supposed to be like this. He should be happily married with two, maybe three, children. He should be busy enjoying them, watching them mature and grow, not worrying about whether his and Monica's mistakes would warp his daughter for life.

Absently, he turned the gold band on his left hand. Victoria wanted a mother; she needed a mother. Her own mother didn't want her. Monica was the only woman he'd ever loved. A life and a family with her had been all he'd ever wanted.

Josh rubbed his face with both hands, feeling the stubble on his jaw. He thought Monica's going back to Atlanta alone would make her change her mind. He thought she would miss him. More importantly, he hoped she'd miss her daughter. Nearly a year had passed since she left and, so far, neither had happened.

He heaved a heavy sigh. He was going to have to give up his dream of an ideal family. Somehow, he had to make himself stop loving Monica. It was obvious she didn't want his love. He had Victoria and she had him. That would have to be enough.

He prayed, and for the first time in a long time, instead of praying that Monica would change her mind, he prayed that God would show him what would be best for him and his daughter. After a few moments, Josh stood, stretched, and made his way to the bedroom that was his when he lived at home years ago.

He went straight to the chest that sat in the corner of the room. He studied his left hand and then wiggled the ring from his finger. It was the first time it'd been off his hand since Monica placed it there more than sixteen years before. A visible impression, paler than the rest of his hand, remained where the ring had been. A small ceramic dish shaped like a baseball sat on the chest. He'd had it since he was a small boy. He dropped the small bit of gold that used to mean so much into it. It made a hollow clinking sound. He sighed again and forced his thoughts toward the future.

For about an hour, he folded and packed his clothes and personal belongings that weren't in storage. Tomorrow he'd move his and Victoria's clothes to the new house. Saturday, Steve was going to help him move the few larger pieces that he'd taken from the old house and were in storage. At least that part of his life was coming along as planned.

Tomorrow, he and Tori would spend the night in their new house. He was determined to make it a home for them.

Chapter 4

Rain beat down on Steven's car when he drove to Food Mart Friday morning. He parked his Honda Accord, pocketed his keys, and flipped the hood of his jacket over his head. He strolled around the grocery service counter and saw Dana in an aisle in front of the pharmacy, talking to a woman who had a child seated in her shopping cart. Steven was watching her, trying to look as if he wasn't watching her, when someone asked if he needed help.

Startled, he turned to face a young woman. Her smock told him she was one of the pharmacy technicians. "Uh, no, thank you. I'm waiting for Dana."

"Hey, Steven," Dana said from behind him. "How are you today?"

He turned toward her. She was smiling, and he returned the gesture. "I'm doing great. A little wet, but still great."

She stepped back into the pharmacy area, pushing through the swinging half door between the waiting area and cash register. "Everything's together for Grandma Farris."

"How did you know I was here for her?"

"She called me this morning." She walked behind the counter, returned with a bag, and started ringing up his grandmother's prescriptions. "It's so good of you to do things for her. I know it means a lot to her."

Steven shrugged and gave her a grin. "What can I say? I'm a nice guy."

Dana laughed.

"Hey, Dana," the other pharmacist said after Steven had paid, and he and Dana had been talking for a few minutes. "Kim called. She's sick and can't close tonight. Elizabeth will kill me if I don't go to Missy's piano recital. Is there any way you could work?"

"I'd have to pick up Patrick from school," she said after a moment. "I could come back after that as long as I can find someone to watch him until I get off. Let me make a call."

When she turned away from the counter, Steven reached out and gently held her arm. "Let me watch him."

She smiled and shook her head. "Steven, a nice-looking guy like you has better things to do on a Friday night than baby-sit a second grader."

"It just so happens that my calendar is free this evening. I would love to help you out. Besides, I still need to hook up his game systems. Come on; he'll have fun with me."

"Well, if you're sure. I'll owe you one."

His smile broadened.

"Okay, Craig," Dana said. "Your wife won't have to kill you. Just know I'm doing this because I hate the thought of visiting Elizabeth in prison."

After they arranged a time to meet at Dana's house, Steven left. Before he backed from his parking space, Steven made a call.

"Steve! Whuzzup?" Matt said.

"I'm gonna have to cancel on the Fourth Street Live thing tonight," Steven said.

"What is it this time?"

"What do you mean 'this time'?"

"Well, you missed Katie's party, you missed Les's party, you missed several of Western's basketball games this winter, and now this. What's going on?"

Okay, so maybe Matt had a point, but he was getting tired of parties and going out. Besides, Dana needed him. That was more important than club hopping in Louisville. "I'm helping a friend out tonight. She's in a bind."

"A friend," Matt said crossly. "And what am I?"

"A friend, but you're not in a bind."

"You said 'she.' Who is it?"

"She's a friend, a friend of the family. I've known her for years."

Matt didn't say anything for a minute. "It's not that pharmacist you stop to talk to every time you're in Food Mart, is it? The one with the kid? The one you do stuff for all the time?"

Steven cleared his throat and gripped the steering wheel a little tighter. "Yes, it's her. She's working tonight to help someone else. She needed someone to keep her little boy, and I volunteered."

"You're passing up going to Fourth Street Live with a group of your friends—several of those being hot, single women—to babysit?" Matt sounded flabbergasted.

"I guess I am."

"And she's only a friend," Matt said flatly. "Why don't I believe that?"

Josh made three trips to the new house after taking Victoria to school Friday morning. He moved their clothes and things he could carry without help. Thankfully, the rain hadn't lasted long, and the new furniture for their bedrooms had been delivered without any problems.

Once the delivery men left, Josh headed to Food Mart so that he could stock the pantry and fridge. He noticed Craig working and went by the pharmacy to speak to him. He saw Dana Bradley, too, who gave him a wave and a smile from the other side of the work area. Josh knew he must have seen her at the pharmacy before but hadn't put it together that he should know her. How he'd missed making the connection he didn't know.

He had everything in Tori's room ready for her, and when he drove to school to pick her up, his excitement grew. This would be a fresh start for them both. He had a good feeling about it. A very good feeling.

Tori began talking a mile a minute before she even got in the truck. Josh couldn't help laughing at her. She fired off questions faster than he could open his mouth to answer. He gave up and simply listened, enjoying her enthusiasm.

He noticed a Toyota Avalon behind them as he drove from school to the house. It turned into his subdivision and then into his cul-de-sac and finally into the driveway of the house beside his.

Curious about who followed him home, Josh walked through his garage and out into the backyard. Tori tagged along, still chattering.

She paused in mid-sentence and then said, "Look, Daddy, a puppy! And Patrick!"

Patrick came to a halt near them. He smiled broadly. "Hey!"

"Hi, buddy," Josh said. "I didn't know you lived in this neighborhood."

The dog's entire body wagged with excitement. Laughing, Tori dropped to the ground and tried to capture it in her arms.

Patrick pointed next door. "I live there. This is Zoe. But she's not a puppy. She's as big as she'll get."

"You're so lucky! I've never had a dog. Monica—I mean my mom—wouldn't even let me have a fish." Tori squealed with delight when the dog licked her face.

Patrick looked confused for a moment. Then his grin returned. "If you're gonna be my neighbor, you can play with Zoe anytime you want. She likes you."

Josh looked up to see Patrick's mother making her way toward them. She smiled.

"Mom! Guess what. Tori and Mr. Peters are our new neighbors."

Tori hopped from the ground, skipped to Dana, and took her hand. "Wanna come see my room?"

Josh cringed inwardly.

Dana looked at her watch. "I wish I could, but I have to go back to work. How about later tonight?"

"Okay," Victoria said and then ran off with Patrick.

The kids chased the dog around the joined yards, or maybe the dog chased them. Either way, they were laughing. Josh took it as a good sign that Tori wasn't disappointed about Dana's not taking a room tour.

"I thought you didn't work nights," Josh said.

"I don't, not usually. But the pharmacist scheduled to close is sick, and Craig's daughter has a piano recital this evening. I told him I'd come back after picking up Patrick and close this evening."

"Do you need someone to watch Patrick? I'd be happy to do it."

"That's nice of you, but, no, I've already made arrangements. In fact, I'm sure you know him since you design most of the houses Tom Farris builds. Steven was in the pharmacy this morning when Kim—that's the pharmacist who's sick—called. He offered to come out and watch Patrick. He always has a blast with Steven."

"How do you know Steve Farris?" Josh asked.

"Oh, I've known Steven since he was a kid. His grandmother has been one of my regular patients almost as long as I've been a pharmacist. He used to come shopping with her when he was younger. He helped me with electronic devices and odds and ends at the other house after Brandon . . ." She cleared her throat and looked away for a moment. "Brandon always took care of stuff like that." She cleared her throat again. "Steven was here for most of the construction when Tom built my house, and he helped me move in."

"So your husband was good with gadgets?"

Josh was relieved when she gave him a small smile. "He was definitely a gadget man. He could build or fix about anything."

She was quiet for a moment and had a far-off look in her eyes. "It's weird, but Patrick's the same way."

She was smiling more when she looked at him again. Josh smiled back. It was good to know the woman had pleasant memories of her husband. Maybe he could help her.

"I'm glad we're neighbors," he said. "It'll be good for Tori to have a friend close by to play with."

"Absolutely," Dana agreed. "If I can help you get settled, please let me know. Maybe we could take turns running the kids to school and picking them up."

"Sounds good. I guess we can talk about it when you get off work. You'll come over later? Tori really does want you to see her room."

"Sure. I'll be back between eight and eight thirty." They both turned toward the sound of a car door closing. "There's Steven now. I better get going."

Josh followed a few steps behind her to greet Steve and gather his daughter. He watched and listened while

Dana gave Steve instructions regarding snacking and TV viewing, said her goodbyes, and made her way to her car.

"Plan to eat dinner with us after work tonight," Josh called. He turned toward Steve. "You're invited, too." The younger man nodded but continued to watch Dana.

"You don't need to feed us," Dana called back.

"I'm cooking tonight, and you're not going to hurt my feelings and refuse to eat with us."

She glanced at Steve, who nodded in agreement. "Well, okay." She waved a final goodbye, got in her car, and drove away.

Josh invited Steve and Patrick to come over later. Then he took Victoria home. First stop was her room. She took a flying leap and jumped onto her bed. Her enthusiasm made him laugh.

"How about a snack?" he asked her.

"In our new kitchen?"

"In our new kitchen." He picked her up from the bed, swung her around, and flung her over his shoulder. She squealed, and he stomped to the kitchen with her upper body hanging down his back. He plopped her down on one of their new stools. She was breathless from laughing, and her cheeks were rosy. He kept a supporting arm on her until he was sure she'd regained her balance.

She was a beautiful child. Except for her dark blue eyes, she was a mixture of him and Monica. Her eyes were so much like his that it was almost scary. Her hair was the closest thing to being like her mother's, but even that was a much lighter shade than Monica's. Lighter than Monica's, but darker than his. Her hair color, like most of the rest of her, was part him, part Monica, but all Victoria.

When he gave her a choice of snacks, he mentally braced himself for a difficult but necessary discussion. He set her chosen granola bar and yogurt in front of her and tried to think of the best way to approach the subject.

"Honey, I want to talk to you about Ms. Bradley," he said after giving up trying to find a way to be subtle.

"Isn't she great? It's gonna be awesome living beside her." Tori's face was so hopeful that it frightened him to think of the plan unfolding in her mind.

"This is important. You need to listen to me."

Wide-eyed, she stared at him.

"Do you remember what you told me the other night? About wanting Patrick's mom to be your mom?"

Tori nodded slowly, the look on her face solemn.

"I don't want you to mention that idea to Ms. Bradley. Or to Patrick."

She looked stricken, and he felt guilty.

"You don't think she'd love me?"

He gave her a tight hug. "It's not like that. She's been through a lot, Tori. She's still sad that Patrick's dad died. Sometimes when someone's husband or wife passes away, the person never marries again."

"Oh."

"Do you know what you can do?"

She shook her head, not quite meeting his eyes.

"You can be her friend. Everyone needs friends. A person can never have too many. I bet she would love to be your friend, too."

Her face brightened, and he could tell thoughts churned behind her eyes. "What if I'm such a good friend she decides she wants me to be her little girl?"

At that moment, Josh Peters wanted to throttle the woman he'd spent most of his life loving. He struggled to maintain his composure and took a deep breath to keep from taking his frustration out on Tori.

"I know you feel you're missing something because your mom isn't part of your life. Kids need moms. Kids need dads. But life is rarely all we think it should be, and loving families come in all shapes and sizes, even little ones like ours."

"Why can't things be the way they're supposed to be?"

Josh took a deep breath and let it out before he wrapped an arm around her shoulders. How do you make up for a woman's rejection of her own child? "People make choices; sometimes accidents happen and people die."

"Like Patrick's dad," she said sadly.

"Yes. Like Patrick's dad. What I'm trying to tell you is that bad things happen to everybody. Even to people who don't deserve to have bad things happen to them, like you and Patrick. The way you handle those bad experiences determines what kind of person you are. If you dwell on the bad parts of your life, you'll be unhappy. If you try to find the good in things, you have a chance at being happy. Things happen that we can't possibly understand, but God has a plan. If you can trust him, it makes life so much better even when things seem messed up. Does any of this make sense to you?"

"I think so. I shouldn't feel bad that I don't have a mom. I do have you, Daddy, and I think you're the greatest dad in the world." She threw her arms around his neck and squeezed. "I won't think anymore about not having a mom. I'll be thankful that I have such a great dad. And I promise I won't say anything to Ms. Bradley about wanting her to be my mom."

"Good girl."

She pulled away from him. "Daddy, do you think we could help her not be sad anymore?"

"We can try."

"By being her friends?"

"That would be a good start," he answered.

"You're gonna be her friend, too?"

"Sure."

She smiled at him—making him wish he could read her mind—and took a bite of her granola bar.

Chapter 5

Dana was exhausted when she pulled down the gate that separated the pharmacy from the twenty-four hour grocery. She was also hungry. The only thing she'd eaten all day was a banana. Hunger was a vast improvement over vomiting. Maybe tonight she could eat a decent meal and keep it down.

After locking the gate, she walked to the service counter to wait while Carrie, the pharmacy technician closing with her, turned in the till from the cash register. Carrie came through the office door and gave Dana a tired smile.

"That was a rough one, wasn't it?" Carrie said.

"I was afraid it was me," Dana said.

"No, tonight would've been rough for anybody. I mean, third-party problems are enough, but we had the printer jam and then Ms. Tinsley's little fit. When it rains, it pours."

"True," Dana agreed. She was ready to put the night behind her.

By the time Carrie and Dana reached the parking lot and said their goodbyes, it was twenty minutes after eight. Before starting her car, Dana called Steven to let him know she was running late. He told her they were already at Josh's house and that Patrick had been asking when she'd be home.

"Let him know everything's okay. I'm on my way."

"Be careful," Steven said before she said goodbye.

After putting her phone in the console between the seats, she started her car and headed for home. Steven said that Patrick was having a good time playing with Victoria. Dana was glad. Having a friend next door would be good for him.

Dana caught herself wondering about Josh and if the divorce was his idea or Monica's. Something about Monica had always rubbed Dana the wrong way. She never helped with anything at school, and Dana couldn't remember her bringing Tori to even one of the class birthday parties.

The few times Dana had been around her, Monica had looked perfect. Perfect clothes, perfect hair, make-up, nails. Dana sighed and told herself she was being too hard on the woman; after all, she didn't really know her.

"You're jealous," Dana told her reflection in the rearview mirror while she sat at a red light. "You don't get anywhere near perfect, even on your best days."

Something else about Monica Simpson-Peters niggled in the back of Dana's mind.

When she pulled into her garage, it hit her. Why did Victoria live with her father? Rarely did fathers gain primary custody of their children in divorce cases. Tori said something in the library yesterday about her mom being "gone." Come to think of it, she hadn't even called her Mom.

Dana shook her head and told herself it wasn't any of her business. She walked out of her garage and made her way next door. After knocking, she briefly looked away. When she turned back, Josh stood in his open back door. Under the glow of the outdoor light, his blue eyes shone and his smile was wide and welcoming. She couldn't have stopped herself from returning his smile even if she tried.

He grabbed her hand. "Come on in." His hand was warm, and the simple gesture was comforting. He drew her in front of him and then guided her by the shoulders into a brightly lit kitchen.

"We've been waiting for you." He pulled out the chair between Patrick and Victoria.

Zoe, under the table, looked up at her as if to say, *Where have you been?*

After she sat, Patrick leaned into her. She squeezed her son's leg under the table, and he grinned at her. "Hi, Mom."

From her left, Tori gave her a hug. Dana reached over with her left arm and squeezed her in return. She looked around the table while Josh set plates of food in front of each person. First, the children's plates, then hers, then Steven's, until finally Josh sat down with his own plate.

Dana was amazed. "You've been busy. This looks great."

"I fixed the milk," said Patrick.

"And I set the table and got out the salad dressings and stuff," said Tori.

"You two did a great job," Dana said.

"Who wants to say the blessing?" Josh asked.

Both Victoria and Patrick volunteered. They held hands while the children recited the prayer that Dana recognized from lunch at school.

Slight chaos broke out when the salt, pepper, salad dressing, potato toppings, and steak sauce were passed around the table. After she cut Patrick's steak, Dana glanced over at Steven who hadn't spoken since she came in. He was looking at her with an expression she couldn't read.

"Was Patrick good for you, Steven?"

He glanced at Patrick and winked. When he looked at her again, his expression was as it usually was. "Of course. We hooked up the game systems and played a couple of games to be sure everything was running okay. Then we stayed outside for a long time, kicking around a soccer ball and playing with Zoe. I fixed him a snack, and then we came over here. We've been helping Josh and Tori a little and playing some card games."

"I helped with the Wii and XBox," Patrick said. "Steven said I'm a natural. He said when I grow up I might like working with computers like he does, and . . . Hey! I'm always good."

Dana laughed. "I wondered how long it'd take you to catch that."

She turned again to Steven. "Thank you so much for watching him. I appreciate it. I'll fix you dinner soon. I definitely owe you one."

❦

While the five of them talked over dinner, Josh kept an eye on Dana's plate. Tonight she was eating, not merely pushing the food around with her fork. He felt like a spying, overprotective parent.

He felt even more so when she went to the restroom after dinner. He hovered in the hallway listening to be sure she wasn't sick. Suddenly the door opened. Josh backed away but didn't have time to escape. They stood in his hallway, staring at each other.

Her eyes had to be the softest green he'd ever seen. Instead of looking suspicious, her expression was open and questioning. Josh was glad Steve was busy with the kids in the living room.

"Everything all right?" Dana asked.

"Yeah. Sure. It's just that . . ." Josh looked at the wall beside them. She'd probably think he was sticking his nose where it didn't belong if he told her why he was in his hallway. Besides, if he mentioned her being sick, it might make her sick. Still, he didn't want to lie to her. He was bad at it anyway. He cleared his throat before he faced her again. "I was afraid you were sick after you ate. Like you were at the pizza buffet."

She didn't say a word, but her expression changed. It was as if shutters had slapped shut.

"Your friend Jennifer said that you've had trouble eating since . . ." He studied her face. Her jaw tightened. Well, now he had nothing to lose. "Jennifer told me that you've had trouble with vomiting and losing weight since Brandon's accident. I'm concerned about you. I want to be your friend, Dana. I'd like to help you. Please don't be angry with me. I didn't mean to offend you."

Her gaze dropped to the floor. He could no longer see her face, but he could feel her hands in his. He didn't realize until then that he'd moved toward her and grasped her hands. His thumbs stroked her skin. He stopped the movement but didn't let go.

"I can't believe Jennifer told you that," she murmured and then shook her head. After a moment, she looked up at him. Her expression was friendly yet guarded. She shrugged. "Well, it's not like it's a big secret. One look at me is enough to know something's wrong. Normal, healthy people don't look like I do." Her tiny smile didn't reach her eyes. "I appreciate your concern, Josh, but I don't think there's anything you can do."

He squeezed her hands. "Will you let me be your friend?"

"Friend? Well, a person can never have too many of those."

Hearing her use the same words he'd spoken to Tori earlier made him smile. Dana's entire face changed when she returned the expression. The transformation was incredible.

His daughter's voice rang through the house. He dropped Dana's hands and backed two steps away from her. Tori flew into the hall, grabbed Dana, and pulled her past him into her room. Josh followed them, listening to his daughter's cheerful chatter.

"Oh, Victoria," Dana said, "your room's beautiful! This is the rainbow you said your dad painted. What a neat idea."

"My dad's really good at stuff like this. I told him I wanted a rainbow room, and this is what he did."

Dana turned to look at him. "I can't believe you painted this. I would've guessed a professional did it. It's so perfect."

"It wasn't all that difficult—a lot of measuring, taping, and time, but it wasn't hard. It was Tori's idea, and she picked out the furniture and bedding. I only did the labor."

"You have good taste, young lady," Dana said.

Tori giggled, gave Dana a quick hug, and dashed from the room, calling to Patrick as she went.

Dana walked over to the striped wall and studied it. "How long did it take you to do this?" she asked without turning around.

Josh moved over and stood behind her. "A while."

In truth, it had taken many hours over many days to get it done. He had measured, marked off, taped, and painted stripe after painstaking stripe. A professional could have done it in a tenth of the time, but he was pleased with the results. Tori was thrilled with it, and that's all that mattered to him.

"Hey," Steve said from behind them. Josh shifted, and Dana looked over her shoulder.

"What time do you want me to be here tomorrow, Josh?" Steve asked with his gaze focused on Dana. She smiled at him before turning back to the stripes on the wall.

"Are you going to have one of your dad's trucks?" Josh asked.

Steve nodded without looking at him.

"You want to meet me at the storage unit place around ten?"

"Sure. I'll see you in the morning. Thanks for dinner."

"Don't mention it," Josh replied. "Thanks for all your help." He glanced from Steve to Dana. She seemed unaware that Steve couldn't take his eyes off her.

"No problem," Steve said. He looked at Dana as if he were willing her to turn around. "Dana, will I see you tomorrow when I help Josh move the rest of his things?"

Dana turned. "I don't know." She looked at Josh. "Would you like my help? I could at least keep Victoria entertained while you two carry things in."

"I would appreciate that," Josh said. "Thank you."

Steve cleared his throat. "Well, I'm gonna take off now if neither of you needs anything else tonight."

Dana moved past Josh. "Let me walk you to your car. Would it be okay if Patrick stays here? I'll come right back. I'd like to see the rest of your house."

"That's fine," Josh said.

Steve's eyes met his when Dana passed between them. He dropped his gaze from Josh's and turned to follow her. In the living room, Patrick and Tori were playing Go Fish on the floor. Dana told Patrick what she was doing and that she'd be right back. The kids joked with Steve when he told them goodbye and then resumed their card game. Josh walked Steve and Dana to his back door and opened it for them.

Feeling nosy and intrusive once again, Josh watched them through the window. Steve held Dana's arm when they maneuvered around muddy areas in his yard where the grass wasn't established. He couldn't see them when they moved into the shadows beyond the light from his porch, but Josh caught sight of them again once they moved close enough to Dana's garage.

When they reached her driveway, they faced each other, talking. Dana took a step toward Steve and raised on tiptoes. Josh let out his breath when she gave Steve only a quick hug and a kiss on the cheek.

Steve waved, got in his car, and backed out of her driveway. He didn't drive out of the cul-de-sac until Dana reached the circle of light from Josh's porch.

Josh glanced at the kids who were intent on their game and stepped outside. Quietly he closed the door behind him. Dana was looking at the ground and didn't seem to notice him.

"You do realize he's got a thing for you," Josh said right before he took her hand to help her navigate the muddy path.

She looked up at him with an expression of complete surprise. He wasn't sure if his presence or his words were what shocked her, and her expression became neutral before he could decide.

"I beg your pardon?" Dana said after they reached his porch.

"He's attracted to you."

She laughed. "That's one of the most ridiculous things I have ever heard!"

He couldn't help smiling at the warmth of her laughter. "What's so ridiculous about it?"

She shook her head and smiled with disbelief. "I'm a widowed mother who is almost fifteen years older than he is."

Josh raised his eyebrows. It didn't seem to him that Steve cared about the age difference, but he wasn't going to argue the point. "Never mind," he muttered. "Let me show you the rest of the house."

Chapter 6

Monica scanned the memo on top of the messages her personal assistant handed her. It was from the new chief financial officer, Marcus Taylor, her boss.

"Scott," she said without looking up, "I need twenty minutes free beginning at one fifteen Monday. Arrange my schedule to accommodate that."

"Yes, Ms. Simpson-Peters. Will there be anything else?"

"No, Scott. That's all. You may leave for the day."

Even though her eyes never left the work on her desk, it didn't escape Monica's notice that he checked his watch and shook his head as he walked through her office door. She'd let him off easy tonight; he was leaving before nine. She worked him hard, but it wasn't anything she wasn't willing to do herself. Hard work never killed anyone.

She'd been expecting the meeting with Taylor. He liked to have personal relationships with his employees, or, in Monica's estimation, he pretended to. She'd done her homework. Taylor marched to the beat of a different drummer. He was fifty-seven years old, had been married to the same woman for more than thirty years, and had four stable adult children. She could find no hint of scandal in her research on the man. Everything indicated that Taylor was a family man all the way and that he attributed his success to making his family a priority over work. She didn't believe it for a minute. In Monica's opinion, it was merely public relations rhetoric. If Taylor's family was that important to him, Monica resented him for it. The corporate world would never allow a woman devoted to her family to get ahead. In Monica's experience there had been no room for the distractions of a family.

Her mama had told her she couldn't have it all. "When the babies come, you won't care about climbing ladders, getting promotions, or earning raises. I gave up my career for your sisters and you, and I've never regretted it."

But Mama lived a life that Monica despised. She depended on Daddy for everything.

Monica had convinced herself that she could have both a career and a family by keeping the emotional upper hand. As long as Josh needed her more than she needed him, she would stay in control. That worked for her until Victoria was born. When the sweet, tiny bundle that was her daughter was placed in her arms, Monica knew she was in trouble. The love she felt for her helpless infant would be her undoing if she allowed it. So Monica hardened her heart and refused to allow Victoria to distract her.

She stopped working the figures on the spreadsheet before her and tapped her pencil against her chin. She had to admit, the marriage part hadn't been all bad. Josh had adored her. What woman didn't love having an intelligent, sexy man adore her? And Josh was most definitely sexy. He always had been.

She hadn't given Josh much thought since leaving Kentucky. It was odd that she was thinking about him tonight. It must be because she'd cooled things down with Ross. She was simply missing intimate male companionship. Josh had always been an extremely thorough lover.

Still, Ross was close by. Good old Ross. She pulled her phone from her leather bag. She could give him a call. Invite him over for the weekend. He would drop everything else if she asked him to, but he'd been hinting at marriage. She never wanted to be married again. What kind of woman wants to saddle herself with only one man for the rest of her life? She laid the phone on her desk.

Admittedly, she hadn't been at all good at the one-man thing. Oh, Josh had been her first. God, they'd even waited until they were married. That fact still amazed her. He'd been the only one, too—for a while. They'd been married three years the first time she'd been unfaithful. When an opportunity presents itself, what's a woman to do? The reward for that escapade had been her first big promotion, and Josh had never been the wiser.

Josh was so good and so noble that he couldn't imagine others not being the same way. To Monica, that was naïve. Extremely naïve. And foolish. She figured if Josh hadn't come home and found Ross and her together, he still wouldn't have that one figured out.

Even after that, after seeing her with another man, Josh wanted to save their marriage. Monica agreed to counseling, but it finally became too much. She simply did not want to be married.

She ran her manicured fingers over her phone. Maybe she should give Josh a call, let him know she'd been thinking about him. But then he'd start talking about Victoria. Whenever she called about the house, he never failed to bring the conversation around to their daughter. He couldn't grasp the fact that she didn't care.

From what Monica could tell, Victoria hadn't suffered from her lack of interest. She was pretty, and she did well in school. Many children weren't that fortunate. She'd been careful before and during her pregnancy. No extramarital activity and she'd taken care of herself. She'd owed Josh and their child that much. Now Monica was done. She didn't owe Victoria anything more.

No, she wouldn't call Josh tonight, but soon. She had a feeling they would be seeing each other before long, and her intuition was rarely wrong.

Monica placed her paperwork back in the proper portfolio, straightened her desk, logged off her computer, gathered her belongings, and left her office. On the way out of the building, she punched a button on her phone.

"Ross. Darling. How are you? Why haven't you called me? I've missed you."

Saturday morning Dana started her day in the usual way. She put a Zofran tablet in her mouth before she got out of bed. She swallowed the medication with a sip of water and realized she hadn't taken her dose the night before. She'd also eaten a meal without being sick. She couldn't remember the last time that had happened.

Humming, she went to the kitchen. She craved coffee, something she'd given up when the vomiting got the best of her. When she moved to this house, she bought a new coffeemaker and coffee with the hope that she'd soon be able to tolerate it. She sang while she started it brewing.

"Mom?" Patrick said from behind her.

Dana turned and her smile broadened. He was barefoot and in his pajamas, looking at her through one eye and rubbing the other with his fist. His short-cropped hair was pushed over to one side. He looked especially like his daddy this morning. She knelt and gave him a hug. "Good morning, honey."

Patrick wrapped his arms around her. Dana closed her eyes and held him close, soaking up his embrace.

"I heard you singing," he said.

Dana pulled back. "Did I wake you?"

"No. But have I heard you sing before? I mean, except in church?"

She gave that question some thought. "It's been a while, but you've heard me sing. Perhaps I sing so badly that you've worked hard to wipe it from your memory."

It took Patrick a second, but then he realized what she was saying. He grinned. "You're not a bad singer. I like it."

She stood. "Thank you. Maybe I'll start doing it more often. How would that be?"

"Good."

"Are you hungry?" She opened the refrigerator. "I feel like bacon, eggs, toast, maybe some hash browns, orange juice." Dana pulled the things she needed from the refrigerator and turned to set them on the counter by the stove. Patrick stared at her. His eyes were wide, and his mouth was open.

"What is it?" she asked.

"You're gonna eat with me? More than a piece of toast or a banana?"

She cracked eggs into a bowl. "I'm hungry this morning."

From the direction of Patrick's room, Zoe wandered in. She stretched, yawned, and gave Dana the look that said she needed to go outside.

"Honey, let Zoe out while I fix breakfast."

Patrick walked toward the back door with the dog trailing behind. "Hi, Tori. Morning, Mr. Peters," Patrick called a moment later.

Dana glanced out the window to see Josh and Victoria walking toward her back door. She looked down. She was still wearing her pajamas. She hadn't even thrown on her robe. At least she'd brushed her teeth and her hair. She'd have to go by the back door to get to her room, and Patrick was inviting them in. She positioned herself so that her kitchen island would at least partially block their view of her and busied herself with her eggs.

"Hey, Patrick," Dana heard Josh say. "Would you and your mom like to go with us to grab some doughnuts?"

"I don't think we can. My mom's cooking breakfast right now."

Dana sighed with relief. They wouldn't come in if they were on their way to get doughnuts.

"She's happy this morning," Patrick said in a lower voice. "She told me she was hungry."

Dana made a face. She thought she was doing a decent job hiding the sickness from her son, but evidently not. And why was he saying something to the neighbors about it?

"We're having eggs and bacon and a bunch of other stuff," Patrick said. "You could eat with us."

Dana wished at that moment that she hadn't taught her son to be so friendly and polite.

"Hey, Mom," he called. "How 'bout Tori and Mr. Peters eating with us?"

Patrick walked into the kitchen with Victoria and Josh right behind him. Josh wore worn blue jeans and a T-shirt that hugged his chest. He had a UK baseball cap on his head, and he had obviously skipped shaving that morning. The man looked good. Dana felt like an idiot and wished she'd dressed. She applied her whisk to her already well-scrambled eggs.

"Maybe now isn't a good time," Josh said.

Dana wasn't sure if he sensed her discomfort or if the sight of her scared him. It wouldn't surprise her if the man was frightened. Women in baggy PJs and no makeup would be enough to frighten most anybody.

"Nonsense," Dana said, her manners overriding her common sense. "Give me a minute to make myself presentable. I'll be right back. Make yourselves at home." She hurried from the room.

She washed her face, slipped into a pair of jeans that weren't too baggy, and put on a T-shirt. She'd bought new clothes when she'd dropped a couple of sizes, but she refused to do it twice. She was determined that these clothes, better yet the next size up, would someday fit properly again. She put on a little makeup and pulled her hair back before sliding her feet into flip-flops.

A sense of guilt washed over her when she left her room. She was attracted to Josh Peters.

Standing in the hallway, she convinced herself it was a normal female response to notice a handsome man. Even Jennifer commented the other day about how handsome Steven was, and she was a happily married woman.

She could hear Patrick talking with Josh and Tori. She took a deep breath and walked back to the kitchen; their conversation lulled. "Would you like a cup of coffee, Josh?" she asked without looking toward the table where he sat.

"Yes, please."

She poured two mugs. "How do you take yours?"

"Black with extra sugar."

Dana put two spoonsful of sugar in one cup and one in another. She added skim milk to hers. She handed Josh the black coffee and watched him taste it.

"Perfect," he said after taking a sip.

When he smiled up at her, something fluttered inside her. She had to smile back. She cleared her throat and turned toward the kids who were playing on the floor with Zoe. "How about you two? Orange juice, apple juice, skim milk, or chocolate milk?"

Patrick nodded at Tori.

"Chocolate milk," Tori said.

"Patrick?" Dana said, moving her eyes from Victoria to her son. She could sense Josh's gaze, and it gave her an odd sensation.

"Orange juice."

"Run and get dressed. Then you and Tori can play until breakfast is ready."

Patrick took off toward his room.

"Don't forget to wash your face and brush your teeth," she called after him.

"Can I help with anything?" Josh asked.

"No, thank you," she said without looking at him.

Dana fixed the drinks for the kids and cracked more eggs into her bowl. She looked in Josh's direction when he stood and walked into her living room. She couldn't see what he was doing.

"How was your first night in your new house?" Dana asked Victoria.

Tori skipped over and stood beside her. She had a chocolate milk mustache that Dana wiped off for her.

"It was nice. I like it. It's much better than our other house."

"Oh?" Dana said and put the bacon in the oven.

"Our other house wasn't very fun, except the basement where Daddy had his stuff. Monica always wanted everything to stay perfect." She wrinkled up her nose. "Perfect's not much fun for a kid."

If Patrick started calling her Dana, she would cry. "No, I don't guess it would be," Dana said. She poured frozen hash browns into a preheated skillet.

"Monica hardly went to the basement. That space was mine and Daddy's. Now we have a whole house that's our space."

Dana glanced into the living room where she could now see Josh looking at the framed photographs she had on display. She wondered again what had happened to his marriage.

Steven had worked up the nerve to take the plunge. He'd thought about it last night after leaving Dana's house. He'd thought about it all morning and afternoon while he helped Josh move. Today was the day because Dana seemed different. The smile she gave him when he got out of the truck in Josh's drive told him something had changed. She was brighter, more alive, more like her old self. They'd talked and teased while he'd gone in and out of Josh's house. He planned to ask her out for dinner, on an actual date. With Josh right here, Steven figured he could keep Patrick while he and Dana went out.

In the afternoon, after he (with Patrick's eager assistance) finished hooking up the Wii to the television in Josh's basement, Steven went up the steps to look for her. Josh said he'd last seen her in the laundry room folding the bath towels she'd washed for him. Steven checked that room first. She wasn't there. He went to the bathroom near Victoria's room to look for her. She wasn't there, either. Steven heard noise from Josh's bedroom and followed the sound into the master bath.

When he walked through the open door, he stumbled over towels scattered on the floor. Then he realized what the noise was. He looked toward the commode. Dana's back was toward him, her hands braced on the open toilet lid and seat. Steven had never seen someone vomit. A wave of nausea washed over him. He swallowed hard before he walked toward her.

"Dana?" he murmured.

"Please," she said weakly without turning around. "Don't."

Steven stopped moving. "Let me help. There must be something I can do."

She reached for some toilet tissue and used it to wipe her face. Steven heard her blow her nose. "I don't want Patrick to know."

"Okay," Steven said. "He's in the basement. He won't know." He found a washcloth, dampened it with cold water, and held it out to her.

She took it without turning around or looking at him. She held it to her face and then on the back of her neck. She flushed the commode and leaned against the wall. Her eyes were closed. Steven had never seen someone so pale.

He felt helpless. "Can I get you something? Anything?"

She didn't answer, and Steven thought she might vomit again.

"In my bedroom," she murmured after a few moments. "On my nightstand, there's a bottle of medicine."

"I'll get it. Do you want me to help you lie down?"

With her eyes still closed, she moved her head slightly as if attempting to shake her head no. He was afraid she would collapse if he left her, but he didn't want to move her in case she needed to throw up again.

"I'll be right back," he said after a few moments and hurried out of the room.

In the hall, he collided with Josh. "Dana's sick," he said in a rush, "in the master bathroom. I'm going next door to get her medicine." He moved toward the back door. "Don't let Patrick know," he said over his shoulder.

Steven ran across the yards and burst through Dana's back door. He found the bottle, ran back to the other house, and fixed a glass of water in the kitchen. When he reached Josh's bedroom, Dana was on the bed. Josh sat next to her, mopping her face and neck with the washcloth. Her eyes were shut, and she was as pale as before.

Steven moved next to the bed. "Here's the medicine."

Josh pulled back, and Dana opened her eyes. Steven placed a tablet from the bottle in her open palm. She looked at it, placed it between her lips, and swallowed it while Steven held the glass for her.

She let her head fall against the pillows propped behind her and closed her eyes. "I skipped taking it this afternoon. I felt so much better this morning, and I thought maybe I was getting over it, that it was finally going to stop."

Steven looked at Josh. He looked as grim as Steven felt.

"Maybe you should let us take you to the emergency room," Josh said.

She pulled away from the pillows and opened her eyes. "No!" she said with more force than Steven thought she was capable of. "I can't go there. I haven't been there since . . ." She closed her eyes and lay back again. "I can't go there."

She took a breath and let it out slowly. "There's nothing else modern medicine can do for me anyway. I've had all kinds of tests run, upper GIs, lower GIs. I've been poked, stuck, prodded, scanned, and nothing has ever been found.

"I have a broken heart," she whispered. "Science can't fix a broken heart."

"Have you given up ever being well?" Steven asked.

Dana looked up at him. "No. I keep praying. I take the Zofran." She motioned toward the bottle still in his hand. "I ate too much today is all. And skipped my medicine. But I know I'm getting better. I won't give up."

Steven set the prescription bottle aside and reached for Dana's hand. He ran his thumb against her skin. He wanted so badly to tell her how he felt about her.

"Thank you, Steven. You're such a good friend." She gave his hand a weak squeeze. "You're better to me than any brother ever could be."

Steven swallowed, squeezed her hand in return, and forced himself to smile. He wanted to be more than her friend and way closer than a brother.

Josh cleared his throat. Steven laid Dana's hand on the bed and took a step back.

"Do you know what triggered this episode?" Josh asked. "Is it always the same?"

Dana shook her head. "It was silly. The double sinks in the bathroom made me think of how I have double sinks and how, at our other house, one was mine and one was Brandon's, and how Brandon's not here to use his anymore, and . . ." She sounded like she was close to tears. She waved her hand and took a deep breath. "Like I said, it was silly."

Steven knew there was more to it than his-and-her sinks but didn't push the issue. From the look on Josh's face, he didn't buy it either.

Chapter 7

Sunday after church, Josh changed out of his suit into shorts, a T-shirt, and running shoes. After eating, cleaning up the kitchen, and going through the paper, he found himself knocking at the Bradleys' back door. He thought he wouldn't bother them today. He didn't want to be a pesky neighbor, but still, here he was, knocking. He'd convinced himself that checking on Dana was the neighborly thing to do. It didn't matter that she was fine last night when he'd walked her and Patrick home.

He heard barking and saw Patrick through the window. Patrick called out that Mr. Peters was at the door and then opened it. Josh bent to pet Zoe. Patrick looked at him, looked around him, and looked to the left and right of the door.

"Where's Tori?" he asked.

"She went home with her grandparents after church today."

"Oh," Patrick said, obviously disappointed. "Do you want to talk to my mom?"

"If she's not busy."

"She's not. She's puttin' stuff in the Crock-Pot for supper. Come in." Josh stepped in, and Patrick shut the door. "Mom," he yelled, "Mr. Peters wants to talk to you."

Patrick led him into the kitchen. Dana placed the lid on a slow cooker and turned toward him. When she gave him a warm smile, Josh couldn't help but think how pretty she was.

"What's up?" Dana asked.

He wasn't going to tell her that he was checking on her. "I was wondering if you two would like to go for a walk. Tori's gone, and I'm kind of lonely."

Dana crossed her arms over her chest and eyed him skeptically. A spark of humor flashed in her eyes. "A walk? Somehow, Mr. Peters, you strike me as a runner, not a walker. We would slow you down."

Josh smiled at her. "I do usually jog, but I've been too busy lately. Walking will get me limbered up." He smiled more broadly. "I really would enjoy the company."

"Come on, Mom," Patrick said. "Let's go. I can ride my bike."

Patrick pedaled off when the three of them left Dana's drive. She warned him not to get too far ahead, and he stopped occasionally and rode back toward them. After a few minutes, Dana picked up her pace from their initial stroll, and the two of them hit a brisk, even tempo that was enough to get Josh's heart rate up.

"Brandon and I used to jog every day," she said after they'd walked for a few minutes in silence. "We had a jogging stroller for Patrick when he was little. We took turns pushing him."

Josh glanced over at her. She watched her son with a wistful smile.

"You miss him, don't you?"

She sighed. "Every day, but it gets a little easier as time passes."

Josh didn't believe it had gotten easier for her at all. "Have you seen a counselor?"

"I went through several months of grief counseling. Before that, I couldn't eat at all, and I had horrible nightmares. I don't have the nightmares anymore.

"I'm determined to get through this," she said after a couple of minutes. "I don't want to leave my son alone in the world."

"You two don't have any other family?"

"Jennifer and her bunch are like family. My mom and dad both died a few years ago. Brandon's family is all gone, too."

It seemed that sad events had permeated her life, and the last thing Josh wanted to do was make her think of her problems.

"My family's great," Josh said. "My parents live in E-town—in Indian Hills. I have a younger brother named Jordon who lives near Atlanta with his wife, Abby. They're expecting a baby."

"That's exciting! There's nothing like children to make life complete."

"I totally agree. I couldn't imagine life without Victoria."

They continued to walk the neighborhood. Dana kept a watchful eye on Patrick when they crossed streets and approached others on the sidewalk. The two of them talked about what Patrick and Victoria were like when they were babies, Josh talked about growing up in Elizabethtown, and Dana told him that she grew up a few miles from E-town in LaRue County.

"Is Victoria spending the day with your parents?" Dana asked when the conversation lulled.

"No, Monica's parents. My mom and dad are traveling near the Mediterranean right now. Victoria wasn't thrilled about going, but the Simpsons are her family. There's not much for her to do there. She has cousins who will be there, but they're all older than she is. She says they're not much fun."

"You're not the one who wanted the divorce, are you?"

The question caught Josh off guard. He focused on the sidewalk. "No, I didn't want to get divorced."

Dana squeezed his elbow. "I didn't mean to pry." After a second, she eased her hand away.

"You didn't pry. It's just . . ." He didn't know how to explain it. "I like being married, but Monica apparently doesn't, at least not to me." He glanced at her. She was studying him.

"Maybe Monica will change her mind when she realizes what she's missing."

"She left almost a year ago, and it hasn't happened yet. I've given up hope of her changing her mind."

"I'm sure you wouldn't have any trouble finding a woman who would love you and Victoria. Lots of women want to be wives and mothers."

"That would mean dating," he said.

"That is a socially accepted means of getting to know a prospective spouse."

He looked down at her. She was grinning. The woman was teasing him.

"It's been years since I asked a woman out. I wouldn't know where to begin."

She motioned toward Patrick. "It's like riding a bike. Once you learn, you never really forget. Even a child can ride a bike."

"Is that so? How many dates have you been on in the last couple of years?" Josh regretted the words as soon as they were out of his mouth. He glanced at her and was relieved to see that she was still smiling.

"Me?" she said with a dismissive wave of her hand. "I didn't date much before I married. Unlike you, I've had very little practice."

"Unlike me? What do you mean by that?"

She scanned him critically from head to toe and then tapped her chin with an index finger. "In high school, were you homecoming king or prom king?"

He cleared his throat. "Both."

"Ah," she said with a knowing smile. "I heard you tell Mark about playing baseball in college. I bet you were in some kind of fraternity, too."

"No, only baseball. That and classes were enough to keep me busy."

Even though she was smiling, she looked at him as though she didn't believe him.

"I did go to a lot of parties," he said after a moment.

"Of course you did. I bet you had your own fan club, too. And I bet that most, if not all, of that fan club was female."

He shrugged, and she laughed. The woman had a laugh that was open and sincere. Josh enjoyed the sound of it.

He pushed Patrick up a steep section of sidewalk. "So, what are you saying?"

"You're the friendly, popular type," she answered after her son pedaled away. "Popular people don't have problems finding dates."

"Oh, really? So what were you in high school? Homecoming queen or prom queen?"

She laughed and waved her hand again. "Neither. I'm more of a behind-the-scenes person. I was class president, student council secretary, National Honor Society member. Does the term *nerd* mean anything to you?"

"I don't believe you."

"You can ask Jennifer if you doubt it. I had friends who were guys, but not one boyfriend until Brandon. I didn't meet him until my junior year of college. We started pharmacy school the same year."

They had completed the circuit through the subdivision and were back in Dana's drive. Patrick parked his bike in the garage and hung his helmet from the handlebars. Josh watched him open the door and let the dog out. He ran after Zoe into the backyard.

"Lazy dog," he heard Patrick call. "You should've come with us."

"I think that does it for me today," Dana said. "I'm not used to exercising. I haven't had much energy since, well, you know. But this felt good. Thank you for asking us along."

"Thanks for coming," Josh said.

He waved and called out a goodbye to Patrick before starting off at a jog. As he made his way back through the neighborhood, he wondered what Dana would say if he asked her out to dinner.

Steven was thrilled when Dana called and invited him to dinner Sunday. She told him they would eat about six but for him to come anytime he wanted. He pulled into her drive at four o'clock.

Dana and Zoe greeted him at the door. The dog did her usual dance around his feet until he rubbed her behind the ears. Dana gave him a hug when he was upright again. Steven wanted to hold her and not let go, but he made himself release her.

Dana looked so much better than she had yesterday. There was a glow in her cheeks that had been missing for far too long.

"Where's Patrick?" he asked.

"In the basement. We're playing a game on the Wii. Would you like to play?"

"I'd love to."

On one of Patrick's turns, before a mini game started, Steven asked Dana if she had any plans the following weekend.

"Other than church on Sunday morning, no. Why?"

"I was wondering if you'd like to—"

Zoe barked and ran up the stairs. Dana stood. "Hold on. I think someone's at the door."

Steven watched her walk away. After a moment, he heard voices. From the sounds, he could tell Victoria and Josh were coming down the stairs with Dana. Steven stifled a groan and forced himself to smile at Josh's greeting.

"I'm sorry to intrude a second time today," Josh told Dana, "but Tori begged to see Patrick even if it was only for a few minutes."

"That's no problem," Dana said. "You all are welcome here anytime."

"Mario Party 8! Can I play?" Tori asked.

"Sure," Patrick told her.

"Here, Tori, take my remote," Dana said. "Patrick, fix the other one for Mr. Peters. You four play. I'll watch."

Dana teased and laughed with them while they played. Steven could tell she was enjoying herself. She looked good, better than he'd seen her look in a long time.

"Hey, Mom," Patrick said while he shook his remote and watched the screen during his turn. "How 'bout if Tori spends the night with me Friday?"

"Friday?" Dana asked. "Oh, that reminds me, Steven, you were saying something about the weekend before I went upstairs. What was it you were going to ask?"

Steven kept his eyes fixed on the TV screen. "It was nothing."

"What do you think, Josh? Would you mind if Tori stays over?" Dana said after a moment of silence.

"Please, Daddy."

"This would be a good opportunity for you to pursue what we discussed earlier today," Dana told Josh.

"I guess, but, I . . ."

Steven looked back and forth from Dana to Josh. He glanced at the kids who were whispering to each other. The abandoned game's music continued to play in the background.

"Surely you have someone in mind to ask," Dana said. "Don't be nervous. When you get back out there, it'll be easy for you."

"Well, I . . ."

Steven had never seen Josh Peters unsure of himself, but he looked as nervous as a twelve-year-old asking a girl to dance for the first time. Victoria crawled into her father's lap.

"I'll be right next door," Victoria said. "If you get lonely, I bet Ms. Bradley would let you stay, too."

Steven coughed.

Josh cleared his throat.

Dana laughed softly.

"It's a little different for grown-ups, honey," Josh told her after clearing his throat again. "But if Ms. Bradley doesn't mind, it's okay with me."

They moved upstairs. The kids took off toward Patrick's room after Josh accepted Dana's invitation to stay for dinner. Steven and Josh sat at the kitchen table while Dana finished the meal. She had refused their offers of help.

"Steven, Josh needs some ideas for eligible dates. Can you think of anyone?"

"Dana!" Josh said.

Steven laughed. Josh gave him a dirty look, and Steven laughed harder.

"It's not funny," Josh said. "It's been a long time since I asked a woman on a date."

Dana winked at Steven. "You're young. Prime dating age. Give the old guy some pointers."

Steven laughed again, and when Josh gave them both dirty looks, Dana laughed, too. After a moment, Josh broke down and laughed with them.

Josh leaned toward him. "Okay, Stevie boy. Whatcha got?"

"I don't date a whole lot. I never have."

"Really?" Josh and Dana said at the same time.

Steven shrugged.

Dana washed dough off her hands and put the pan of biscuits she'd been working on in the oven. Then she walked to the table and sat next to Steven. "I bet you'll be like Brandon."

"How's that?" Steven asked.

"When you meet the woman you're meant to be with, you'll just know. He didn't date much, but he told me that when he met me, he knew I was the one."

Steven wondered what Dana would say if he told her he already knew that she was the one for him, too.

"But, back to Josh's dating dilemma," she said.

"I do not need help here," Josh grumbled.

Dana waved off Josh's comment. "Don't be silly. All men need help when it comes to women. So, who do you know who would be a good match for Josh?"

Steven rubbed his chin and tried to look thoughtful. "Hmm."

"You and your dad both work with him," she said. "Surely you have mutual acquaintances who would be good date material."

"Let me think," Steven said. "He might like—"

"I'm sitting right here," Josh said.

Dana waved a hand in Josh's direction again. "Shh. Let Steven concentrate."

Josh shook his head. "This is ridiculous."

"Go ahead, Steven," Dana said. "Who did you have in mind?"

"She lives in this subdivision."

"Oh?" Josh asked with sudden interest.

Steven turned toward him. "Yeah. You designed her house for her. Ms. . . . Ms. . . . I can't remember her name. Her last name was a common first name. I remember that much."

"Not Ms. Shirley!" Josh said.

"What's wrong with her?" Dana asked.

"She hates children. She told me so herself. She said they're loud and messy and anybody who had one was crazy."

"Oh," Dana said. "Being one of the crazy ones, I completely understand your feelings on that. Who else?"

Steven thought for a minute. "How about that Jessica girl at the bank? I've seen her checking you out when we've been in there together. She always seems happy to see you."

"Jessica?" Josh said. "What is she? Twenty-five?" He shook his head.

"What's wrong with that?" Dana asked. "How old are you?"

"Forty. Too old for a twenty-five-year-old."

"I don't know about that," Dana said. "Mark's ten years older than Jennifer."

"Ten years is not fifteen years," Josh said.

"Age shouldn't matter if two people care about each other," she said.

Steven silently celebrated.

Josh narrowed his gaze on Dana. "That's not what you said the other night."

Dana stared back. "That's a completely different issue."

Steven looked from Dana to Josh, wondering what in the world they were talking about. Just when it started to feel tense, Dana looked at Steven and smiled.

"Can you think of anyone else?" she asked.

He thought for a minute and slapped the table when a name came to him. "Tammy Windsor."

Josh gaped at him.

"What?" Steven said. "I don't know her exact age, but I'm pretty sure she's somewhere in her mid to late thirties. She has kids. Two boys, I think. She's divorced, has been for a while."

Dana rubbed her hands together and wiggled her eyebrows. "Now we're getting somewhere. Is she nice? Attractive?"

"Sure," Steven said.

"There you go," she said to Josh. "How often do you see Tammy?"

"I'm going to see her tomorrow," Josh said, not sounding at all excited. "She's the real estate agent who sold my last house. She has a check for me to pick up."

"Perfect," Dana said. "You can ask Tammy on a date, take your check to the bank, and give Jessica a second look."

"Are you insane?" Josh said.

Steven used his hand to hide his smile.

Dana's expression looked grave. "Maybe a little, but there's something you should know about me if we're going to be friends."

"What's that?" Josh asked.

"I have a twisted sense of humor, and I love giving people a hard time."

Even though she didn't crack a smile, Dana's eyes sparkled. Steven was glad to see so much of the old Dana.

"That's true," Steven said. "Sometimes it's hard to tell when she's joking and when she's serious."

Josh spread his arms. "So all this was to torment me?"

Dana smiled innocently and then stood. With deliberate movements, she removed her biscuits from the oven. "It's not any of my business, but I do think you should ask Tammy out. It sounds like she'd be perfect for you."

Josh looked at her, moving his head slowly back and forth.

Dana left the room to gather the kids for dinner.

"How long have you known Dana?" Josh asked Steven after she was gone.

"Ten years."

"Did you know she was pulling my leg?"

"Not at first," Steven said. "It's been a long time since I've heard her joke around like that. Before the accident, she did it all the time."

Steven didn't get the chance to ask Dana out Sunday night, but he did enjoy the time with her, Josh, and the kids. He'd waited years. A little while longer wouldn't kill him.

Monday, after Patrick left with Josh and Victoria for school, Dana stripped the sheets off the beds, made them up with clean ones, started the washer, unloaded the dishwasher, and left the house to go for a walk. Sunday she ate three meals without being sick. The walk with Josh had made her feel so good that she wanted to make walking part of her daily routine.

Maybe exercising would help increase her appetite and keep the nausea at bay. It was worth a try.

She hadn't gone far when she heard rapid footfalls approaching from behind. She moved to the far right of the sidewalk to give the person room to pass. She was surprised when Josh fell into step beside her.

"Hey. Mind some company?" he said after catching his breath.

"No, not at all, but you probably want to finish your run and get to work, don't you? I think it'll be a while before I'm up for jogging."

"I'd like to walk with you if you don't mind."

"All right," she said.

He smiled that great smile of his, and she couldn't help returning it. She faced forward, trying to hide her reaction to him. "Walking yesterday felt so good, I decided to try it again today."

"Let's do this every day then, either in the morning after the kids are at school or in the afternoons when they get home. I'm sure they'd like riding their bikes along with us."

She glanced at him. "Now why would you want to go slow with someone as out of shape as I am?"

He shrugged, and his smile broadened. Dana figured out what was so captivating about his smile. He had dimples, wonderful dimples, on each side of his nicely formed mouth. She turned away again.

"If you prefer to be alone, I can go away," he said in a subdued tone.

Dana was glad he'd misread her. She didn't want him to know she thought he was attractive. Another part of her felt guilty. She didn't want to make him feel bad. He was only trying to be a friendly neighbor.

"Oh, not at all," she said without looking at him. "I like having company. I spend a lot of time alone since Brandon died." They continued to walk and she glanced at him. She could see the pity in his expression.

"Don't you dare feel sorry for me."

"I don't. I admire you, Dana."

Surprised, she studied him. He seemed quite sincere, but Dana knew she was no one to be admired. It had been two years since Brandon's accident, and she still puked when something sparked memories of him lying bloody and dead. She shook her head before the horrible picture could form in her mind.

"Did you get a chance to see Tammy Windsor today?" she asked.

"Not yet. I'm going to run by her office on my way to pick up the kids from school."

"Are you going to ask her?"

"I don't know. It seems weird to be forty years old and thinking about dating. I never envisioned my life being like this. What about you?"

"No," she answered, trying to not sound bitter. "I never considered the possibility of being a thirty-eight-year-old widow and single mother." She took a breath and let it out. "It's better not to know what life's going to deal out to us. Of course, even if I had known it would be this way, I would have married Brandon. He and Patrick are the best things that ever happened to me."

Remembering that kept her from completely losing her mind.

They walked in silence for a few minutes.

"Would you date if someone asked you?" Josh asked.

She turned to look at him. She knew her expression was sarcastic, but she couldn't help it. "I don't know if you've noticed it or not, but I'm not exactly the epitome of a man's dream date." She stretched out her arms. "I mean look at me. I wasn't much to look at before I lost so much weight, but now—"

"You didn't answer my question."

"No one is going to ask me to go on a date," she insisted.

"What if they did?"

She turned to look at him, laughed, and wagged a finger at him. "I know what you're doing, Josh Peters. You're giving me a hard time, trying to get even with me for how Steven and I did you yesterday."

He shook his head but didn't say anything. They were quiet for a while.

"You could practice on me, if you want," she said.

"Huh?"

"Practice on me. Pretend I'm Tammy. It'll be like rehearsing a scene in a play or something. It's been a while, but I've helped guy friends before. Mark practiced proposing to Jennifer on me."

"You're kidding!"

"No, he did. Brandon shot video of it, and the four of us watched it together after they were engaged. It was a hoot. Jennifer said he blew the whole thing, tripped over his words, did it nothing like he had rehearsed. Of course, that—and the fact that we laughed through most of the rehearsal—made it that much more hilarious to watch."

They had gone through the neighborhood and were approaching her driveway. She figured Josh would rather continue at a faster pace without her. She needed to build up her stamina before she'd be able to do more than one lap through the subdivision anyway.

She turned toward the house and was preparing to tell him goodbye, when he took her hand in his. Gently he pulled her until she faced him and held both her hands in his. She looked up at him, into his amazing blue eyes.

"Dana, we don't know each other well, but I'd very much like to spend more time with you. Would you like to have dinner with me this weekend?"

She swallowed. It took her a moment, but she suddenly realized what he was doing. She smiled.

"That's good! Just one thing, be sure to use her name. Other than that, it was perfect." She pulled her hands free of his grasp, crossed her arms over her waist, and tilted her head while she looked at him. "You should definitely ask her in person. You have a powerful presence. She would miss that on the phone."

When Dana turned and made her way toward the house, Josh stood rooted in her driveway and watched her. Either the woman had no idea that he wanted to date her, or she was skilled at gentle rejections.

He shook his head before heading off at a jog back over the path he and Dana had walked. He took two more laps through the neighborhood, went inside his house, showered, and sat at his computer to work. When he finished and saved the latest plan he'd been working on for Tom, his phone rang.

"Hello, Bradley, D.," he said after seeing her name on the caller ID. He heard her laughter over the line. She had a truly great laugh.

"Hello," she said. "Am I interrupting you?"

"Not at all. I'd just finished up something when the phone rang. It wouldn't matter if I was busy. A neighbor's call is welcome anytime."

"Ah, that's sweet. I wanted to know if you had any lunch plans."

Josh looked at his watch. He hadn't realized the morning was gone. "I don't. Do you have something in mind?"

"I thought I'd warm up the stew left over from last night. I, uh, don't do well eating alone and usually skip lunch unless I'm at school and eating with the kids. I thought since you were next door, you might like to eat with me."

Her asking him to lunch surely meant she didn't find him or his company unpleasant. "I'd love to," he said.

"Would you like to come over, or would it be more convenient if I brought the food to you?"

"Why don't you bring the stew over here? That way at least I'll be cleaning up the mess after you supplied the food."

She laughed again. "That seems fair. I'll be right over."

Josh greeted Dana at his back door, took the pan from her hands, and started heating it on the stove. "Would you like to see what I was working on?"

"Absolutely," she said.

Josh led her to his office and pulled up the file he had recently finished. He brought up each part, and explained the different elevations of the plans. She seemed interested and asked several questions about symbols and notations. When she asked to see the file for her house, he brought that up on the monitor so she could see it.

"Wow. So when you draw these plans, do you envision the finished home, or do you see it only in lines and angles?"

He thought about it. "Both."

"Mmm. I suppose you have to see it both ways to be able to do what you do. It amazes me that you can create all that out of your head. You're extremely talented. I love my home. It's as if you knew me when you designed it, even though I know you drew the plans for the site and not for me specifically."

"I'm glad you're happy in it." It always made him feel good to know a person was pleased with what he had designed, not only with the building itself but the home they made of it. As corny as it would sound to say aloud, he often thought about the lives of the people who would occupy the houses he designed.

He pulled up the plans he'd been doing for Tom and sent the file to the printer. Dana turned toward the machine once it started running. He laughed at her comment of how different his printer was from the ones used in the pharmacy.

They went back to his kitchen. He pulled out one of his stools and held it for Dana. He stirred the stew, set out dishes, and fixed them both a glass of ice water. All the while, they talked about the children.

"The other night after dinner, your friend Mark asked me if I'd be interested in helping him coach baseball. I'm considering telling him yes, and I was wondering if you'd let Patrick play on the team."

Dana looked at him quizzically. "You'd do that without having a child of your own playing?"

Josh nodded. "I love baseball. I have since I was a kid. I think it's a great sport for kids to learn. It teaches teamwork and cooperation. And it's fun." He smiled at her. She smiled back. "The only problem I would have is keeping Victoria occupied. She has no desire to be on a baseball team. I thought if you wanted, we could sort of trade off children."

She didn't say anything, and her expression became difficult to read.

"I don't know if you can tell or not, but my daughter adores you. Monica was never very . . ." He looked away while he searched for the right word. ". . . nurturing. I think Victoria would benefit by being around someone who is a good mother. I thought Patrick might miss having a dad as much as Tori longs to have a mother."

Dana's eyes grew wide.

"We live next door to each other. They go to school together. It makes sense for us to help each other."

Dana tilted her head and studied him. He had no idea what she was thinking.

"Victoria's a wonderful child," she said after a few moments. "I would love to spend time with her. I don't know about Patrick and baseball, though. I mean, I think it would be great for him to play. Mark and the boys tried to get him to play last year, but he wouldn't."

"Does he like sports?"

"Oh, sure. He started playing soccer before he was in kindergarten. Brandon coached him, but when he died, that changed many things for us, including soccer. Patrick still likes it and will fool around in the yard with a soccer ball, but he won't play on a team. I've tried to talk to him about it, but he insists it's because he doesn't want to. He says he'd rather be at home."

"Would you mind if I ask him?"

"No, not at all." She studied him again. "You're a very kind man."

He let his smile express his thanks, and she smiled back.

91

Monica covered her surprise with a cool smile when Marcus Taylor, not his secretary, met her and escorted her into his office. He greeted her cordially, asked her to make herself comfortable, motioned toward the leather chairs in the corner, and offered her a drink.

"I'll have a Perrier, please, Mr. Taylor."

He poured her mineral water over ice. "Please, call me Marcus. May I call you Monica?"

Monica nodded and accepted the offered glass. She took a sip to hide her smile. She was quite accustomed to welcome and not-so-welcome advances. She prided herself in her ability to deal with such situations and to use them to her advantage.

She took measure of Marcus Taylor. He pulled a plain bottle of water from his mini fridge and sat down opposite her. He was an attractive man, not exactly handsome, but he had an air of refinement about him. He still had a full head of dark hair with a touch of gray at the temples that added to his distinguished appearance. He was tall, not as tall as Josh, but he was above average. From what she could discern of his physique through his well-tailored suit, she would guess he kept a rigid workout schedule. She was surprised to see that he wore a wedding band on his left hand. Of course, that was part of the whole family-first persona he projected.

They worked through the typical small talk and their educational and professional backgrounds that she guessed they both already knew about each other. When he asked personal questions about her family, her parents, and where she grew up, she was apparently unsuccessful at hiding her surprise.

"Don't misunderstand me, Monica. It is not my intention to pry. If you're a private person, I completely understand. Please don't feel interrogated. I simply like to know about the people I work with. I have no ulterior motive apart from my own curiosity. I'm a people person. Always have been. Hannah, my wife, is constantly chastising me for being too 'chummy' for a man in my position. She laughs when she tells me this. Everyone, including her, knows she's even more interested in people than I am. Our kids call her nosy."

The man laughed and smiled easily, and Monica found herself relaxing. She listened while Marcus told more about his wife and his four children, and described his two grandchildren, both born within the last year. The man's open admiration and enthusiasm for his family amazed her.

"My husband is a talented architect," Monica said with pride she didn't have to feign. "He's at least partially responsible for many of the notable structures throughout Atlanta and the surrounding areas."

Marcus looked troubled, and his smile faded. "At which firm does he work?"

"Atlanta Architecture." That wasn't a complete lie. Josh was no longer on their regular payroll, but he had continued to do consulting work for the firm after they moved to Kentucky. As far as she knew, he still did that.

"Monica, surely you're aware that Atlanta Architecture is one of the firms bidding for the contract to design our new corporate offices. One of our employees being married to one of their employees may constitute a conflict of interest."

She sipped from her glass. "Of course I know they're one of the firms. Since I'm not on the board of directors and have no influence over the board's decisions, I didn't think there was any conflict. Otherwise, I would have said something earlier. I'm almost positive Josh told me their legal department had already checked into the issue."

"To be on the safe side, I'll have our lawyers double check. I look forward to meeting your husband, Monica. If he's as talented an architect as you believe him to be, I have no doubt that he'll be our main man on this design."

Monica smiled.

Chapter 8

"Are you too busy to talk?" Josh asked when Craig answered his phone Tuesday morning.

"No, just running refills through before we open. What's up?"

"I want to know what time would be good to come by the store with lunch for Dana."

"Lunch? For Dana?"

"Is that a problem?" Josh asked.

"She always works through lunch. From what the techs say, she doesn't even eat when she's here all day on Saturday."

"That's why I want to bring her food. And I want it to be a surprise. If she knows I'm coming, I think she'll try to stop me."

"It won't work. Elizabeth has tried to take her to lunch. She won't go."

"That's why I'm coming with food. She won't say no if I've already bought it. Help me out, here, will ya?"

Craig was quiet for a while, and Josh wondered what was going through his mind.

"Why are you doing this?" Craig finally asked.

"Why?" Josh hadn't expected Craig to ask for a reason. "Well, we're neighbors. Our kids go to school together. It's obvious she needs to eat, and I think I can help her get over this sickness. I want to try anyway. She's a nice person."

"That's true," Craig said. "She's the best pharmacist I've worked with. Even difficult patients love Dana." He was quiet for a minute. "I'd hate to see her get hurt. She's been through an awful lot."

"You think I'd hurt her? I'm trying to help her."

"I don't mean to offend you, Josh, but I thought you still cared for Monica."

"Monica is gone," Josh said after he loosened the tightness in his jaw. "All I'm trying to do is find out what time to bring lunch to my neighbor."

Several moments of silence followed. Then Craig said, "It's a good idea. Maybe you'll be able to pull it off. Be here by noon. That'll give you two thirty minutes and me enough time to take my lunch after she comes back. I'll talk to the other pharmacist about it, too, but I won't say a word to Dana."

After dropping off Patrick and Victoria at school, Dana drove to work. On her way through the store to the pharmacy, she greeted store employees and familiar customers. She put her purse in the closet and grabbed her pharmacy smock.

"Good morning," Craig said.

She finished logging her credentials into the terminal she usually operated and gave him a smile. "Morning."

"Carrie told me Friday night was rough. I hate that you got stuck with a mess."

She waved a hand. "Don't worry about it. How was Saturday?"

"Smooth as silk, believe it or not. I was surprised after the notes you left Friday."

Dana picked up the first prescription on the pile and began inputting the information in her computer. "How was Missy's recital?"

"The recital was long, but Missy did great. She didn't make a single mistake. Thanks for covering so I could go. Elizabeth wants to take you for a manicure sometime to make it up to you."

Dana grabbed a stock bottle off the shelf and set it on the counter along with the prescription and label she had printed. "No mistakes? Isn't that unusual for a first recital?"

"I know I'm her father, but she was so much better than any of the other kids. I think she may have a gift."

Dana patted Craig on the shoulder. "Missy's a special young lady."

They worked without conversation for a while. Carrie and another technician ran the register and counted while Craig and Dana processed prescriptions. Between checking and filling, Craig took phone calls and Dana counseled patients with new prescriptions or questions.

"How do you like having Josh for a neighbor?" Craig asked when he and Dana were both in the processing area again.

"Oh, he's great." She kept her face toward her computer monitor because she could feel a huge smile spread over her face.

"We went to high school together," Craig said.

"Yeah, he told me."

"He's a super guy. He was always popular and athletic, but he was friendly, too. Everybody liked him."

She processed a set of refills for a patient. "What do you know about Monica? She went to school with you, too, didn't she?"

"She was a year behind Josh and me. I'm not gonna lie to you. That's a relationship I never understood. In high school, Monica was the type to take care of herself regardless of how it affected anyone else. From what I can tell, she still is. I've always thought Josh was too good for her. They'd date, and she'd break up with him. They'd date other people, but when Monica decided she wanted him back . . ." He snapped his fingers. ". . . she'd get him. I think she wanted to keep him from being happy with anyone else, wanted to prove that she wielded some sort of power over him.

"I've never once heard Josh say anything against her, though. And I'm pretty sure the divorce wasn't his idea. Even before they married and moved to Atlanta, Monica acted as if E-town wasn't good enough for her. If you ask me, her going back to Atlanta was the best thing that could happen to Josh and Tori. It'd be great if he could find someone else, someone as good as he is."

"Do you know Tammy Windsor?"

"Who?" Craig asked with a blank look.

Dana waved a hand. "I don't know her either. Steven Farris and Josh both do. She's a real estate agent, and Steven thought she'd be a good match for Josh. She's also divorced and has a son or sons; I can't remember if it's one or two. Anyway, I'm trying to persuade Josh to ask her out. I thought if you knew her, we could move the process along a little bit."

She checked the refills that the techs had filled before turning to Craig again. "Can you think of anyone else who would be good for Josh to date?"

Craig stared at her a moment before he shook his head. "Well, I thought I did," he muttered.

Dana wasn't about to go there. Thankfully, business picked up, and the conversation ended.

They stayed busy for the next hour. Then a third technician came in, and the five of them worked steadily, processing, counting, answering phones, and running the register. The workflow backed up when Carrie went to lunch at eleven, but by ten minutes or so before twelve, they were caught up again.

Dana finished checking the filled prescriptions on the counter and was placing the stock bottles back on the shelves when she heard a familiar voice say he was here to see her. Her heart kicked up a notch, and she remained hidden for a few seconds.

When she came out from the bay of shelves, Craig and Josh were talking over the half wall between the waiting area and filling area. Josh gave her one of his amazing smiles. Of course, she smiled back, and her heart rate picked up again.

"Hey, Dana," Josh said before she could ask what was going on. "I was out and decided to drop by with some lunch for you. It's out in my truck."

She didn't eat at work. She couldn't run the risk of being sick here. She opened her mouth to offer an excuse.

"I wanted to thank you for having Tori over Friday and for helping me move in and for being such a good neighbor," he said before she could speak.

She waved a hand. "Oh, that's not necessary. Besides, I don't eat lunch when I'm working."

"The man brought food," Craig said. "From that bagel place you're always talking about trying."

"But we've been so busy this morning," she protested.

"We're caught up now. You always cover my lunch. Go!"

"Fine."

"You won't need to bring a thing," Josh said. "We won't even leave the parking lot. Everything's out in my truck."

Josh mouthed thank you to Craig when Dana went to the closet and left her white jacket. Holding Dana's elbow, he led her through the store and out into the parking lot. Josh asked how her day had been and listened while she told him about the flurry of business they'd had that morning. When the two of them reached the truck, he opened the passenger side for her and helped her into the seat.

"What?" he asked in response to the look on Dana's face.

"I'm not helpless. I can get into a truck."

"I'm sure you can, but my mama raised a gentleman." He bowed with exaggerated gallantry before shutting the door. The sound of her laughter reached him from inside the truck.

When he got to the driver's side and opened the back door, he pulled the bags containing their lunch from his cooler and passed everything between the seats to Dana. Then he joined her in the front.

He picked up one of the bags. "I wasn't sure what you liked, so I got three different sandwiches. You pick first. I like them all. There's chicken salad, ham and Swiss, and turkey breast with white American cheese. All of them are on whole-wheat bagels. Which would you like?"

"Could I have the chicken salad? I don't suppose you got pickles on it, did you? I love pickles."

He pulled a small container of pickles from the bag in his lap and handed it to her. "Your wish is my command, madam."

She took the container from him and laughed.

"I brought salads for both of us, too. I had them throw in a variety of dressings."

Josh handed Dana one of the salads and a fork, then spread the salad dressing packets on the console between them.

He made a point of keeping the conversation going. He'd always been interested in other people, but he found he was especially interested in Dana. They talked about the kids, their jobs, and her work in the library at school. Josh was pleased to see that she'd eaten most of her sandwich and her salad. He was feeling more confident in his plan. She didn't look nauseated.

Together they gathered the trash and stuffed it into one of the empty paper bags. Josh looked down when he felt Dana's hand on his arm. He resisted the urge to place his other hand over hers. It struck him that he might be in trouble. She didn't seem to be attracted to him at all, and he found himself more attracted to her every day.

When she thanked him for lunch, he lifted his gaze from her hand to her face.

"You really didn't have to do it," she said. "I enjoy Tori and helping you. I'd be happy to help you anytime."

Josh continued to gaze at her. It took a moment for what she said to register. After all, the thanking-her thing was merely a ploy to get her to eat with him.

"Oh, well, that's what friends do. Nice things for each other, I mean. Besides, eating here with you is better than the canned whatever or the frozen dinner I would have had at home alone. Let's do it again tomorrow."

He could tell she was trying to think of an excuse. "Please," he added, along with his best smile.

She laughed. "All right." She looked out into the parking lot. "Well, I better get back to the grindstone. I'll take care of the trash on the way in. Thanks again, Josh. Remember, I pick up the kids this afternoon. See you later."

With that, she was out of the truck, trash in hand, headed across the parking lot. She hadn't even given him a chance to walk her back into the store. He looked at his watch. That was the fastest thirty minutes he could remember spending.

Wednesday evening after he and Tori finished dinner, Josh sat in his office rolling a baseball in his hand. Victoria was in her bathtub. He could hear her singing. She loved to sing in the tub. Monica had always hated it.

Josh's thoughts weren't focused on his ex-wife or even his daughter. He was thinking about his neighbor. Thoughts of her occupied his mind more every day.

Tuesday afternoon when Dana brought Tori home from school, he asked again about afternoon walks. Shamelessly, he'd asked in front of the children. He knew Patrick and Victoria would want to ride their bikes together every day while he and Dana walked. He wasn't opposed to using their powers of persuasion. It worked; they did one lap through the neighborhood yesterday and two today.

They'd had lunch together Monday, Tuesday, and today, and she already looked better. She hadn't noticeably gained weight, but her color had improved and she seemed to have more energy than she had had a few days before. She'd even told him that she hadn't been sick since Saturday at his house. Apparently, that was a record number of days without vomiting for her.

More than once he'd tried to bring up the subject of dating. Except encouraging him to ask Tammy, she politely evaded it. He didn't understand it. She seemed to enjoy the time they spent together but must still be so in love with Brandon that she wouldn't entertain the thought of involving herself with another man.

Josh tossed the signed and worn baseball from his last year on the UK team from one hand to the other. He was going on a date Friday. He didn't want to go. That was terrible. Why had he asked her if he didn't want to? He couldn't help but think how differently he'd feel if it were Dana going to dinner with him Friday instead of Tammy. That was completely unfair to Tammy, and he felt guilty.

"What are you thinking about, Daddy?"

Josh held the ball in his fist and turned toward the doorway of his office. Tori stood in her nightgown with her brush in her hand. He smiled at her. "Why do you think I'm thinking?"

She walked over and climbed into his lap. He wrapped his arms around her and inhaled the strawberry scent of her shampoo.

"You're always thinking about something when you toss one of your baseballs that way."

He leaned forward and placed the ball in the holder on his desk. He took her brush out of her hand and shifted her in his lap so that he could brush the tangles from her damp hair. "I was thinking about this and that."

She was quiet while he worked the brush through her hair.

"I know something," she said after a while.

"Oh? What do you know?"

"I know that Patrick wants to play baseball even though he told you he didn't. I know why he said no, too."

"How do you know Patrick wants to play ball?"

"He told me so," she said.

He finished with the brush and set it on his desk. He leaned back in his chair and pulled Tori against him. Her hair made his shirt wet, but he didn't care. He knew her crawling into his lap would stop before he was ready for it to. She'd be grown before he knew it. He savored moments like this and often wished it were possible to freeze time.

"Tell me what you know about Patrick and baseball," he said.

"He misses playing soccer with his dad. Patrick's really good at soccer. He's always the best when we play in PE."

"Hmm."

"He doesn't like to leave his mom alone. He knows he has to go to school and on the weekends when his mom has to work, he spends the night with Alex on Friday. He thinks practice would leave her alone too much. He said she would come to the games, but he's afraid she would be alone while he's at practice." Tori twisted so that he could see her face. "I told him I would stay with her so he could go to practice. I told him how I really like his mom." She shifted her head back and forth. "I didn't tell him that I wanted her to be my mom. I promise."

Josh rubbed her arm reassuringly. "I know you didn't, honey."

"Tomorrow, could you ask Patrick again? I think he'd say yes this time. And talk to Ms. Bradley so I can be with her when you and Patrick are gone? I really like her, Daddy."

She snuggled closer to him, and Josh tightened his hold on her. He kissed her strawberry-scented hair. "I know you do, sweetheart. I like her, too. I'll talk to Patrick after school tomorrow."

On Friday, Dana saw Josh's truck turn into the sub-division ahead of her. She parked in her drive and walked across the yards. The kids both waved before taking off into Josh's house. Josh waited for her in his drive. When she drew close, he smiled. She felt a tingle inside and told herself the response was ridiculous. She smiled back at him anyway. Smiling at the man was like a reflex.

"How was the pharmacy today?"

"Steady." She walked through the door he held open for her. "How was the architectural business?"

"It was good. Would you like to see what I've been working on the last couple of days?"

"Absolutely."

She could hear the kids' squealing and turned toward Victoria's room when she and Josh walked by.

"They've made some major plans for tonight," Josh said. "I hope you don't expect to get much sleep."

"They won't bother me. I always lock Patrick and his friends in the basement when he has someone spend the night."

Josh's head jerked around. His eyes were wide.

"I'm joking," she said, without cracking a smile. "I'm a pharmacist, for heaven's sakes. I drug them to get them to go to sleep."

"Uh, maybe I should call and cancel this evening."

She waved her hand and made a face. "Nonsense. Can't you take a joke? I stopped drugging Patrick when he picked up on it at the age of four. He can smell it when I put it in his drink. I can't get it by him."

Josh laughed that time, shook his head, and sat down at his desk. What he brought up on the screen didn't look like any building she'd ever seen. Dana leaned forward to get a closer look. It was amazing, kind of a mix of modern and classic styles. Dana knew nothing about architecture, but she knew that whatever this building was, it was original and creative. "Wow! What is it?"

She turned to look at his profile. He had laugh lines at the corners of his eyes and a few gray hairs mixed with the light brown hair that thickly covered his head.

He had a freckle on his left earlobe. He turned and caught her studying him. His face was close to hers. If she moved a few inches, she'd be able to kiss his cheek.

She pulled back, stood, and cleared her throat. "What is it?" she asked again.

He continued to look at her for a moment before turning to face the computer screen. "It's an idea for the firm I worked for in Atlanta, for an office building. They're putting together a proposal to bid for a design contract. The man who was my supervisor there emailed me Tuesday and asked for my input."

"Do they pay you for that?"

He nodded and stood. "I've consulted for them several times since I moved back to E-town."

They both turned when Victoria and Patrick came into the room. They struggled with an overfilled pink duffle bag.

"What do you have there?" Josh asked his daughter.

Tori grunted when they dropped the bag on the floor. "My stuff to stay over at Patrick's."

Josh looked down at the bag's overflowing contents and grinned. An army of stuffed animals, a puzzle, Uno cards, and a Nintendo DSi were visible.

"Do you have any clothes in there?" Josh asked.

Tori looked at Patrick who shrugged. Tori looked back at her dad and shook her head.

"Pajamas? Toothbrush?" Josh asked.

Tori shook her head again. Josh picked her up and tickled her. She giggled and squirmed.

"Maybe I should help you pack another bag," Josh said after he set her back on the floor. "Go change your clothes if you want, and I'll fix us all a snack before we pack it." He turned toward Dana. "Would you and Patrick like to stay and have an after-school snack with us?"

"Patrick can stay, but I need to run home and let Zoe out." Dana noticed the look on her son's face. She patted his back. "It'll be fine, honey. You stay as long as you want. Well, as long as Mr. Peters says it's okay."

"You sure, Mom?"

"Absolutely."

Dana looked at Josh when he cleared his throat. "I've been meaning to talk to you about the Mr. Peters thing. It makes me feel old. Would you mind if Patrick calls me Josh?"

"I don't mind," she said, "as long as Tori calls me Dana."

It was eight thirty when Josh took Tammy home. He opened the door of his truck, helped her out, and walked with her to her porch.

"Would you like to come in for a while?" she asked. "My boys are with their father."

Josh smiled. "I should get back home. Victoria's at a neighbor's. She's never stayed there without me before."

"Oh."

Her obvious disappointment didn't make Josh change his mind.

"I completely understand about kids," Tammy said. "Seems they're always needing something. At least my ex is around to take them off my hands once in a while. It must make it rough on you with Monica living so far away."

Josh gave her a noncommittal smile. "Thank you for understanding."

"Oh, thank you, Josh. I had a great time tonight, even if it has ended too soon."

Tammy rose up and pressed her lips against his. He hadn't expected that. He returned the kiss with slight pressure and eased away before it moved into anything more.

He backed toward the steps. "Good night."

"Good night, Josh. Thanks again."

She waved goodbye when he backed from her drive. Even though he didn't want to spend more time with Tammy, he wasn't ready to go home, not alone. For more than thirty minutes, he drove around. Then he parked in his garage, walked across the yard, and knocked on Dana's back door.

He heard Zoe bark, but it was several minutes before the outside light came on and Dana's face was in the window. She looked surprised to see him. Josh wasn't sure, but he thought she looked happy, too. She smiled at him anyway.

"Is everything all right?" she asked. "I didn't expect to see you until tomorrow."

He stepped in and closed the door. "Everything's fine. I . . ."

"Missed Tori," she said. She placed a hand on his arm and squeezed. "Come on in. We're hanging out in the basement. I'm painting Tori's nails. She said you wouldn't mind. It's a pale pink polish. If you think it's too much, I can take it off before she goes home tomorrow."

"I'm sure it's fine, if you think it is."

Motioning for him to follow, Dana walked toward her basement door. Suddenly she stopped, turned, and looked at him. Her head was tilted to the side. "Your date didn't go well, did it?"

Josh didn't know how to explain how he felt, except he felt like a failure. He was supposed to be happily married with a family—settled, not dating, not kissing women on their front porches. "It didn't feel right. I don't know how else to explain it."

She gave him a sympathetic smile. "You'll find her. I'm sure she's out there." She studied him for a moment. "Do you want to stay for a while? You're more than welcome. The kids would love it, especially Patrick. I think he's feeling a little outnumbered. Nail polish is not his thing."

Josh smiled and nodded. How in the world this woman, who had so much wrong in her life, could make things feel so right was beyond him.

She moved behind him and pulled his sport coat from his shoulders. "The first thing you need to do is get comfortable." He shrugged off his jacket, and she hung it over the back of one of her kitchen chairs. "Now untuck your shirt."

"My shirt?"

"Yes, of course. You look fabulous and all, but this is about comfort. Look at me." She put one hand on a hip and struck a silly pose for a second.

He let his gaze move from her head to her toes. She had on green flannel pajamas with sheep on them and matching green socks. She looked cute—very cute. He smiled. She hadn't run and hid this time when he caught her in her PJs.

"See," she said, "not at all fabulous but extremely comfortable."

He disagreed. She looked fabulous and comfortable.

By the time he followed her down the basement steps, his belt was off, his shirt tail hung over his slacks, and he was in his sock feet. Tori didn't seem at all happy to see him until he assured her she didn't have to leave. After that, she was fine and jabbered about her nails, the pizza they'd had delivered for supper, and the banana splits they made together.

"I hope you don't mind junk food," Dana whispered. "I think a good junk food night every now and then is good for the soul."

"I agree," he said.

When Tori's nails had dried, the four of them snuggled on the couch with pillows and blankets and watched a movie. The lights were dim, and partway through the movie, both children fell asleep. Somehow, Patrick's head rested on one of Josh's legs, Zoe's rested on the other, and Dana held Tori across her lap. Josh hadn't felt such a sense of home and belonging the entire time he and Monica were married. He envisioned Brandon and Dana spending many evenings like this one. He studied Dana whose gaze rested on the children. She reached out to lift a strand of hair off Victoria's cheek.

"Did you slip the drugs into the pizza or the ice cream?" he asked.

She laughed quietly but didn't say anything.

"They grow up so fast, don't they?" she said after a moment.

"Too fast."

She caressed Tori's hair. "Did you and Monica ever think about having other children?"

"I did. Monica didn't. She had her tubes tied after Victoria was born. She didn't like being pregnant."

Dana looked at him. "Did she have trouble?"

"No."

She looked from Patrick to Tori. "That's too bad. I would love to have had more children."

"Why didn't you?"

"Gestational hypertension. I was on bed rest for about a month before Patrick was born. Even with bed rest, I went into pre-eclampsia, and Patrick was born four weeks early. I had to have a C-section on top of it all because he was breech. Brandon said he wasn't putting me through that again. He had a vasectomy before Patrick's first birthday."

"I'm sorry."

She leaned her head on the back of the sofa. "There's nothing to be sorry about. I have a son who, for the most part, is healthy and happy. A lot of people don't have that."

Dana Bradley amazed him. Josh wished he'd spent his entire evening with her.

Dana had just finished showering and dressing Saturday morning when she heard the sound of a mower outside her bedroom window. She pulled back the curtains and looked outside. Josh drove a shiny, bigger-than-necessary piece of lawn equipment over her recently established lawn. Josh said something last night about using Mark's trailer to pick up a new lawn mower. Nothing had been said about it being used to mow her grass.

Something was wrong with this picture. It was one thing for the man who had been her husband's best friend and who also happened to be married to her best friend to insist on mowing her grass, but she was not going to accept the charity of the next-door neighbor.

Dana checked to be sure Victoria and Patrick were occupied before she stepped out onto her back porch. Mark waved and jogged over.

"Dana, my love, how are you this morning?" When his eyes met hers, he stopped and the smile left his face. "What's the matter?"

"Why is Josh mowing my grass?"

"Because it needs to be mowed?"

She crossed her arms over her chest. "You know what I mean, Mark. It's one thing for me to accept charity from you, but I'm not going to accept it from my neighbor."

"He's a good guy. He only wants to help. Besides, that mower's too big for his small yard. He needs your yard to be able to turn it around. You know how guys are. With age, the toys we buy get bigger."

She couldn't help smiling.

Mark stepped up next to her and put his arm around her shoulders. "It's not like you to get angry. What's going on?"

She dropped her arms and sighed. "I don't know. Maybe I'm tired of feeling helpless."

He squeezed her. "Helpless? You and my wife are the least helpless people I know. Men. Now men are helpless. I couldn't get dressed without Jennifer telling me what to wear. Tell me Brandon wasn't the same way."

She stared at Mark, her eyes wide.

"Oh, Dana, I am so, so sorry."

"Why are you sorry?"

"Well, I mean . . . Jennifer and I decided we shouldn't talk about him. We thought it would help you not be sick."

"I miss talking about him," she said. "I want us to talk about him again."

"Okay." He dropped his arm and shifted to face her. "Don't be mad at Josh. I don't know the man well, but something tells me . . . Oh, I don't know what I'm saying, but be nice to him. Okay?"

Josh drove up and cut the engine. He swept an arm above the mower and looked at her. "How do you like it?"

"It's big."

He laughed. "Mark told me he mowed your lawn. I thought since I'm right next door that it would make more sense for me to mow it for you. I hope you don't mind."

Self-pity and pity from others were things she despised, and she wanted to tell him she didn't need his. She glanced at Mark and then back at Josh. She'd never been good at confrontation. It was easier to let things slide.

"I hope you'll let me," Josh said. "I haven't mowed grass since I lived at home with my parents. In Atlanta, I lived in apartments. At our house here, Monica wanted everything to be professionally done. I'm looking forward to taking care of things myself."

Her shoulders sagged; she'd lost another battle. "I don't mind if you mow my yard. It's very kind of you. You need to think of some way to let me repay you."

Darn the man if he didn't give her a huge smile. And of course, she had to smile back. It was so unfair that he had such an affect on her.

Less than an hour later, Josh was at Dana's back door asking if she and Patrick would like to go shopping with him and Tori for baseball gear.

"I can't," Dana told him after she invited him inside. "I have some housework I need to get done. I don't mind if Patrick goes with you, if you don't mind my not going along."

"No, I don't mind. I'd like for you to go, but I understand if you can't."

Dana excused herself, went to her laundry room, and pulled her wallet from her purse. She turned around to find Josh standing in the entry of the small room.

"You don't need to send money, if that's what you're doing," he said.

Trying to keep a rein on her temper, she took a deep breath and slowly released it. "I am not a charity case. I am not financially strained. I do not need you to buy my son's baseball equipment."

He gave her a grin that made her anger evaporate. "There's something you should know about me if we're going to be friends."

"And what's that?"

"I like to do things for people. I'm a nice guy."

She shook her head in defeat and returned the wallet to her purse. "All right, but I don't understand why you're doing all of this."

He stepped closer to her. "All of what?" he murmured.

A freshly showered, masculine scent surrounded her. She dropped her gaze to the floor. "The walks. The lunches. Mowing my grass. Buying baseball stuff for Patrick."

Dana was stunned when Josh wrapped his arms around her. For a second, she couldn't breathe. She wouldn't allow herself to return his embrace, but her cheek rested against his chest.

"Why do you work in the library at school?" he asked.

"What does that have to do with anything?"

"Why did you work so Craig could make Missy's recital Friday? Why did you help me move in Saturday?"

"I—"

"You're a nice person, Dana. You do nice things for people. Let me do a few nice things for you. We're friends, aren't we?"

A friend's hug had never caused her heart to pound in her chest. She heard the kids coming up the basement stairs. She pulled away from him and moved out of the laundry room before the children came into the kitchen.

When she told Patrick that Josh wanted to take him and Victoria to look for the things he needed for baseball, she could tell Patrick didn't want to leave her at home. She did her best to reassure him. She needed time alone, time away from Josh, and time to figure out what was going on inside her. She wasn't supposed to feel this way. She loved Brandon; she would always love Brandon.

While she scrubbed the bathrooms and picked up around the house, she kept telling herself that the way Josh treated her was nothing special, not for him anyway. He was simply a good person who went out of his way to be kind and generous to those around him. The idea of falling in love with Josh Peters scared the hell out of her. By the time she finished cleaning, she had convinced herself that they would be no more than friends.

Later that evening, Jennifer, Mark, and their kids came over. Dana invited Josh and Tori. It would have been rude not to.

Josh ended up manning her grill while she got the other food together inside. She studied Mark, Jennifer, and Josh through the window. The three of them talked and laughed while they watched the children play in the yard. It was so much like when Brandon was here.

She couldn't help wondering if Josh was the reason she hadn't been sick this last week. That hadn't happened since the accident. She hadn't taken any Zofran today either. She'd thought about Brandon, too. She always thought about him. Her thoughts hadn't included the end, though. She'd been able to keep those visions pushed to the far reaches of her mind. She wondered how long she'd be able to do that. She shook her head. She certainly didn't want to bring the horrible images to the forefront on purpose.

"He's something else, isn't he?"

Dana hadn't noticed Jennifer's entrance, and she felt a hint of shame because she'd been caught gawking at a man. She jerked her gaze away from Josh, turned from the window. and cleared her throat. "Who?"

"Your neighbor," Jennifer said.

She walked across the room and pulled hamburger and hot dog buns out of the pantry. "Oh, yeah. He's great."

"Uh-huh. He's good-looking, too."

"Is he? I hadn't noticed."

"Liar," Jennifer said.

Dana opened the refrigerator, pulled out bottles, jars, and bowls, and set them on the counter. "How are the kids doing in school?"

Jennifer walked across the kitchen and shut the refrigerator door. "Brandon wouldn't want you to stop living."

Dana looked at her. She refused to let herself cry.

"We messed up," Jennifer said. "We thought not talking about him would be the best thing for you. I see now how wrong we were. You know we love you, don't you?"

Dana hugged her. "Of course I do. I never would have made it through the past two years without you and Mark. You're the best friends anyone could hope to have."

"This could be a second chance for you, Dana. I don't think you should ignore it."

She pulled away. "Josh?"

Jennifer nodded. "His daughter thinks you hung the moon, and Josh is good with Patrick. I saw all the things he bought so the four of you can play ball together. Can you believe he's going to help coach the ball team?"

"No, not really," Dana murmured.

"I'm not saying you should run out and marry the man or anything. Just keep an open mind."

Chapter 9

Steven hadn't seen Dana for more than a few minutes in nearly two weeks. He'd been busy working on his term programming project and had only seen her the couple of times he'd run into the grocery to pick up something quick for dinner.

With his project completed, he called her at work Friday and arranged to pick up her and Patrick after school so they could visit Grandma Farris with him. His grandmother loved Dana.

Steven pulled into Dana's drive behind her Avalon. He saw her in Josh's drive and walked over. The kids were climbing out of the truck; Josh and Dana were grabbing lunch boxes and backpacks.

"Hey, Steve," Josh said. "How's it going?"

"Great. My project's finished. It's downhill now. Next stop, graduation."

Dana gave him a hug. "Good for you, Steven."

After talking for a few minutes, the three of them said goodbye to Josh and Tori, and walked across the grass with Zoe trailing behind them. After Patrick changed clothes, they got into Steven's Accord and headed for his grandmother's house.

Grandma Farris met them at the door, delivered and received her customary hugs and kisses, and ushered them into her kitchen. They settled around the table with a plate of homemade cookies, sweet tea for the adults, and a glass of milk for Patrick.

"Young man, you grow at least a foot every time I see you," Grandma told Patrick.

Patrick grinned at her. She patted his hand and asked him to tell her what he'd been up to. The three adults listened to Patrick talk about Tori and Josh moving next door and how he was going to play baseball.

"I bet you'll be the best one on the team," Grandma told him. That earned her another big grin. "Be sure your mom lets me know when your games are, and I'll come and watch you play."

Grandma pulled out a puzzle for Patrick, and Dana and Steven helped him with it while they visited. When the puzzle was complete, Grandma took Patrick to her butler's pantry so that he could get a treat. It was a tradition. Steven remembered getting goodies from the treat jar on every visit when he was a kid.

"Is Patrick spending the night with your friend tonight?" Steven asked Dana when they were alone in the kitchen.

"Yes."

"I was wondering if I could bring a movie out tonight and test your surround sound in the living room. The subwoofer needs to be tried out. *Jurassic Park* would be a good movie for that, and I thought it would be good to watch while Patrick's gone. It's kind of violent."

"I'm staying for dinner when I take Patrick to Jennifer's. After that, I have no plans, but I don't want you wasting your Friday night on my sound system."

He smiled at her. "What time would be good for you?"

Alone in his office, Josh leaned back in his chair and tossed his baseball back and forth between his hands. He let the events of the week, more specifically the time he'd spent with Dana, run through his mind.

He'd spent time with her every day. They walked and talked together, usually with the children, a couple of times without them. The four of them spent hours since Saturday playing ball together. He'd persuaded her to let him continue to bring her lunch on the days she worked. The more time he spent with her, the more time he wanted to spend with her.

Something had changed between them Saturday. Something that told him the attraction wasn't one sided, but since Saturday, she'd been careful to avoid any physical contact with him. When he tried to talk to her about it, she skillfully avoided the subject.

Josh placed the baseball back on his desk and ran a hand through his hair. This was ridiculous. He knew she was home and that she was alone. He'd heard her pull in a few minutes earlier, returning from taking Patrick to stay the night with the Morgans. His parents were back from vacation and after dinner with them, he'd left Victoria to spend the night at their house. Maybe if he went over now, he'd be able to get her to talk about whatever was going on.

He left his house and strode across the grass to her back door. He smiled when he saw her through the window and felt his smile widen when she smiled in return.

"Did your parents have a fun trip?" she asked after he stepped inside.

"I think so. They're happy to be home, though." He heard the sound of a car in the drive. "You expecting company?"

"That's Steven," she said.

"You have plans to spend the evening with Steve?"

Dana nodded and waved a hand toward her living room. "He wants to test out my subwoofer speaker thingy or something like that. He's bringing a movie for us to watch."

"You two have a date?"

She looked at him with an expression of stunned disbelief. "No! Steven's like a brother to me. What's wrong with you?"

He pulled her away from the door. "I need to talk to you, but it will take longer to tell you than it will take Steve to get to the door."

"All right," she said slowly. "Would you like to stay and watch the movie? We can talk afterward."

"Yes," he said without hesitation. He leaned down, kissed her cheek, and brushed his skin against hers when he eased away from her. She blushed and looked flustered. He smiled. She was attracted to him.

She moved away from him to answer the door. Josh watched Steve's face while Dana greeted him with a friendly kiss and hug. When Steve saw him, his expression changed.

"Josh," Steve said with surprise.

"Hey," Josh said, smiling. Steve returned his smile halfheartedly.

The three of them sat on Dana's sofa—Steve on her left and Josh on her right. No one spoke. About halfway through the movie, Josh's phone rang.

He pulled it out and silenced it. "Sorry." He checked the display and then told Dana he'd be back. He moved through the kitchen and slipped out the back door.

"Hello, Josh," Monica said when he answered.

"What do you want?"

"It is so good to hear your voice."

"What do you want?" he repeated.

"To talk to you. It's been a while. Have I caught you at a bad time? You sound upset."

"No, I'm not upset, but I am busy."

"Surely you're not too busy to talk to me."

"Actually, Monica, tonight I am. Why don't you get to the point?"

She sighed. "I miss you."

If she'd told him she'd sprouted wings and could fly, he wouldn't have been any more shocked.

"I want to see you." She paused as if she expected him to say something. "I thought maybe you were doing some work for Abe. I was hoping you might be coming to Atlanta sometime soon."

Josh walked in a circle through the grass of Dana's backyard. He looked at her house and wondered what she and Steve were doing.

"Josh? Are you still there?"

"I'm here."

Monica talked a few more minutes, but Josh wasn't listening, not really. His mind was trying to process the fact that she'd called in the first place, not to mention the fact that she wanted to see him. None of it made sense. The sale of their house, specifically the money involved, had been the focus of all her other phone calls.

Once the call ended, he glanced again at the windows of Dana's house, checked his watch, and went home.

Steven left Dana's less than an hour after the movie was over. He drove around for a while before parking his car. Sitting in a driveway, he could see lights on in the house and people moving around inside. Instead of going in, he sat and thought. Finally, he closed his eyes and let his imagination have free rein.

In his mind, he mustered the courage to do what he hadn't yet been able to accomplish in reality. Deciding it was now or never, he strode to the door and gave a quick knock. Sooner than he expected, the porch light came on and Dana stood in the open doorway inviting him inside.

"Is Patrick in bed?" he asked after he followed her into her living room.

She nodded. "He's been asleep for a while."

Steven put his hands in his pockets and paced back and forth.

Dana leaned on the door frame between her living room and kitchen with her arms crossed over her chest. "Okay, Steven, what is it? Are you having girl trouble? Do you need some female advice?"

With a groan, he crossed the room and stood in front of her. He put his hands on each side of her face and pressed his lips to hers. After the kiss ended, he pulled away far enough to look into her face. Shock was apparent in every part of her expression.

"I've wanted to do that for ten years," he murmured.

She touched her fingertips to her lips. "I don't understand."

"I love you, Dana. I have for a long time."

"You love me?" she said in disbelief.

"I do. I loved you even before Brandon died."

Dana pulled out of his grasp and put a hand to her head. "Okay, Steven. I'm having a hard time getting my brain around this." She walked over and dropped onto her sofa.

He sat down next to her. "Why?"

She looked at him with wide-eyed wonder. "I'm so much older than you. I have a seven-year-old."

He took her hands in his. "I like children. I think Patrick's a great kid, and he likes me, too.

"I've been in love with you since I was fourteen. I used to sit and watch you working in the pharmacy. I think about you all the time. The more I'm with you, the more I want to be with you." He ran the back of his fingers over her cheek. "I think you're beautiful."

For several moments, she sat with her head tilted to one side, looking at him as if she'd never seen him before. Steven leaned forward to kiss her again, but she jumped up and paced as he'd done a few minutes before.

"This cannot be happening," she muttered. "This is not possible." She stopped moving and looked at him. "Steven, you're twenty-four."

"So?"

"Twenty-four," she repeated and began pacing again. "I'm thirty-eight. Thirty-eight, Steven. When I was learning to drive, you were probably still in diapers. When I graduated from high school, you weren't even in kindergarten. When I—"

He stood. "Stop it! Just stop it. I know there's an age difference, but I don't care." He walked toward her and wrapped his arms around her. "I'm a man now. I'm not a boy anymore."

"I know that," she said in an understanding tone. She looked up at him and placed her hands on his arms. "You are a kind, handsome, and wonderful man. You have your whole life ahead of you. I've already lived much of mine. I'm a widow, for heaven's sake, with a son."

"It's not like you have one foot in the grave, Dana, and I already told you, I like Patrick. I could learn to be a father."

She pulled away and paced again. He stopped her, pulled her close, and lifted her chin so that he could look into her eyes.

"Dana, the age difference doesn't matter to me. We could work through all that. Tell me. Do you think you could love me?"

Steven opened his eyes with a start when he heard someone pound on his car window. Oh, well, his encounter with Dana probably wouldn't turn out any better in reality than it had in his mind. He turned the key in his ignition and pushed the button to lower his window.

"I thought it was you," his friend Brett said. "Hey, I just got back from a beer run. Help me pack it in."

Steven got out of his car and pulled out his wallet. "I didn't have a chance to pick up anything. Put this toward what you bought." Steven handed him a twenty and some smaller bills.

Together the two of them took four cases of Bud Light from the bed of Brett's truck and carried them into the house. Music was playing, and people were everywhere. Steven recognized most of them, and he heard shouts of varied greetings from every direction. He forced a smile and called back hellos.

He followed Brett into the kitchen. At Brett's direction, he put the cases he'd been carrying in the refrigerator. A bottle of mustard and a bottle of ketchup were the only signs of food. Everything else was a drink of some sort and most of it was alcoholic. Steven couldn't imagine why Brett needed more beer. He turned from the fridge and helped Brett empty his two cases into the sink and cover the cans with ice.

Brett handed him a beer and opened one himself. "I haven't seen you in a while. Glad you came by."

"It's good to be here." That wasn't a complete lie. It was good to see Brett. What did it matter if he'd rather be with a woman nearly fifteen years older than he was? Especially since she only had eyes for Josh. Steven shook his head. Man, he was messed up.

He and Brett were talking in the kitchen when, out of the corner of his eye, Steven caught someone looking at him. He turned toward her. The face was familiar, but Steven couldn't place her. She smiled, waved, and made her way across the open space between the kitchen and living room.

"Hey, Steven," she said when she reached him. "How are you?"

"I'm okay. How are you?" He hated when people knew him and he had no idea who they were. She couldn't be anyone he'd had classes with, not calling him Steven.

"It is Steven, isn't it?"

"Most people call me Steve."

"You don't recognize me, do you?" she asked.

He gave her an apologetic smile. "Sorry. No."

"Carrie, that's not fair," Brett said. "You know everybody."

She laughed warmly. "That's true."

"Okay," Steven said. "How do you know me?"

"I work at Food Mart."

He still wasn't making a connection.

"I work with Dana in the pharmacy. I'm one of the technicians."

"Oh, okay."

"I have spoken to you before, but you always tell me you're waiting for Dana."

"She's a family friend."

After a while, Brett wandered off, and Steven and Carrie walked over to a corner of the room and sat down. They'd been going through the normal small talk when Matt came over. He sat on the arm of Carrie's chair and draped a possessive arm across her shoulders. It was obvious he was loaded, which was bad. Matt was always an ass when he'd had too much to drink.

"Steve," he slurred, "how is it that I try and try to get you to come to parties and when you finally do, I find you sitting alone with my date?"

"We're hardly alone," Steven said. "We're in a room full of people. Besides, I didn't know she was your date."

Carrie ducked out of Matt's embrace. "We're talking, Matt. You need to chill. Steve's a friend of one of the pharmacists I work with."

A gleam came into Matt's eyes that shone through the drunken glaze. "Ah, Steve's pharmacist friend. She must be something else."

Carrie glanced from one man to the other, clearly not understanding Matt's comment. "Yeah, she is," Carrie said. "She's great to work with, and she's super nice."

Matt leaned toward Steven. "What I want to know is how she is in bed."

Steven glared at him. "If you know what's good for you, you will shut your mouth now."

"I must've hit a nerve, huh, Carrie, to get him so ticked off."

Carrie stood and tried to pull Matt up off the arm of the chair. Instead, he fell over, landing sideways on the seat Carrie had vacated. Most of his drink spilled onto the floor. Carrie slipped the cup from his fingers and set it aside. "Come on, Matt, it's time for you to go home. I think you've had enough fun for one night."

Matt brushed Carrie off and struggled to sit up in the chair. After muttering that he wasn't leaving and spouting a few curses, he finally sat upright. "Did you know that Stevie boy here babysits for that super-nice pharmacist of yours? He helps her all the time. Why would he do stuff like that if he wasn't getting something out of it?"

The muscles in Steven's jaw tightened and his hand balled into a fist. Carrie tried again to persuade Matt to leave, but he refused.

Instead, Matt scooted closer to him. His breath reeked of whiskey.

"Tell me, Stevie, how is it with a woman who misses her husband and has experience satisfying a man?"

Steven grasped Matt by the neck and pushed him against the back of the chair. The force moved the chair against the wall. Carrie gasped and jumped back. People who had only been giving the three of them curious glances stopped their conversations and moved closer.

"I told you to shut up," Steven said in a hard, low voice. "You don't even know Dana, and I'm not going to let you talk about her like that."

Matt stared at him. It wasn't until his face turned purple that Steven realized he was cutting off most of his air. Steven released him and stood up. The group that had formed around them began to murmur and move away. Steven saw Brett making his way through the parting onlookers.

"Oh. It's Matt," Brett said when he reached Steven's side. He kicked Matt's foot. "Man, I don't know why you think you can drink whiskey. All you do when you drink that crap is piss people off. You must really be sloshed if you said something bad enough to get Steve mad at you." Brett kicked him again. Matt grunted. He rubbed his throat and glared at Steven.

"I think I'm gonna take off," Steven said. "Sorry for the disruption. I didn't mean to cause any trouble."

Brett walked with Steven toward the door. "It's no problem. I wish you wouldn't go. Everybody knows Matt deserved what you gave him—that and more."

Sensing movement behind him, Steven turned in time to see Matt lung at him. His face was red with rage, and he was swinging wildly. Carrie was backed against the wall with Matt's wayward fists coming close to her face. Steven moved to shield her, and Matt's knuckle caught him on the cheek, right below his left eye. It hurt, but more than the pain, Steven was aware of his exploding anger.

He grasped the front of Matt's shirt, swung him around, and rammed his back into the wall beside the door. Matt's head made a loud thud when it hit. Before Steven realized what he was doing, he had his arm drawn back, intending to plow his fist into Matt's face.

Steven stopped. The drunken fool wasn't worth it. He lifted Matt until his feet hovered over the floor. "If I hear a hint of a rumor even close to what you were saying about Dana tonight, I will finish this. Do I make myself clear?"

Wide eyed, Matt nodded. Steven gave him one more push against the wall before releasing him. Matt staggered, but made no move to strike him.

"If I've made any dents in your wall, call me and I'll fix them," Steven told Brett.

Brett slapped him on the shoulder. "Don't worry about. You probably ought to put some ice on that eye. I think you're gonna have a shiner. Come on in the kitchen; I'll fix you an ice pack."

"No, thanks. I'm going home."

Steven pulled his keys from his pocket and made his way to his car. He stopped when he heard someone call his name. When he turned around, he saw Carrie weaving around parked cars, coming toward him.

"Hey, could you give me a lift?"

Steven turned and continued walking. "What about your date?"

She fell into step beside him. "He wishes we were dating. He offered me a ride to the party and I accepted, but we are not dating. I don't want to leave with him. Please. I don't live far away."

"All right."

Once she'd given him the address and they were on their way, it became quiet in his car.

"Thanks for protecting me," Carrie said after a few minutes of silence.

"It's what any red-blooded American guy would've done."

"Ha! I doubt that." She shifted in her seat so that she faced him. "Does it hurt?" she asked.

"I think I'll make it." Steven stole a glance at her. The entire side of his head hurt, but he was glad he took the punch. "One thing about it, and I mean no offense by this, but I'm sure I'll look better with a black eye than you would."

She laughed. Before long, they were at her house.

He looked through his windshield at the two-story brick structure. "Nice place."

"Thanks." She leaned forward and studied him in the dim light from the dash. "I think Brett's right. You need some ice on that, the sooner, the better. You should come in and let me fix you an ice pack. My parents are out and won't be home tonight."

His face was throbbing, and it would take him a good twenty minutes to get home. He went inside with her. Under the lights in the kitchen, Carrie examined his cheek.

"There's a little blood."

Steven sat still while she cleaned his face with a damp cloth. She set out a bottle of ibuprofen and a glass of water. "Dana and the other pharmacists recommend this a lot for pain. I think you should take a couple."

Steven opened the bottle and took two tablets while she put ice cubes in a Ziploc bag and wrapped the bag in a towel. She held it to his face. He reached up to hold it. Their fingers brushed together when she removed her hand. Their eyes met and held. She smiled at him. She had a great smile.

Not long after Steven left, Dana got ready for bed, even though she wasn't the least bit sleepy. She paced near the foot of her bed, worrying because Josh had failed to return. She pulled back the draperies in her bedroom and peered into the darkness. Lights were on in Josh's house, and she could make out a shadow moving inside from time to time. Surely if something was wrong with Tori, he would've gone to her.

Dana had called when the movie ended to check that everything was all right. She'd only reached his voicemail with his cell number and his answering machine with the house number. She'd left messages, but he hadn't returned her calls. Maybe it was something with work, and he was too busy to call her. She thought about going over to check on him, but decided against it. He'd call back if he wanted to talk to her. Apparently what he planned to tell her before Steven arrived wasn't as important as the phone call that caused him to leave.

She climbed into bed, and Zoe snuggled next to her legs. She picked up her book, but put it back on the nightstand when she realized she'd read the same paragraph three times. Slowly she massaged lotion on her hands, paying deliberate attention to her cuticles. With a final glance at her phone, she flipped off the light and tried to get comfortable.

Zoe made a dissatisfied groan and moved to the opposite side of the bed. Soon the dog was breathing in a soft, restful snore. Giving up sleeping, Dana tossed back the blankets and put on her robe. Zoe raised her head, gave Dana a sleepy look, and let her head drop back down on the bed. Dana left the beagle and padded into the living room. She turned on a lamp and pulled the photo albums from the bottom bookshelf. She sat down on the floor, her legs tucked under her with the albums stacked around her. Dana started with the college album.

After she and Brandon met, she took pictures of everything—trips they took together, special occasions, not-so-special occasions, and the two of them being silly. She had placed the photographs in albums, and written dates and details to document it all. She took photos the whole time they dated and throughout their marriage. Before Patrick was born, Brandon surprised her with a new camera.

She kept up with the albums until Patrick was a toddler and wanted to "help." For several years, all she'd done was take pictures, but none of them had been placed in albums. After the accident, she took a six-month leave of absence. During that time, she spent hours on end placing photographs into albums. It had been painful at times, but mostly it had been therapeutic.

With the sleeve of her robe, she wiped away tears. She should start taking pictures again. After the funeral, she'd printed the photographs on her memory card and put her camera away. She sighed and opened the album with the last pictures she'd taken before Brandon died.

The flow of tears grew heavier as she caressed the page protector over the pictures of her husband. A smiling Brandon held Patrick. Brandon's arm was around her in the photograph of the three of them dressed for church on Easter Sunday. She closed her eyes for a moment, remembering his touch, the feel of him next to her. When she studied the pictures of Brandon helping Patrick hunt Easter eggs, she could hear Brandon's voice hinting to Patrick about where he should look.

Patrick had changed so much in the two years Brandon had been gone. Her husband would be so proud of his son if he could see him now.

She was thankful she had captured the memories of Brandon's last days and thought again about how much she needed to get out her camera. She was missing a period of Patrick's life that she'd never get back. She sighed and flipped through more pages. She'd get it out soon.

She'd looked through all the books at least once when she heard a soft knock. She got up, shook the kinks out of her legs, swiped a sleeve across her face, and made her way to the back of her house. Zoe met her in the kitchen. The outdoor light was on, and even before she reached the door, Dana could see Josh standing on her step. His expression was troubled, and his hair looked as if his hands had plowed through it over and over.

Not trusting her voice, she opened the door and motioned for him to come inside. Without a word, Josh closed the door, turned toward her, pulled a handkerchief from his pocket, and pressed it into her hand. For a moment, she stared at it. She didn't know men still carried around handkerchiefs. She couldn't help the pull that lifted the corners of her mouth.

A small smile broke his defeated look. "What? I told you. My mama taught me to be a gentleman."

She used the handkerchief to wipe her eyes and nose. She could feel Josh studying her.

"Why are you crying?" he asked.

Dana was tempted to tell him. Instead, she shook her head, wishing she hadn't allowed him to see her when her emotions were unchecked. She took a deep breath and, without making eye contact, asked about Victoria.

"Victoria?"

Dana toyed with the handkerchief. "The phone call, during the movie, when you left. I was worried that something happened to her. I thought it was either Victoria or work. Was it work related then?"

"Not exactly." He took a breath and slowly released it. "I know it's late, but I've been on the phone. That's why I didn't call you earlier. I need to talk to you, Dana. Could I stay for a while? Please."

She nodded, and Josh followed her to the next room. He stopped and looked down at the albums spread on the floor. Hurriedly, Dana bent to close the books. She tried to ignore the odd look Josh gave her and refused his help when she stacked them out of the way.

"I think I'd like something to drink," she said when she'd finished with the albums. "Do you want something? Is lemonade all right? I've got some in the fridge."

"Sure. That's fine. Don't go to any trouble."

She walked away. "It's no trouble. Please, make yourself at home."

In the kitchen, Dana moved so that Josh wouldn't be able to see her. She was overwhelmed. She wasn't supposed to have any desire to share her feelings with a man other than Brandon. She didn't want to care about what bothered Josh, at least not as much as she was beginning to care. Something inside her had come back to life. She thought that part of her died with Brandon. She told herself how ridiculous the whole thing was. Josh was her neighbor, her friend, and he was here because he needed someone to talk to. She poured two glasses of lemonade, wishing she had something stronger in the house. After several deep breaths, she walked back to the living room.

Josh stood when she entered the room. She held out his glass. He took it, and their fingers touched. He held her gaze for several moments, until she looked away.

She sat down on the couch and took a drink. He sat beside her, a tired smile on his face. Zoe balled herself on the floor between them. Josh reached down and rubbed her behind the ears. An uneasy quiet filled the room, and Dana grew more nervous.

She stared at the glass in her hands. "So. What did you want to talk about?"

"Would you show me your albums and tell me about the pictures?"

"You didn't come over here to look at my photo albums."

"No," he said. "I didn't."

She looked at him and waited. He stared at the floor.

"Why don't you start with the phone call you got during the movie?" she prompted.

"Did you and Steve have a good time?"

Dana tilted her head and continued to look at him. "Yes, I guess so. He said my surround sound seemed to be working fine."

"Oh."

He continued to focus on an unknown point on the floor. Dana was too aware of him physically and shifted to put more space between them.

He seemed to catch the movement and turned to face her. "Monica called me," he said. "The phone call during the movie was from Monica."

Dana studied his face. He didn't look happy about it.

"Do you want to talk about what she said?"

"She said she misses me. She wants to see me. Do you remember the plans I showed you last week, the ones for the office building?"

Dana nodded.

"It turns out the firm I consult for in Atlanta is trying to get the contract to design the new corporate building for Southern Finance, the company Monica works for. That design could possibly become the building where Monica works."

"How does her missing you have anything to do with the design for the new building?"

He ran his hand through his hair. "That's just it. I don't know, but somehow it's all connected. Monica wants me in Atlanta for some reason, and I think she's using this design as a way to get me there. I tried to make some calls to find out what she's up to, but all I learned was that the plans were for the company she works for."

"Why do you think she's up to something? Couldn't this be the change of heart you've waited for? If not that, maybe she wants you to take Victoria to see her."

Josh shook his head. His eyes bore into hers. "Monica hasn't seen or talked to Victoria since she left. She didn't even ask about Victoria. She never asks about Victoria."

Dana clamped her lips together. She feared the words that would spill from her mouth if she allowed them to. The two of them sat motionless, looking at each other for some time. The only sound in the room was Zoe's soft snoring.

After a while, she cleared her throat. "What happened to your marriage, Josh?"

He took a deep breath. "To tell the truth, I'm not sure when the trouble started. We grew up together, right next door to each other. We went to church and school together. We dated off and on during high school and college. It seemed natural for us to wind up married to each other. I think everyone—our families and friends—expected it.

"When I graduated from college, I got the job at Atlanta Architecture. After Monica graduated, we were married and lived in Atlanta. The plan, one we both made, was to work in Atlanta for a few years before starting our family. We agreed to move back home to raise our children.

"Her career became more important to her than I did, or maybe I was jealous that she seemed to enjoy spending more time at work than she did with me. Looking back, we should have divorced then, but I was determined to make our marriage work and our dreams come true. The problem was that my dreams and Monica's dreams had become different.

"She kept putting off starting our family. She wanted to get that next promotion, and then she'd be ready for children. But a better position was always on the horizon. She eventually consented to not using birth control, and before long, she was pregnant with Victoria. I thought that having a baby would bring Monica back to me. If anything, it pushed us further apart.

"I insisted we follow through on our plan for coming back here before Victoria started school. Monica agreed, but I think her mother and sisters had more to do with her decision than I did."

Dana waited while Josh took a drink of lemonade. He ran his hand through his hair again and blew out a long breath. "This is difficult to talk about," he whispered.

She set her glass aside and eased closer to him. She put a hand on his back. "Don't talk about it if it's painful for you."

"I need to, Dana. I need you to know."

She placed her other hand on his arm. He set his glass on the table and covered her hand with his. Dana studied his eyes and tried to figure out why Monica would leave him.

"The worst happened on our sixteenth wedding anniversary." He looked away and stared at the floor. "I thought things were going well between us. We had a beautiful home that I designed and she had it decorated exactly the way she wanted. Our businesses were both successful. We had Victoria, who was healthy and did well in school. I thought everything was the way it was supposed to be. I thought Monica was happy.

"I closed the office early that day so I could go home and get the house ready to surprise her. I'd made plans with my mom to pick up Tori from school and keep her for the evening. I had flowers, candles, a special dinner planned. When I got to the house . . ." He pulled Dana closer and sandwiched both her hands between his. "Monica was already at the house when I arrived." He locked his gaze with Dana's. "Do you have any idea what it's like to see the person you love with someone else?"

Dana's eyes widened. "Oh, Josh. No."

With a nod, Josh gave her a pained and bitter smile. "She was in bed, our bed, in the house I designed for her, with her accounting partner."

"What happened?" Dana whispered.

"Let's just say I won't be the poster boy for anger management after what I did that day." He hung his head.

Dana moved her hands so that hers held his. She squeezed them. "I'm so sorry, Josh."

He gave a bitter half laugh. "Oh, that's not the end of it. After that, I still didn't want to end our marriage. I begged her to go through marriage counseling with me. We went through weeks of it. I felt that Monica wouldn't have needed someone else if I'd been the husband I should have been. I wanted to fix whatever was wrong between us. I thought the counseling was making a difference, but out of the blue, in the middle of one of our sessions, Monica announced that she was finished. She wanted a divorce. She'd already seen a lawyer and had everything drawn up. All she wanted was to keep the money from her business and a third of the sale of our house."

"A third of it?"

"Oh, yes, Monica has always been more than fair when it comes to money," he said cynically. "Because I designed it and we paid for the house together, she thought it would only be fair for me to receive a greater portion of the money from it. She wanted nothing else from me."

"What about Victoria?" Dana asked.

"Monica didn't want her. She signed over custody to me."

Something inside Dana snapped. Like a spring wound too tightly and released, emotions that had been bottled inside her for two years sprang free. Monica had willingly given up everything that Dana had lost—a husband who loved her, a family, and opportunities to have more children.

Brandon was gone, and she would never have him back. She wouldn't see his smile, feel his touch, hear his laugh, or ever again awake in his arms. Dana tried to take deep breaths in an attempt to calm herself, but she began to shake and her breaths turned to gulps. The day of the accident came rushing back. She braced herself for the nausea, but it didn't come.

More than anything, Dana was angry. Furious, because Monica could have all that she'd lost. Life was so unjust, so unfair. Dana wanted to know why she'd been forced to suffer so much, while someone like Monica threw away her family.

She was vaguely aware of Josh pulling her onto his lap and cradling her in his arms. Her sobs broke free.

"Oh, Dana."

"Monica . . . gave up . . . so much. I'll . . . never have . . . Brandon back."

"I shouldn't have dumped all this on you. I didn't think about how it might affect you."

All Dana could do was cry. Josh held her against him. She felt him caressing her hair and heard him murmuring words of comfort in her ear. When the tears slowed, she felt Josh pull his handkerchief from the pocket of her robe. He gently wiped her face.

"Tell me about the accident, Dana. Tell me what happened to Brandon."

She buried her face in his shirt. "I can't," she said against his chest. "It hurts too much."

Dana felt his hand on her cheek. He eased her away from him. "Trust me. I want to help you. I think it's time to let it go."

She looked into his eyes and felt her resolve disappear. She dropped her gaze and absently picked at one of the buttons on his shirt.

"It was raining that morning when he left for work." To her own ears, her voice sounded far away, and she could see the events unfold in her mind like a movie. She closed her eyes.

Brandon knelt down and kissed the top of Patrick's head. "What time will you be home tonight, Daddy?"

"Four o'clock. Wanna practice in the yard when I get home?"

"Yeah!" Patrick turned from his breakfast and hugged Brandon's neck. "Have a good day at work, Dad."

"Have a good day at school, son."

Dana laughed at their routine. Every day, it was the same words exactly. Patrick hugged his dad again. Then Dana walked with Brandon to the garage. He drew her close and kissed her goodbye before he got into his car.

"Be careful driving to school today," he told her through the open window. "It's supposed to be nasty all day."

"I will be. You be careful, too. What do you want for dinner?"

"Meat loaf. Mashed potatoes. Surprise me with the vegetable."

She laughed, leaned inside the car, and kissed him again. "Love you."

"Love you, too."

"Dana?" Josh whispered.

She took a deep, shuddering breath, opened her eyes, and focused on the button under her fingers.

"I hadn't been home long from taking Patrick to school when the doorbell rang. When I answered it, there were two police officers waiting for me. One of them told me there had been an accident and they needed to take me to the hospital to see my husband. I was too afraid to ask if Brandon was all right. I kept thinking that if I could get to Brandon, everything would be fine.

"The officers pulled up to the emergency room entrance, and one of them walked with me into the hospital. When we went through the corridors of the ER, I glanced in room after room expecting to see Brandon. The officer held my arm and led me down a back hallway. When we reached the morgue, I still wouldn't believe it. The officer told me to wait in the hall, but I pushed passed him into the room. I heard someone yell that they weren't ready, to get me out of there. The officer tried to stop me, but I went in anyway.

"Brandon was in a half-zipped body bag. He was bloody and twisted. His shirt." She gulped back a sob. "I'd ironed it that morning. It was torn and soaked with blood."

Dana's lip quivered. She bit down on it and breathed slowly until it stopped.

"Then I was by the gurney. I tried to wipe the blood from his face with my hands, but there was so much of it. It had started to dry. I couldn't get it off."

She took some deep breaths. "I can still feel the eerie coolness of his skin. That lifeless chill convinced me that he was gone." She cried, and Josh wiped her face again.

"I'm not sure what happened next," she said when she could speak again. "I remember the stickiness of his blood on my hands, the smell of death. I vomited on the floor of the morgue. I think I may have passed out. Then I was sitting in another room—it was an office of some sort—and the same police officer was telling me about the accident and asking me questions to verify that the . . . the body was Brandon."

Dana sobbed again. She had held that day in for so long. She'd never talked about the morgue, about identifying Brandon's body.

Josh wiped her face again. He shifted her and held her against his shoulder. He told her to cry all she wanted, to let it out, to let all the hurt go. She did; for a long, long time she cried. When she was drained, Josh continued to hold her. He wiped her face once she grew quiet.

She sat up and moved away from him. "I apologize," she murmured hoarsely. "You came here to talk to me about something, and I end up crying like some kind of emotional basket case."

"That's all right."

Dana stood. Josh did, too. "I'll be back in a minute," she said.

She hurried through her bedroom and into her bathroom. She blew her nose, splashed her face with cold water, dried it, and ran her brush through her hair. Several minutes later, when she had her emotions under control, she returned to the living room. She sat on the sofa, but left a generous amount of space between the two of them.

She made an attempt at a smile. "Let's get back to what you needed to talk about."

Her smile disappeared when he moved next to her and laid a hand on the side of her face. His thumb brushed back and forth over her cheek.

"You are so lovely."

Her eyes grew wide and her mouth fell open.

"When I came over earlier, before Steve got here, I wanted to talk to you about how I feel about you, and I wanted to see if you feel the same about me."

"You? Me? You can't possibly . . . You're so . . . and I'm—"

"You're not making sense, Dana."

He smiled, and she felt even more confused.

"Maybe now is not the best time for words," he murmured.

He moved even closer. His breath on her face caused her heart to slam against the inside of her chest. "What about Monica?" she whispered.

He shook his head and kissed her, first one cheek and then the other. Dana closed her eyes.

"I don't love Monica anymore."

His lips touched lightly all over her face. Then she felt his lips on hers. The kiss was soft, gentle, but it caused feelings inside her that she had long forgotten. Without thinking, she kissed him in return. The kiss grew deeper, and it felt so unbelievably good.

Suddenly she came to her senses. She pushed away from him and stood. She was breathing hard and struggling with her emotions. It wasn't right for her to be acting this way, to be feeling this way.

She turned her back to him and covered her face with her hands. She felt Josh moving behind her. "Dana?"

"I'm not ready for this."

"I promise I won't do anything to hurt you. Please, let me spend time with you and Patrick. I won't ask for anything you aren't willing to give."

He rubbed her shoulders. She didn't understand why his touch had to feel so good.

"What time can I bring lunch to you tomorrow?"

"Lunch? Tomorrow?" she said through her hands.

"Yes. I know you won't be able to leave the pharmacy and eat with me, but I wanted to be sure you had something to eat."

Taking two steps away from him, she dropped her hands and turned around. "Why?"

"I don't want you to go all day without eating."

She motioned toward the sofa. "So all of this is because you feel sorry for me?"

"I told you before that I do not feel sorry for you."

"Then why do you care whether I eat or not?"

"Because I care about you," he said.

She glared at him, crossed her arms over her chest, and waited for more of an answer.

After a moment, he cleared his throat. "Victoria told me that you only eat yogurt at school. Then, like I told you before, when we were at the pizza place, Jennifer told me how you had trouble eating and keeping it down. After I found out you lived next to me, I wanted to help you. I talked to Craig and arranged to bring you lunch on the days you worked. After spending time with you, I have to admit my motives became more selfish."

He moved toward her, unhooked her arms, and stood directly in front of her. Both of his hands caressed her face, one on each side.

She opened her mouth, but no words came out. Her thoughts were a jumbled mess. It was impossible to think when he touched her. She wanted to be angry because of his pity, but she couldn't help being grateful.

"The more time I spend with you, the more time I want to spend with you."

All she could do was shake her head.

"I know you still love Brandon. I'm not asking you to stop. Just give this a chance."

For a long time they gazed at each other.

"One o'clock," she said. "I should have time to eat after one o'clock."

Chapter 10

Saturday morning, Josh alternated between humming and singing the whole time he shaved, showered, and brushed his teeth. For the first time in longer than he could remember, he felt a sense of promise.

He dressed in pair of Levi's, a long-sleeved, blue oxford shirt, and his leather loafers. He ran a comb through his hair, splashed on some cologne, and checked his appearance in the mirror. He hoped Dana would like the way he looked. He laughed at himself. He was forty years old, and he felt like a high school kid getting ready for his first date.

When he got to his parents' house, he found his mom and Tori in the kitchen. Tori was still in her nightgown, her hair in a frazzle, and her legs swinging from the stool where she was perched watching Grammy flip pancakes.

Tori's face lit up when she caught sight of him.

He moved behind her and gave her a raspberry on her cheek. She giggled.

"How's my girl?" he asked her.

"Great. Mmm, you smell good."

He thanked her and then moved around the counter. "Morning, Mama," he said before kissing her cheek.

"Good morning. Mmm, you do smell good. What's the occasion?" She looked at him with a mischievous gleam in her gray eyes.

"I'm spending the day with the prettiest girl in town."

Victoria bounced on her stool. "Who's that?"

"You, silly." He rubbed his nose against hers. "Run and get dressed while Grammy finishes breakfast. Bring your brush back, and I'll untangle your hair."

He and his mother watched Tori, her shoulders hunched with disappointment, trudge from the room.

His mother studied him while she poured a cup of coffee for him and passed the sugar bowl. "Your attitude and cologne wouldn't have anything to do with your new neighbor, would it?"

With his hand suspended above the sugar bowl, Josh caught his mother's watchful expression. A sly smile spread over his face after he looked away from her. He gave extra attention to sweetening his coffee. "Now, Mama, why would you ask me that?"

She placed pancakes from her griddle onto a warming tray in the oven and poured out more batter. "It might have something to do with your daughter talking constantly about the woman, her son, and their dog. At least I assumed Zoe is the dog. It took me a little while to figure that one out. Victoria seems to be quite taken with the lot of them."

Josh sipped his coffee and settled onto the stool his daughter vacated. "Oh? What did she say about them?"

"Everything, I think," his mom said with a laugh. "I know her name is Dana Bradley. She's a pharmacist. Her son, Patrick, is one of Tori's friends from school. Patrick's dad died a couple of years ago, and your daughter's plan is for the four of you to make a family." She gave him a pointed look. "According to Tori, Dana is intelligent, nice, and 'too skinny.' Those last words are Victoria's, not mine." She went to the refrigerator and pulled out maple syrup and orange juice. "Oh, and she works in the school's library on Thursdays. Did I leave off anything?"

Josh looked at the mug positioned between his palms and shook his head. He had asked Victoria to avoid mentioning her plan only to Dana and Patrick. He'd have to be more specific in the future.

He studied his mom while she loaded a platter with enough pancakes to feed an army. Her sharp, intelligent eyes peered at him through her silver-rimmed eyeglasses.

"She's a special person, Mom," he said. "When Victoria first told me that she wanted Dana to be her mom, I told her there was no possible way. Now that I've spent some time with Dana, I think Victoria's idea is a very good one." He sipped his coffee. "But she still loves her husband. I don't know that she'll ever want to remarry."

"What about Monica?"

His mother was adamant in her devotion to her family and had worked hard to instill those qualities in her two sons. In her opinion, people should marry for love, and they should love for life. He knew his mom hoped for him and Monica to reconcile, but she didn't know about Monica's accounting partner.

"I loved Monica, Mom. I tried hard to make our marriage work. She left even though I begged her not to go. She wants nothing to do with our daughter, and I'm finished with her."

She wrapped her arms around his shoulders from behind. "I'm sorry. I know how painful this has been for you." She released him after one last squeeze. "I don't understand Monica," she said after she poured four glasses of orange juice. "It's hard to believe the girl who grew up next door is the same person as the woman she has become."

"Tell me about it," he muttered.

Victoria skipped into the room. "Tell you about what?"

"Tell me how I'm going to get these tangles out of your hair," Josh said when he took the brush from Tori's fingers.

"Very carefully, Daddy, so you don't hurt my head."

"I never hurt you." Josh gave Tori a wounded expression that made her laugh.

He gently worked the tangles from her hair. He wasn't at all skilled with doing hair, but he had become a pro at brushing. Thankfully, Tori was happy to wear her hair straight and loose. He could do that.

While he worked on Victoria's hair, his mom slipped out of the room. A moment after Josh finished, his mom returned with his father. The two of them were smiling and talking. Josh stood from the stool, and his dad embraced him.

"It's just like your mother to keep you all to herself instead of letting me know you were here."

"Oh, Joseph, hush and sit down for breakfast."

Joseph Peters gave his wife's behind a smack when she walked to the counter to replace the carafe in the coffeemaker. Tori laughed. So did Josh. His mother said, "Joseph!" but was smiling when she took her place at the table opposite her husband. When the four of them held hands while his father said the blessing, Josh couldn't help but think how wonderful it would be to be married for forty-three years and still be crazy about each other.

After breakfast, Grammy helped Victoria pack her things. When Josh and his father cleared off the table, Josh asked him about coaching baseball.

"I enjoyed it," his dad said in his deep, rumbling voice. "I wouldn't trade that time with you and your brother for anything."

Josh rolled up his shirtsleeves to scrape the dishes. "I'm going to help coach a team this season. I've got a friend who coaches his two sons. I've convinced a boy I know to play."

His dad paused in the open door of the refrigerator, orange juice carton in hand, and looked at him. "You'd be a great coach. Who's the boy?"

"My neighbor's son. He's a friend of Victoria's."

"Ah," his father said.

Twenty minutes later, Victoria waved from the back seat of Josh's truck. His mom and dad stood arm in arm in the driveway waving in return. After Josh turned onto the next street and his parents were out of sight, Tori settled back in her seat and sighed.

"It's good to spend time with them," she said, "but I'm looking forward to being with people my own age. Will I be able to see Patrick today?"

Josh almost laughed but controlled himself when he looked in the mirror and saw her serious expression. "Well," he said in an equally serious tone, "I have a surprise for you."

She quickly reverted to little girlness by bouncing in her seat. "You do? What is it?"

"How would you like to go with me to take Dana lunch? While we're there, we'll invite her and Patrick over for movie night tonight."

"Are we gonna see her at the pharmacy?"

He braked at a stop sign. "Yes."

"Can I go back and watch her work?"

"I'm not sure about that. I don't know if people who don't work in the pharmacy are allowed to be back there. We'll see."

"Can we get some movie candy?"

"Sure. What's movie night without candy?"

"Have I ever told you that you're the best dad in the whole world?"

"Oh, a time or two."

"It's true," she said.

"And you're the best girl in the world."

A little later, Josh and Tori walked around the customer service area of Food Mart. It wasn't until his daughter pulled her hand from his and hurried forward that he saw Dana. She stood in the aisle labeled Cough, Cold, & Allergy with a man who was talking to her. Josh caught Tori's shoulder to signal that they should wait until Dana finished.

"Thank you," the man said. "All these labels overwhelm me. I was afraid I'd pick something that'd raise my blood pressure. I knew you'd know what I needed."

"That's what I'm here for, Mr. Jamison."

"You're a sweet thing," the man said before he walked past Josh and Tori toward the checkout lines.

At the moment Dana turned toward the pharmacy, Victoria hit her full force and wrapped her arms around her waist. The look of shock on Dana's face quickly transformed to a warm, happy smile, and she knelt to Tori's level.

"Hey there," Dana said after she embraced Victoria. "How was your night at Grandma and Grandpa's?"

"Gramps and Grammy's," Tori said.

"Oh, well, how was your night at Gramps and Grammy's?"

"It was fun. I love them a lot, but I miss being around people my own age."

"I completely understand that," Dana replied in a conspiratorial tone after she stood.

"Could you and Patrick come over tonight for movie night? Daddy and I are going to make homemade pizzas and watch a movie. Please say you'll come. We'll have candy. Please, please, please."

"How could I resist?" Dana said.

When Dana looked at him, Josh gave her a smile, and she glanced back at Tori. Something in her expression made him wonder if she was remembering last night's kiss.

"Hello, Josh."

"Hello." He held up the McDonald's cup in his hand. "We brought your lunch. Tori picked the spot, if you couldn't tell. I got a hamburger with extra pickles and a side salad."

Tori handed Dana the bag of food. "And a chocolate milkshake," she added.

"And a chocolate milkshake," Josh said, smiling down at his daughter.

"Chocolate milkshakes are my favorite," Dana told Tori. She turned toward him. "I cannot believe you remembered about the pickles."

He gave her a smug smile. "A gentleman never forgets."

Dana led the way back to the pharmacy with Tori walking along with her, holding her hand.

"Can we come back there with you?" Victoria whispered.

"Absolutely, we're not very busy this afternoon."

Victoria looked as if she were about to enter the vault at Fort Knox instead of a community drugstore. On the other hand, he'd never been in the dispensing area of a pharmacy, either, and he was intrigued himself. Wanting Dana to be able to eat first, he told Victoria to "hold any and all questions until the pharmacist has eaten."

That got a laugh out of Tori, Dana, and a young brunette putting blank labels in a printer. Dana introduced them to Carrie Sims.

Josh watched Dana grab a stool, the only visible seating in the pharmacy. He set her lunch on the counter and moved to take the stool from her hands.

"Where would you like it?" he asked.

"I can move a stool."

"Yes, you can. I, however, cannot fill prescriptions, explain medications to people, or decipher that gibberish that passes for writing on a prescription. You're able to do all those things and have been doing them all day. Let me do what I can and move the stool for you."

"I never thought about it that way," she murmured. "Thank you."

"You're welcome. Where would you like it?"

She pointed to the far side of the filling area. "Over there in the corner, in that last bay. You can sit and keep me company while I eat."

"I don't think so." Once he had the stool in position, he practically picked her up and set her on it. His hands lingered a moment on her thighs before he turned back to the other counter, grabbed her lunch, and brought it to her. "You've probably been standing all day. You sit. I'll stand and keep you company while you eat." Josh could tell he was getting to her by the expression on her face. That knowledge pleased him greatly.

Dana ate, Josh talked, and they both watched while Victoria perused the shelves. Carrie took care of ringing up the few customers they had and answering the phone calls that came in. Josh was glad to see Dana finish the burger, the salad, and most of the milkshake.

After Dana gathered her trash, the phone rang. He took the trash away from her and tossed it in the can nearby. Carrie answered the phone and turned to Dana to tell her that the caller needed her.

"Hello, this is the pharmacist," Dana said. "How can I help you?"

Josh listened to Dana's end of the conversation. She explained dehydration, electrolytes, and something called a BRAT diet to the person on the phone. She finished the consultation and hung up.

When Dana turned around, he was staring at her.

"What?" she said.

"You are amazing," he murmured.

She laughed at him. "I'm not amazing, but pharmacists know how to do more than count pills."

"I knew that. I still think you're amazing. Did you learn all that in college?"

"You know, those pharmacy classes are tough. I think I took pediatrics three or maybe four times. You pick up more when you review the material a few times over."

Josh studied her. He didn't think she could possibly be telling the truth, but she looked and sounded so sincere.

"She's lying," Carrie said in a singsong voice from between the shelving units.

Josh laughed and so did Dana. "Really, though," he said, "how did you know what to tell that caller?"

"Mostly from being a parent. Experience is often the best teacher."

"I don't know how it works, but Dana does," Carrie said from the other side of the shelving.

"No way!" Tori said.

"Take this bottle to her and ask her what the medicine does," Carrie said.

A second later, Tori came toward Dana with a bottle in her hand. Dana explained the use of the medication in amazingly understandable language.

"Of course," Tori said seriously. Dana looked at Josh and grinned.

They went through the exercise several times until Josh heard Carrie giggle from the other side of the shelving. Tori came out with another bottle. After Dana looked at it, she cut her eyes to him. He was sure his face showed the same expression Dana's did. He was trying, without much success, to keep from laughing. Even he recognized this medicine. A person couldn't watch ESPN for ten minutes without seeing a commercial for it. Tori held a bottle of Viagra in her little hand.

Dana leaned toward Tori so that their faces were only inches apart. "This one we will talk about when you are thirty."

"Make that thirty-five," Josh said.

Carrie burst into peals of laughter and took the bottle from Tori. "My bad, but I couldn't help myself."

Victoria looked from one adult to the next and then went on as if resigned to the fact that Dana would explain it to her someday.

After Josh and Tori left, the rest of the afternoon crawled by. Dana told herself it only seemed that way because she was eager to see Patrick. If she'd been honest, she would have admitted that she was eager to see a couple of other people, too.

During her drive to Jennifer's, she couldn't help thinking about Josh. She told herself that he was a kind person doing thoughtful things for a neighbor, that he couldn't possibly have romantic feelings for her.

Then she remembered his kiss. She ran her fingertips over her lips and shifted in her seat. She didn't know what to think about that. It felt good to be held, to feel alive again. But wasn't she betraying Brandon, betraying his memory? She shook her head, trying to clear her mind.

None of this had bothered her when Josh and Tori visited her. She thought she'd be self-conscious around him after last night, but, somehow, he was able to put her at ease. He had a way about him that made her forget her problems. She smiled at the thought and then frowned. It had to be pity that made him do the things he'd done, including kissing her.

But what if it wasn't? Was she ready for this? Would she ever be? Dana wondered if Josh would go to Atlanta and if Monica wanted to reconcile their marriage. Dana didn't doubt that Josh had loved Monica very much. He probably still did. She didn't know if a person could stop loving someone simply because he wanted to.

She sighed, closed her eyes, and let her head rest against the car's seat after she pulled into Jennifer's driveway. She needed a moment to collect herself before she faced Jennifer.

Dana was making her way to the porch when the front door flew open. "What's the matter," Jennifer said. "I can tell something's wrong. Have you been sick today?"

"No," Dana said after she stepped into the house, "not for two weeks, and it's been a week since I've taken any Zofran."

Jennifer's eyes brimmed with tears.

"Don't," Dana said. "If you do, then I will, and I don't want Patrick to see me upset."

Jennifer wiped her eyes and nodded. "Okay. I know. I know. Anyway they're all downstairs."

She grabbed Dana in a fierce hug. When Jennifer sniffed, Dana eased away. If she wasn't careful, Jennifer's emotions would get the best of her and she'd come unglued herself.

"I know," Jennifer repeated, "but I can't help it."

After she wiped her eyes again, Jennifer motioned for Dana to sit.

Dana glanced toward the basement door when she heard music.

"They're playing Guitar Hero," Jennifer said. She smiled and leaned toward Dana. "They make Mark sing. It's awful!

"You have to tell me what's going on," Jennifer said. "Start by telling me why you and Patrick aren't staying for dinner. All I could get out of Paige was that you weren't staying to eat."

"We're having dinner with Josh and Tori."

Jennifer raised her eyebrows.

"When they brought me lunch today, they invited us."

"Lunch?" Jennifer asked. "At work? You ate at work?"

Dana nodded without making eye contact. "Josh has been bringing lunch and eating with me on the days I'm at work."

"Really? The way Patrick's been talking, the four of you spend all your time together."

"Not all of our time, but we've spent time with them every day since they moved in."

Silently, Jennifer studied Dana, and Dana avoided eye contact. "It's obviously been good for you, and Patrick seems happier than I've seen him in a long time. You have no reason to feel guilty."

Dana stared at her hands.

"Brandon would want you to be happy," Jennifer said, "not wasting away to nothing. If Josh makes that possible, then I don't see any reason for you not to spend time with the man, as long as he's good to Patrick and you."

Dana took a deep breath and told Jennifer about the office design in Atlanta, how Monica lived there, and how she had called wanting to see Josh, and about the kiss.

Jennifer leaned forward again. "Tell me about the kissing. How was it?"

Dana stared at the basement door, willing it to open.

"Dana," Jennifer taunted.

"It was a nice kiss," she admitted.

"Nice? Come on. A man who looks like that can surely pull off better than nice!"

"Jennifer!"

It took Jennifer a minute to get her laughter under control.

"What about the deal with the ex-wife?" Jennifer asked. "That sounds like too much for it to be a coincidence. I'd guess she's up to something."

"Josh thought so, too."

"Does he still care for her?"

"I don't know. I know she hurt him terribly. And she left Victoria. Monica hasn't even talked to Tori on the phone, much less seen her, for an entire year."

"Well, I don't need to ask what kind of woman she is. That poor girl. And she's such a sweetheart."

"She is. I don't think her mom was much of a mom when she lived with Victoria. I only know Monica from what little time she spent at school-related functions. I admit that I've never thought much of her. Knowing that she abandoned her little girl gives me even less to like about her."

"This may be God's way of ensuring your son and Josh's daughter have a father and a mother."

That thought had crossed Dana's mind, but she wasn't ready to admit it, not even to herself. Thankfully, she didn't have to respond. The group from the basement tromped up the stairs.

Patrick walked straight to Dana's side. "I was wondering when you'd get here."

"I've been here for a little while. I didn't want to interrupt your jam session." She reached over to pat his back. Patrick still liked to be hugged, but she knew he wouldn't want her showing that much affection in front of his friends.

Patrick leaned into her leg. "Mark is a terrible singer," he said in a loud whisper.

Mark stalked toward Patrick. "I heard that, boy." He grabbed Patrick and wrapped an arm across his shoulder and chest. He rubbed his head with his other fist. "Do you need me to rough you down and teach you a lesson?"

Patrick squirmed and laughed. "No! No!"

When Patrick had his breath back, Dana sent him to gather his things. Wesley and Alex went along. Mark gave Dana a hug and headed up the stairs after the boys. Jennifer walked with Dana to the door.

Paige breezed into the room, iPod in hand with wires stretching from it to her ears. She grunted a greeting to Dana who laughed. Jennifer sent Paige on her way when she started making herself comfortable on the stairs near where they were talking.

Paige rolled her eyes. "Whatever." She turned and left the room.

"Things will work out," Jennifer said. "Just don't move too fast. You've been through a lot, and I don't want to see you hurt. If you were to fall in love again, it wouldn't mean you loved Brandon any less. Like I said before, he wouldn't want you to stop living."

Jennifer leaned her head in the direction of her daughter's exit. "Victoria will be a teenager someday. Be sure you think long and hard about that one before you get in too deep."

Dana couldn't help laughing. When Patrick came down carrying his suitcase, they said their goodbyes and left.

"Why didn't we stay for dinner?" Patrick asked.

"I forgot to tell you. Tori and Josh invited us over for homemade pizza and a movie. How does that sound?"

"Good."

"When we get home, you let Zoe out while I change. Okay?"

"You think it'd be all right if she went with us? I took her over before. Tori likes her."

"I guess it's all right. We'll make sure with Josh, though."

"Okay." He was quiet for a minute. "I like Josh. He's nice. Don't you think he's nice?"

"Yes, honey, he's very nice. I'm glad they live next to us."

By the time Dana and Patrick had done what needed to be done at home, they arrived at Josh's back door ten minutes before the scheduled time.

"We're a little early," Dana said when Josh greeted them.

He graced them with one of his fabulous smiles. "All the better."

"We brought Zoe. Is that okay?" Patrick said.

"Sure." Josh ushered them into the kitchen. "She's always welcome."

Tori popped into the room. She gave Dana a quick but tight hug around her middle before grabbing Patrick by the arm and pulling him in the direction of her room. They jabbered their way down the hall with Zoe right behind them.

Josh drew Dana toward him. Warmth spread through the hand he held and up her arm. His gaze dropped to her mouth.

"I'm not sure this is such a good idea," she whispered.

He inched closer, pinning her with intensity of his expression. "Why? Our kiss last night wasn't nearly long enough. I've thought of little else today except kissing you again."

"Oh, come on, Josh!"

He nuzzled behind her ear. "You've been on my mind all day."

"What about the children?"

He stopped what he was doing, but his face hovered at her neck. His breath gave her goose bumps. She tried to pull away, but his arms were wrapped around her.

"They sound occupied." His cheek brushed hers. "They're playing. Besides, I have nothing to hide. We're not doing anything wrong."

His lips were close to hers. His hands caressed the length of her back.

"I'm scared."

His hands stilled. He didn't release his hold but eased back and studied her. "I'd never hurt you, Dana."

His hurting her wasn't necessarily anything he could control. After all, Brandon hadn't meant to die. She stared at one of the buttons on his shirt. "I believe you would never intentionally hurt me," she murmured, "but what if things don't work out? What would that do to the kids? We live next door to each other. It would be awkward."

Josh nudged her chin up and studied her face. Dana saw varying emotions play across his features. She feared she'd made him angry or hurt his feelings.

"We're not kids anymore, Dana. Life's too short for 'what ifs.' You know what? You think too much."

Then he kissed her. She resisted for only a second. The warmth and security emanating from his body seduced her. Her arms wrapped around him, and she pressed closer into his embrace, into the kiss. The pain, hurt, and loneliness of the past two years melted away.

When the kiss ended, they clung to each other. They were both breathing hard.

"My God," Josh whispered against her hair. "Please tell me that felt as good to you as it did to me."

Unable to speak, she nodded her head, her forehead rubbing up and down against his shirt.

"Will you give this a chance? Spend time with me and Victoria?"

She nodded again.

He tilted her head and gave her another kiss.

"Let's go tell the kids," he said after she eased away from him. He pulled Dana by the arm and he started toward Victoria's room.

She didn't move. "Wait. What are we going to say?"

He stopped. "I want to make sure they're okay with the idea. They're going to see us touching each other—kissing, holding hands. I don't want them to freak out when that happens."

"What if one or both of them are against the idea?"

He pulled her against his body and placed his lips next to her ear. "Then we'll have to sneak around." He kissed her down the line of her jaw and pulled away to give her a grin. "Until they get used to the idea, anyway. Besides, I think they'll be happy with the situation."

When Josh and Dana reached Victoria's room, Zoe was belly up on the floor with her tongue lolling out of her mouth. Victoria examined the dog while Patrick gave a list of symptoms.

"What's the diagnosis, Dr. Peters?" Josh asked.

Victoria turned toward the two of them. "She's going to be fine," she said with confidence. "She has a very good owner."

Patrick smiled.

"That's good to know, doctor," Josh said. He smiled and squeezed Dana's hand. "I'd like to talk to the two of you about something. It's something important. Okay?"

Patrick and Victoria looked at each other, then turned toward Josh. "Okay," they said in unison.

Josh glanced at Dana and intertwined his fingers with hers.

"How would you feel if the two of us . . ." He lifted their joined hands. "Spent a lot of time together and with the two of you?"

The children glanced at each other again.

"Don't we already do that?" Patrick asked.

"Well, yes," Josh admitted. "But we would spend even more time together. And your mother and I might want to hold hands or hug or even kiss. Would that bother you?"

"You mean like she used to with my dad?"

Josh nodded.

Victoria ran toward them, threw her arms around both of them, and jumped up and down. Patrick stood still, staring at the floor. Dana stepped toward him, but Josh shook his head. He moved forward, knelt in front of Patrick, and placed a hand on one of Patrick's shoulders.

"I will never try to take your dad's place, Patrick. Not in your heart or your mom's. He will always be your dad. I only want to help take care of you and your mom."

Patrick looked into Josh's eyes as if he were weighing his sincerity. "Would you ever hurt her?"

"Never," Josh answered.

"Would you help her so she won't be sick anymore?"

"I will do everything in my power to help her not be sick anymore."

The two of them studied each other for several moments more. Josh must have seen something change in Patrick's expression because he let go of Patrick's shoulder and held his arms open to him. Patrick hesitated only momentarily before he fell into Josh's embrace. Josh's arms folded around Patrick, and Patrick wrapped his arms around Josh's neck. Tori hopped up and down again, squealing with delight. She rushed toward Patrick and Josh, tugging Dana along with her. The four of them ended up in a heap on the floor. Zoe waggled excitedly around them.

Later that night, after the pizzas, the movie, the popcorn, the candy, and a little more kissing, Dana lay in her bed in the dark. She'd taken a humongous leap off a cliff, and her mind reeled.

The peaceful comfort she'd felt snuggled with Josh on his couch when the four of them watched the movie had faded. Worry crept into her mind.

Patrick and Victoria would be affected by this relationship. It would change their friendship. They might fight if they were together all the time.

Dana tossed in the bed and rearranged her pillows. Maybe Josh was right. Maybe she did think too much.

When she remembered the kissing that followed that statement, another thought hit her. A burning heat spread through her body. Josh would have certain expectations.

Brandon was the only man she'd been with. When they made love the first time, she'd had a twenty-three-year-old body. Her thirty-eight-year-old body was a great deal different from her twenty-three-year-old one. Not only was there the obvious damage from the weight loss, but time, gravity, and motherhood had shifted things. Dana didn't know about Josh's sexual past, but she did know what his ex-wife looked like. Monica Simpson-Peters probably looked as perfect without her clothing as she did in her clothing.

This wasn't going to work. She groaned, threw her covers over her head, and mentally scrambled to figure out a way to reestablish her footing on that cliff.

Chapter 11

Josh was ecstatic. He hadn't been this excited about anything since the day Victoria was born.

It was crazy. He knew it didn't make sense. He'd only known Dana, really known her, for a short time. He didn't even know her middle name, when her birthday was, or her favorite color. None of that mattered, because what he did know—the kind of mother she was, the way she cared for other people, even her fondness for pickles—he loved.

Whistling, he knotted his tie, picked up his jacket, and headed to Victoria's room. She was slipping on her shoes when he walked through the door.

"Ready for me to brush your hair?" Josh asked after he laid his jacket on the end of her bed.

"Yep." She bounced over and stood in front of her dresser. He slowly ran the brush through her hair. "Do you think Dana would fix it?"

"I'm not sure if she knows how, honey. I doubt she's had much practice doing Patrick's. His is awfully short." Tori made a face at him in the mirror. "I'm kidding. I'm sure she'd love to help you with your hair. If you're ready, we'll go on over to their house. We may be early enough that she could do something this morning before church."

"I'm ready," she said eagerly.

When Josh and Tori reached Dana's back door, Patrick opened it. Zoe went out; Tori and Josh went in.

Josh rubbed the boy's head. "Morning, Patrick."

"Morning," Patrick said. He ran his gaze from Josh's tie down to his shoes and then back to his face. "You're dressed up."

Dana walked into the kitchen. "You look great."

The kids took off to the laundry room. Josh could hear Patrick explaining about feeding and watering the dog.

Josh moved toward Dana and snaked his arms around her waist. He dropped a soft kiss on her lips. "You look pretty good yourself. I like this dress."

She tried to wiggle out of his arms.

He hugged her closer. "It's going to be hard to focus on a sermon with you sitting beside me." He brushed his lips against her cheek.

She maneuvered out of his embrace and skipped away so that her kitchen table was between them. "Josh Peters, would you be serious?"

He strode toward her. "I am very serious. I find you quite irresistible."

Patrick and Victoria returned to the room. Tori walked up to Dana and took her hand. "Would you fix my hair for church today?"

"Of course," Dana answered, sounding relieved. She glanced at the clock on her microwave. "I have time to do a French braid. How does that sound?"

"I don't know what that is, but if that's what you want, it's okay with me."

When Dana moved around the table, Josh gently gripped her forearm. "We'll finish this discussion later," he whispered.

Josh's eyes remained on Dana while she walked from the room.

After the girls were out of sight, Josh sat down at the table with Patrick. "Am I too dressed up?" Josh asked.

"I don't guess so. Some guys at our church wear suits and stuff. Some people wear jeans. Most people are kinda in the middle."

"That's good to know. Do you like church?"

"It's okay, but big church gets boring after a while. That's why I usually go to kids' church. Tori can go with me. Alex and Wesley go. We have Sunday school first. There'll be other kids there from our school."

Patrick went to the back door to let Zoe inside. When he returned, the two of them talked about baseball. Josh told Patrick that he played first base and talked about his dad coaching him and his brother.

Tori rushed into the kitchen. "Look at my hair, Daddy!"

Josh stood. Patrick watched him and stood, too. Dana had done Tori's hair in a smooth French braid, leaving wisps of loose hair that curled around her face, showing off her blue eyes.

Josh bent and kissed her cheek. "You look beautiful, sweetheart."

"Look at Dana's hair. It matches mine."

He straightened and looked at Dana. Their eyes locked until Josh took her hand and turned her in a circle so that he could see the back. Like his daughter's, Dana's hair was pulled back into a smooth braid. Wisps of hair drew attention to her cheeks and eyes. Dana had definitely gained weight. Her face was fuller than it had been.

Then he noticed something else. Dana's hair and Victoria's hair were almost the same shade of brown. He looked back and forth between the two of them. With the sunlight coming through the windows, they both had hints of gold in their hair. Their coloring, the shapes of their faces, even their noses were similar. The only difference was their eyes. Josh was struck by the fact that Victoria looked more like Dana than she did her own mother.

"Hey, Mom, you look like you could be Tori's mom!" Patrick said.

Victoria didn't say a word, but her face spoke volumes. If she'd been any happier, she would've burst.

Josh parked Dana's car at the church and went around the vehicle to help Dana out. She didn't give him a chance. When they made their way to the children's Sunday school room, Josh caught curious glances from several people. Dana gave friendly hellos but didn't stop to introduce him to anyone. Explaining the process to Josh, Dana signed both the children in when they reached their room. They watched Patrick introduce Tori to his teachers. After waiting a few minutes to be sure Tori was okay, Dana and Josh made their way to Dana's class.

When they returned home, the kids took off, leaving Josh and Dana alone in her car. He leaned over to kiss her, and Dana's phone buzzed. She pulled away and examined the display.

"It's Jennifer."

He pulled her toward him. "You can call her back later."

"I can think of much more comfortable places to do this."

"Really? By all means, ma'am, lead the way." He followed her into the house. As soon as they were in the laundry room, he pulled her against him. "We have a discussion to finish."

"We do?"

"It seems you have some doubt about the degree of my attraction for you."

She dropped her gaze.

He lifted her chin so that he could look into her eyes. "I think you're beautiful, inside and out. I am extremely attracted to you." He could see doubt in her eyes so he kissed her. "Do you believe me now?"

She shook her head. He kissed her again, thoroughly and with determined slowness. He ran his hands down her sides to her hips and then pressed her against him. He felt and heard the sharp intake of her breath.

"Now do you believe me?" he asked in a husky voice.

"Yes," she whispered.

He held her close and caressed her back. "Good." After a moment, he cleared his throat. "I need to run home and change. Would you send Victoria over before she ruins her dress?"

"Sure, but aren't you coming back? I thought you were going to have lunch with us."

The sound of desperation in her voice made him smile. "Wild horses couldn't keep me away." He gave her another kiss, lingering after it to gaze into her eyes. He went out the garage door and made his way to his house, hoping he'd have time for a cold shower before Tori got there.

Dana stood at the sink peeling carrots when she felt Josh lace his arms around her waist. He hugged her to his body. She dropped the carrot and vegetable peeler in the sink. "Oh," she said right before he turned her around and kissed her.

He placed kisses all over her face. "I love kissing you. Did you know that?"

"I'm beginning to get that impression," she said between the kisses he delivered across her lips. She pushed against his shoulders with her hands. "But if you don't stop, I'll never get lunch finished."

He let out an exaggerated sigh before letting her go. Then he helped prepare lunch. They worked well together without needing words, the way she and Brandon had. That realization startled her.

"Tell me about yourself," Josh said after they'd been working in silence for a while.

"What do you want to know?"

"Everything."

"Okay. . ."

"Start by telling me more about your parents."

"Like I told you before, they both died a few years ago." She remained quiet while she chopped celery and carrots into sticks. "First my mother, then a few months later my father was gone, too. My mom had lung cancer. After she was gone, my dad gave up living."

"I'm sorry."

"I've come to terms with it. In a way, I'm glad she got sick."

"Why is that?" Josh asked.

"I was never close to my parents growing up. They didn't mistreat me or anything. I always had enough to eat and decent clothes to wear. They were just . . . there. They weren't discouraging or abusive, but they never said anything encouraging either. They never came to school to see me in anything, not even my high school graduation. It wasn't their thing, I guess. After graduation, I moved out and seldom saw them."

"What about college?"

"I always did well in school. My high school guidance counselor encouraged me to go to college. I did well in science and decided to be a pharmacist. I got some help through financial aid and some student loans, but mostly I worked my butt off to pay for it. I shared an apartment in Lexington with Jennifer and two of her sisters. She has a bunch of sisters." She looked up from the counter to give Josh a smile.

"How many?"

"Six. And one brother. Jennifer and I were the youngest of the whole crew. We were abused a lot over the years, but they always took care of us, too. No one at school ever picked on us and got away with it. Her family treated me like I was one of them. There were so many that one more didn't make a difference."

"You're serious? This isn't one of those times you keep me going before finally telling me the truth?"

She shook her head and smiled.

"So how did your mom's illness change your relationship with your parents?" he asked.

"The change started, for me anyway, when I met Brandon. He never knew his parents, not that he remembered. Ironically, they were also killed in a car accident. He was only three. Like me, he was an only child. He was raised by his grandparents. He was very close to them. Grandpa Bradley died right after we started dating. I only got to be with him a few times. Brandon was a lot like him, I think. His grandmother died after we'd been married for a few years, when I was pregnant for Patrick. Both of us were disappointed that she wasn't able to see Patrick before she passed away.

"Anyway, it had always bothered Brandon that he couldn't have a relationship with his parents. Even before we were married, he encouraged me to develop a better one with my mom and dad. I tried. I called regularly. I would visit. I took Brandon to meet them. It never seemed to make any difference. They never told me not to phone or visit, but they were never what I'd call excited to hear from me either. Not once did they call or visit me. So many times, I wanted to give up, but Brandon kept encouraging me. He was confident my efforts would make a difference someday, and even if they didn't, he said that at least I wouldn't have any reason to feel guilty when they were gone. He almost changed his mind when I began to have trouble during my pregnancy."

"The gestational hypertension?" Josh asked.

"Yes."

They had lunch ready, and Josh pulled out two chairs from the table. They sat facing each other, their knees touching and their fingers intertwined. Through the window, Dana could see the children playing.

"I take it your mom and dad were not supportive during your complications with Patrick."

"You could put it that way. When Brandon called them to let them know that I'd been placed on bed rest, my dad simply said, 'Okay.'"

"Okay?" Josh repeated.

"Yeah. Brandon explained to him how serious my condition was and that I couldn't be left alone. They didn't offer to come stay with me, no 'keep us informed of her condition,' no phone calls or visits from them to check on us. My mom wasn't working, and she wasn't sick yet. I didn't know of any reason for her not to come other than the fact that she simply didn't want to.

"That was the only time I saw Brandon truly angry. He slammed down the phone and used a few choice words that I'd never heard him use before. Shortly after that, Jennifer came over, and Brandon left. When he got back to the house, he was breathless and sweaty. I knew he'd gone for a long run. Brandon loved to run. It was his stress reliever.

"It was a difficult time, but he never once lost his patience with me or expressed any other frustration to me about my parents or the situation. He wasn't able to take time off work to stay with me every day. I was only about thirty weeks along. There was over two months left until the baby was due, and we didn't know what other complications might arise once Patrick got here that would require Brandon to be off work. He was the one who arranged for someone to stay with me and take me to my appointments, which were two to three times a week. Mark, Jennifer, and Elizabeth, Craig's wife, helped a lot, but Brandon took over the day-to-day things that I was no longer able to do. He did all the laundry, the cleaning, and most of the grocery shopping."

Dana and Josh sat in silence for a while. When she heard Josh clear his throat, she looked at him. She wasn't sure how long she'd been staring into space.

"You said before that Brandon 'almost changed his mind' about your reconciling with your parents. What happened?"

"Oh," she said, feeling embarrassed. "I'm making a muck of getting to the point of this story, aren't I?"

His finger traced the line of her jaw. "Not at all. This is exactly the sort of thing I want you to tell me. I told you I want to know everything, and I meant it."

"Well, after Brandon talked to my dad, neither of us made any more attempts to contact my parents. We didn't even call them to let them know Patrick had been born. Not right away, at least. Because of my C-section and the condition Patrick was in, the two of us had to stay in the hospital for a few days. Brandon stayed with us most of the time, but he went home to shower and change. They have really comfortable, private rooms at the hospital here, and they encourage dads to stay." She smiled apologetically. "I got off track again."

"It's fine. Go on."

"Going in and out, Brandon said he noticed people at the windows looking at the babies. He knew some of them had to be grandparents. It made him feel bad that his son had no grandparents to come see him. So he called them. My parents, I mean. He told me that at least we would do our part by letting them know their daughter was fine and their grandson was here."

"Did they come?"

"No. They never did, but when I was able, Brandon took us to see them. It was the same as always, no open rejection but no open acceptance either. Neither of them would hold Patrick.

"After that, the three of us would visit them periodically. It was never as often as before, and we never stayed long. My mom was a heavy smoker, and Brandon and I wouldn't stay when she was smoking. When

Patrick got older, we went even less. He was walking and getting into things, and their house was far from childproof. Then Patrick started preschool and had play dates and birthday parties. Brandon and I were both busy with our jobs. I still called them once a week, but we didn't visit much.

"One day, out of the blue, my dad called me at work. I didn't know he paid attention when I told him things about our lives like where we worked, but I guess he did. He described symptoms that my mom had been having and asked me what I thought they should do. It was the first time he asked me for anything. Neither one of them ever went to the doctor, and I set up an appointment for her. Mom's diagnosis turned out to be lung cancer, and after surgery, radiation, chemo, and nearly two years of sickness, she was gone. My dad followed after her a few months later.

"But before they died, we made amends. They both told me that I'd been a good daughter and that they loved me. They apologized for not being there when I needed them. Most importantly, Patrick got to know them and know that they loved him. That's why I'm glad she became ill. I don't think my mom or dad would have thought to change anything about their lives had she not been facing death.

"Mom and Dad didn't take me to church, but I did go with Jennifer and her family. I knew about and believed in God and Jesus, but it wasn't until I knew Brandon that I realized that it took more than believing they existed. Brandon helped me to know how to have a relationship with God. I shared that with my parents, but they weren't receptive until the end of Mom's illness."

"You are an extraordinary woman," Josh said.

Dana shook her head. "There's nothing extraordinary about me. Brandon changed my life; he was the extraordinary one. There's no way to know what kind of mess my life would be had I not known him. I thank God I did."

Dana heard a commotion from the direction of the back door.

"Mom," called Patrick, "I'm starved. When's lunch?"

She mentally gathered herself and stood. "Now. You and Tori run and wash your hands."

Victoria and Patrick talked, one right after the other, about Sunday school and church that morning. It was obvious Victoria liked Patrick's church better than her own. Josh listened and made comments at appropriate times, but in reality, his mind was focused on the time he spent with Dana before the kids came inside.

With all that the woman had endured in her lifetime, she had every reason to be hard and cold. Instead, she was one of the warmest, most caring people he knew. The more he knew about her, the more he was drawn to her.

The kids' voices floated over the table, and Josh caught Dana's gaze. Her expression asked him what he was thinking. With his eyes, he tried to tell her how much he'd like to be alone with her. He watched a slight blush color her face. She glanced nervously at the children. Despite his best efforts, Josh was unable to suppress a chuckle.

"What's so funny?" Tori asked.

He cut his eyes to his daughter. "I'm happy sitting here with you three, and it made me laugh."

All four of them laughed. He looked back at Dana. Their gazes caught and held. If he didn't know better, he'd say the woman was falling in love with him.

When lunch was over, the four of them worked to-gether to clear the table. Dana thanked the kids for their help and sent them back outside to play while she and Josh finished. He loaded the dishwasher while she put the food away. He was standing over the sink scraping the dishes when he felt Dana's arms wrap around him. She pressed her face against his back and murmured thank you. His heart skipped a beat. This was the first embrace she had initiated. He turned in her arms and brought his wet hands to rest on her behind. He pulled her against his body, tightening his grip on her.

"What are you thanking me for?" he asked.

"Everything. Helping with lunch and cleaning up. Mostly for listening to me."

He gazed at her, lost in the depths of her eyes. He wanted so badly to say the words, to tell her he loved her, but he was afraid of pushing her away, of moving too fast. Instead of saying anything, he kissed her. He placed soft kisses on her mouth, her cheeks, and her nose. "There's not much I wouldn't do for you."

When they finished in the kitchen, they went outside and the four of them played tag, chasing one another through the yards of both houses. When he caught one of the children, he would sling his victim over his shoulder and gallop with him or her, giggling and screaming back to base. The process continued until all four of them had several turns to chase the other three. At last, Josh was it again, and he chased Dana to the side yard, where they were out of sight of the kids and the neighbors. He caught her against the house, bracing his hands on the brick on each side of her body.

"You're it, Dana."

It took a minute or two for her to catch her breath. He hoped it wasn't entirely due to running.

"I get the feeling you're not talking about tag." Her gaze dropped from his eyes to his mouth, which was only inches from hers.

"No, I'm not talking about tag."

Dana looked back into his eyes. She placed her hands on each side of his face and closed the gap between them. Josh didn't respond at first, shocked as he was that Dana was the one kissing him instead of the other way around, but it didn't take him long to lose himself.

Chapter 12

Monday morning Josh's cell buzzed when he stepped out of the shower. He yanked on his robe and answered it.

"I'm sorry I didn't get back with you over the weekend," Abe Marcum said. "I'd planned to call you today anyway. We want you to be the lead architect on the Southern Finance presentation. Everyone here loves the preliminary designs you sent."

"Lead architect? But that would mean you'd need me down there. Victoria has school, and I can't—"

"What about spring break? We could schedule the meetings around that, and you could bring her with you."

"Her break is next week. Could you arrange something that fast with Southern?" Josh asked.

"If you'll come, we'll work it out. The finish work and the presentation may not take all week. Then you two could have a mini vacation."

That was true. Of course, he'd have to find someone to watch her while he was working. Josh ran his towel over his damp hair.

"You have a knack for this kind of project," Abe said. "Besides, one of the big wigs at Southern requested you personally."

"Me? But I don't know anyone who . . . Wait a minute. Is it possible Monica had something to do with this?"

"She's not part of the upper management, is she?"

"No, but—"

"That's good. No legal worries then. If she's influenced them to request you, you owe your ex-wife a big thank-you."

Josh wasn't so sure about that. He could hear the sound of papers being shuffled over the line.

"The man at Southern who knows you is . . ." Josh heard more shuffling. "Here it is. Marcus Taylor. He's the CFO over there. I've met him. Seems like a good guy, down to earth. He's big on family, if I remember correctly."

Josh paced back and forth across his bathroom. The chief financial officer—Monica would work for him.

"You've always had great client appeal," Abe said. "You're a talented architect, and you already have a connection with someone there. The board of directors at Southern has all but guaranteed to give us the contract if you're the one heading it up. You'd really be helping us out down here. Promise me you'll at least think about it?"

"I'll think about it."

"We want you on this, Josh. We'll take care of all your travel expenses, and we're prepared to be extremely generous with your consultation fee. Could you let me know what you decide by six this evening?"

❦

Monica was already at the office when Josh called. She smiled and answered her phone. "Good morning, Josh."

"What are you doing, Monica?"

"Right this minute? I'm amortizing funds to pay our taxes. Our fiscal year will be ending soon and—"

"You know what I mean. Why are you pushing so that Atlanta Architecture will make me the lead architect on their bid for your company's office building?"

"Lead architect? Why, Josh, that's wonderful! When will you arrive in Atlanta?"

"I haven't made up my mind that I'll do it."

"Don't be ridiculous. You have to know how much money you'd be throwing away if you don't accept this offer."

"Money isn't everything," Josh said.

Monica took a deep breath and let it out silently. "How long has it been since you've seen Jordon? Mama told me that he and Abby are pregnant again, that she's much further along in this pregnancy than she's been before. From what I understand, things are going well this time. You know they would enjoy seeing you."

She waited a moment. She could sense him thinking it over. "I'd really like to see you, Josh. There's something I need to discuss with you, something I can't talk to you about over the phone. Come to Atlanta. You wouldn't have to be away from Victoria long." She paused again. "Please."

She heard him let out a breath. In her mind, she could see him running his hand through his hair. Monica smiled again.

"Abe said he'd be able to arrange everything for next week," he said. "Victoria will be on spring break. Would you be willing to take time off work to be with her while I'm working? If you could do that, I could bring her with me. I'm sure she'd enjoy being with her mother."

Monica doubted that. Victoria would enjoy spending time with her about as much as she would enjoy spending time with Victoria. "Oh, I wish I could, but there's no way I could take time off, not with the fiscal year coming to a close soon. It's my busiest time; you know that. Why not let her stay with Mama or Margaret? I'm sure they would love having the time to spoil her. She could come on the next trip. I should be able to take some time off later on in the summer, and the three of us could do some fun things together."

The line was quiet. Monica waited a moment. "Josh, dear, I need to get back to work. Call and let me know when you'll be arriving. I can't wait to see you."

When Dana and Josh walked through the neighborhood, she listened to him talk about the two phone conversations he'd had that morning.

"I don't think I'm going to do it," he said a few moments after he finished explaining the situation.

"Why?" Dana asked.

"Victoria won't be happy staying with Mom or Monica's mom as long as I'd need to be gone, not without other kids around for her to play with. I can't take Tori with me. Unless . . ."

Dana could tell what he was thinking. Going to Atlanta with him was not an option for many reasons. "Let her stay with me. I've already taken vacation that week. Patrick and I have some things planned—the zoo, Newport Aquarium, maybe a movie. I'll spend the entire week with them. Patrick will enjoy her being with us, I'm sure."

He smiled, and Dana forced herself to face forward. "I think I'd rather stay here. The four of us could spend the week together."

"I think you should go to Atlanta."

She continued to face forward and was careful to keep her face expressionless.

"Why?" he asked after a several moments of silence.

"It sounds like a great career opportunity for you. You'd be helping out the people you worked for, you'd have a chance to visit with your brother and sister-in-law, and I think it will help you figure out some things."

Josh stopped in the middle of the sidewalk. "Dana—"

She kept walking and motioned toward the sky. "It's getting cloudy. It looks like rain. If we're going to get two laps in today, we better get a move on."

He fell into step beside her and didn't talk anymore. When they finished the walk, instead of jogging as he usually did, Josh followed her inside her house. He cornered her and made her look at him. For several seconds, they stared at each other. Dana swallowed and tried hard to keep her feelings hidden. If Monica had changed and wanted Josh back, Dana was determined not to come between them.

When he lowered his head and kissed her neck, she almost asked him stay. When his lips met hers, she kissed him. She told herself that it wasn't wrong to savor this closeness for a little while, just until he went to Atlanta. Then she could let him go.

Josh was glad he'd persuaded Dana to go out to lunch with him. He stressed the fact that this was their first official date and insisted that she allow him to assist her in and out of his truck, open doors for her, and pull out her chair. He was thankful that she put up no resistance. They lingered at the restaurant.

Hoping he'd be able to get her to reconsider going, he told Dana about activities he knew the kids would enjoy in Atlanta. No matter how hard he tried, Dana wouldn't discuss it.

Instead, she asked questions about Jordon and Abby. Josh described his brother, told her some of the things they had done as boys, and talked about when they both lived in Atlanta. He explained how Jordon and Abby had tried for several years to have a child, how Abby had miscarried twice before, and how this pregnancy was going well.

Dana's expressions told Josh this wasn't her changing the subject from something she wanted to avoid. He got the feeling she was sincerely interested in his family.

"I hope the rest of her pregnancy goes well," she said. "I can't imagine losing a baby."

If she wouldn't talk about going to Atlanta with him, at least they talked about everything else. They discussed their favorite foods, colors, sports, and books. They learned each other's and the kids' birthdays. Victoria and Patrick were both born in May. Dana told him that she was born in February, and Josh told her his birthday was in September.

"Your eyes are the same color as your birthstone," Dana told him.

"Really? What's my birthstone?"

"A sapphire. It's a beautiful blue stone, exactly like your eyes."

He gave her a teasing smile. "Are you saying I have beautiful eyes?"

"Like you've never heard that before."

"I have heard that a few times, but it's never sounded as good as it does from your lips."

She laughed and rolled her eyes. "That's smooth, very smooth."

He laughed with her, then asked about her birthstone, and Victoria and Patrick's.

"Mine's an amethyst, which is a purple color. May's stone is an emerald."

He ran his fingers over the ring she wore on her right hand. "That's this stone, isn't it?"

"Yes," she said, watching his fingers brush hers. "Brandon gave that to me after Patrick was born. He was supposed to be born in June. That's one good thing about his being born early. June is pearls. I don't care for pearls."

He released Dana's fingers to lift his glass for a drink and saw Steve walk into the restaurant. He was with a group of guys who all looked to be in their mid-twenties. Josh waved and smiled, and Steve noticed him. He said something to his companions before walking toward Josh and Dana's table.

"We're about to have company," Josh said. "Steve just walked in."

Dana turned in her seat. Josh could tell the moment Steve realized that it was Dana with him. He froze in mid stride but recovered quickly and continued walking to their table with a smile that Josh knew was forced.

Dana, who seemed oblivious to Steve's discomfort, smiled warmly at him and said hello. When Steve greeted them, Josh noticed that he was holding his head at an odd angle. He leaned so that he could see the left side of Steve's face. He had a black eye, not a bad one, but his face had run into something.

"What's the matter?" Dana asked.

Steve caught Josh's eyes and shook his head slightly. Dana wasn't oblivious to that.

"Steven Allen Farris," Dana said with maternal authority. "What are you hiding from me?"

Slowly Steve turned his head so that Dana could have a view of his left cheek. She gasped and stood. "What happened? Were you in a fight?"

"Carrie didn't tell you?"

Dana pushed Steve into the chair beside hers and studied the purplish green area on his face with clinical acuity. "Carrie?" she asked absently.

"Carrie was there, at the party where it happened. I was afraid she might have—"

Dana looked at Steve with a confused expression.

He looked from Dana to Josh. "One of my friends had too much to drink and started swinging around like a crazy person. I happened to be in the way of one of his fists."

Something told Josh there was more to it than Steve was telling them.

"I'm glad you weren't hurt any worse than you were," Dana said after she sat down again. "Would you like to eat with us?"

"No, thanks. I can only stay for a minute. I came with some other friends."

"Not the one who popped you in the face, I hope," Josh said.

Steve cleared his throat. "No, I doubt the two of us will do anything together again." He looked again from Dana to Josh. "Did you get a chance to go over the revisions to lot 78?"

"I did. I'll run the plans out to your dad's place in the morning along with the plans for the three lots you're scheduled to start on next week. I'm going to

Atlanta a week from today, so I want your dad to have those before I leave."

"Atlanta?" Steve asked.

"I'm going down to present a design for the company I worked for down there."

"How long are you going to be gone?" Steve asked.

"I'm not sure yet. I definitely won't stay past Friday. I can't leave my girl that long." Josh gave Dana a smile that she pretended not to notice.

Steve stood but didn't leave right away. It was clear that he didn't want to go. Finally, he told Dana goodbye and told Josh to have a safe trip.

"You're going to have to talk to him," Josh said after Steve had walked to the other side of the restaurant. "If you don't want to, I will."

She waved a hand dismissively. "What's to talk about? I don't see how he could possibly think of me as anything other than a friend. If I'm right, and I say something to him, it will be embarrassing for him and me."

Josh disagreed but didn't argue. He trusted her.

Tuesday evening Dana and Patrick went with Josh and Tori to Margaret and Joseph's for dinner. Josh's parents were warm and friendly. Their home was nicely furnished and comfortable. It was no wonder Josh was so thoughtful. Margaret and Joseph greeted her and Patrick warmly, making Dana feel like a part of their family.

After they finished eating, Joseph invited Patrick to his work area in the basement.

"Dad has an unbelievable O scale train system down there," Josh said. "He has villages, a wharf area, and broad expanses of countryside set up, all in miniature. There are electric lights, running water, and authentic train sounds."

"Patrick will love that," Dana said. "We may not be able to get him to leave."

"They'll be a well-matched pair," Margaret said. "Won't they, Tori? Gramps is always trying to get you to play trains with him."

Victoria shrugged and then leaned toward Dana. "I think trains are kind of boring," she whispered.

Dana put an arm around her and gave her a squeeze. "I understand, but I bet your grandpa likes having you around."

Patrick stayed in the basement with Joseph for nearly an hour. When the two of them joined everyone else in the living room, Joseph and Patrick were both smiling and talking.

"That's a very bright boy you have, Dana," Joseph said. "Sharp as a tack. I had a bridge problem I've been trying to work out for months. Patrick took one look at it and knew exactly what to do."

Patrick beamed.

Joseph sat next to his wife, pulled a laughing Victoria onto his lap, and asked Patrick about baseball.

"Yes, sir, I'm going to play this year."

"Sir?" Joseph said. He turned Victoria so that he could see her face. "Does that sound right, Tori? Do you think Patrick should call me sir?"

She wrinkled her nose and shook her head. "I call you Gramps. Can't he call you Gramps?"

Joseph looked at Dana. "Is that all right with you?"

Patrick leaned against her leg, and she patted his back. "That's kind of you. My parents and his father's parents have passed away."

"That settles it," Margaret said. "Patrick, call Joseph Gramps and I'm Grammy. Does that suit you?"

He nodded enthusiastically.

"Fine," Margaret said with a smile. "And I want you to come see us whenever Tori comes. Will you do that?"

Patrick looked at Dana. She smiled her agreement. "Yes," Patrick said.

Victoria jumped down from her grandfather's lap to give Patrick a hug, which he returned. "Gramps," she said, "come show me how Patrick fixed your bridge."

Joseph walked out of the room holding Tori's hand in one of his and Patrick's in the other.

A little later, when Josh, Dana, and the children were saying their goodbyes, the sound of "Yoo-hoo, Margaret" came from the kitchen.

Dana caught a knowing glance pass between Josh and his mother before he moved closer to her side. He put a protective arm around her. "Monica's mother," he whispered.

The sound of the voice grew louder. "I saw Josh's truck outside and came to see . . ." Her voice trailed off when she reached the foyer. Her eyes scanned the group until her focus settled on Dana and Josh. She surveyed Dana from head to toe. The flash of disdain evident in her expression was quickly covered by an excessively sweet smile.

She extended a hand to Dana. Dana shook it. "I'm Camille. Camille Simpson. Josh's mother-in-law. You must be the babysitter. Margaret told me that a neighbor or some such nonsense was keeping our little muffin while Josh traveled to Atlanta."

"She's not a babysitter," Josh said. "She's my—"

"Of course, dear," the woman said before pushing her way between Josh and Dana. "Monica is so looking forward to your visit, Josh."

"The purpose of my trip is not to see Monica."

Ms. Simpson went on as if Josh hadn't spoken and rambled on about how wonderful Monica was and how she knew this trip would bring Josh and Monica back together. "You two are meant for each other. You always have been."

Josh opened his mouth but closed it again. Then he shook his head. He gave Ms. Simpson a short goodbye before ushering Dana and the children to his truck.

In the driveway, Margaret caught Dana's hands in hers. "Please don't let what Camille said upset you. She's not very good at listening and has her own sense of reality." Margaret squeezed her hands and pulled her close. "Believe me, dear, I haven't seen Josh this happy in a long, long time." Margaret squeezed her hands again. Dana gave her a weak smile.

Josh helped the kids and her into the truck, then stood outside talking with his parents. Behind her, Dana could hear Tori and Patrick murmuring.

"Is your dad married?" Patrick asked.

"He's divorced. My mom left us."

"My dad left, too," Patrick said.

"But your daddy's in heaven. He didn't want to leave you. My mom wanted to go, and she's only in Georgia."

Dana turned in her seat. Victoria's eyes brimmed with tears. Dana wanted to comfort her but had no idea what to say. Reaching back, she gave them both a pat on the leg.

Josh got in, started the truck, and they drove toward home in silence.

Monica was at a downtown restaurant, waiting with Ross for a table when her phone vibrated. She checked the display.

She passed a hand down Ross's arm. "It's my mother. I'm going to run outside and call her back. I'll only be a minute." On her way out, she glanced over her shoulder. Ross's steady gaze followed her. She smiled.

Outside on the sidewalk, she dialed her mother. "Mama, it's Monica."

"You won't believe who I met this evening at Joseph and Margaret's."

"Oh, who was there?"

"Your daughter and Josh. He had a woman with him. And her little boy. Did you know Josh was dating?"

Monica struggled to keep from dropping her phone. "Dating?" she asked once her grip on the phone was secure.

"Well, he had his arm around her, and he got all huffy when I referred to her as a babysitter."

"Who is she?"

"I don't remember her name, but I bet you know her. Her son and Victoria are in the same class at school. Margaret told me her husband died a couple of years ago. The last name is Bradley. I remember that now. She and Josh are neighbors."

Bradley. Monica tried to remember. She went to the funeral with Josh. What was her first name? Donna? Deanna? Dana? It was Dana Bradley. Monica remembered her. Surely her mother had the wrong person.

"What did she look like, Mama?"

"Well, she's not attractive. She's small and thin. She has mousy brown hair and a fair complexion."

That sounded like Dana Bradley. Monica didn't know the woman well, but what encounters she'd had with her left Monica feeling like the woman put on a goody-two-shoes act. Nobody could be that nice.

"I made sure she heard me tell Josh how wonderful you are and how you're looking forward to his visit," her mother said. "I told him right in front of her how the two of you have always been meant for each other.

"I don't understand why Josh isn't taking Victoria with him. Why is he leaving her with some other woman when she could be down there with you?"

"Oh, Mama, I begged him to bring her. It's been so long since I've seen her, and it's impossible for me to take time off work to come up there. Victoria's going to forget who I am."

"Don't you worry about that," her mother said. "I'll make sure she knows her mother."

After talking a few minutes more, Monica told her mother goodbye. Instead of going inside, she remained on the sidewalk, pacing in front of the restaurant. At least she knew for sure that Josh was coming. He'd have to be an idiot to turn down the senior partnership that she knew Marcum was going to offer him while he was in Atlanta. She bet Josh didn't even know about that yet.

She needed Josh here. He'd always loved her, and Monica wanted it to stay that way. She'd put a stop to Dana Bradley.

Monica took a deep breath before she made her way back inside. She caught sight of Ross when he turned to follow the host away from the bar. She slipped in beside him and eased her arm around his waist.

Chapter 13

"Please drop us off at home," Dana murmured when Josh turned into the subdivision.

He pretended not to hear, pulled into his garage, and shut the door.

"Thank you for this evening," Dana said stiffly. "We better head home, Patrick."

"Come inside," Josh said. "We need to talk."

She turned to look at him, her expression shuttered.

He begged her with his eyes. "Please."

While the children went to Tori's room, Josh drew Dana into the living room. They sat close on his sofa.

"It never dawned on me that Monica's mom would drop in. None of what she said is true. Surely you know that."

She didn't answer, and he couldn't get her to look at him. "Please, Dana, talk to me."

"What do you want me to say?"

He rubbed her hands with his. "Tell me what you're thinking, what you're feeling."

She took a deep breath and released it slowly. She pulled her hands from his grasp and clutched them together on her lap. "Deep down I think you still love your wife." Her voice was so low that Josh had to bend his head until it touched hers to be able to hear her. "I think she wants to see you because she knows she's made a mistake. No woman in her right mind would willingly give you up, and I think once you see her again, the two of you will get back together."

She looked at him, holding his gaze with hers. He started to speak, to contradict her, but she held up a hand to stop him.

"I know that you have feelings for Patrick and me. It's in your nature to want to protect and care for those around you. You possess a noble character. Whatever happens, I will always treasure our friendship. I cannot begin to tell you how grateful I am that you have been so kind to my son, not to mention how you've helped me. I hope you don't move back to Atlanta." She gave him a sad smile. "I would miss Victoria terribly, and I know Patrick would miss you both, too."

Anger swelled inside him. He was angry at his mother-in-law for her lies and rudeness, angry at Dana for thinking he would want to be with Monica, and, more than anything, angry with himself for not telling her how he felt before now. He could tell she wouldn't listen if he told her how much she and Patrick meant to him. He knew nothing he said tonight would change her mind, not completely.

He eased her to him so that she was cradled in his lap. She allowed him to nestle her against him. He whispered that he no longer loved Monica. He only wanted her, needed her. He begged her to give him time to prove himself to her. His whispers became kisses, and Dana kissed him in return.

Her arms came around him, and she brought herself closer within his embrace. He was swept away by the feel of her in his arms. All he wanted to do was protect her, care for her, and love her. Without thinking, he eased his hand under her shirt and caressed her bare skin. She was soft and warm.

It wasn't until Dana tensed that he realized what he had done. He stilled. His hand covered one of her breasts. He lifted his head enough to look into her face. Her cheeks were flushed. Her beautiful eyes were huge. In their depths, he saw desire, but he also saw fear. He caused that, and it broke his heart.

"Josh, I'm not ready for this."

"I understand. I got carried away." He slowly withdrew his hand and smoothed her clothing back into place. "I just need you to know how much I care about you."

For several moments, they remained motionless, staring at one another. Finally, she placed her hand on the side of his face. He covered her hand with his and pressed it against his cheek.

"Dana, I want to tell you how much I lo—"

She placed the fingers of her other hand against his lips. "Please," she whispered. "Let's wait and see what happens in Atlanta. We're moving too fast. This time apart will be good for us both to figure out what we need to do."

"What about before I leave? I want to spend as much time with you as possible before I have to go."

"Why don't we continue the way we have been? Well, except for what just happened."

Josh tried to stop himself from cracking a smile, but he couldn't hold it back. "I enjoyed what just happened, and I would like to do more of it."

It was obvious Dana was trying hard not to smile at him, but she finally gave in. "Josh Peters, you are a very bad man. You know exactly what I mean."

"You mean you didn't enjoy it?" he asked with feigned innocence.

She blushed. "You know I did."

"Good, because we will finish this, Dana. You're the one I want, and I want all of you. I'm going to prove to you that we belong together."

"Mom, will you lay with me for a little bit?" Patrick asked when Dana went to tuck him in.

She climbed into his top bunk and snuggled next to him so they faced each other. She draped an arm over his waist. "Is something bothering you?"

"I want to talk a little. Is that okay?"

"Absolutely. Do you want to talk about anything in particular?"

He hesitated. "Did you and Josh have a fight tonight?"

"No, we didn't fight. We had something we needed to talk about."

"What does 'divorced' mean?"

It took Dana a minute to adjust to Patrick's train of thought. "Sometimes when people get married, something happens and they don't want to be married anymore. Once they stop being married to each other, they're divorced. Does that make sense?"

"I think so. Are you and Daddy divorced?"

"No, honey. If Daddy hadn't died, we would still be married."

"Oh." He seemed to consider his next words and remained quiet for a few moments. "Can people marry somebody else when they're divorced?"

"Yes," she answered slowly.

"Could you marry someone else if you wanted to?"

Dana took a deep breath and released it. "If I fell in love again with someone who loves us. He'd have to be someone special. He'd have to be a good daddy."

"How 'bout Josh? Do you love Josh?"

"I don't know, Patrick. I think I could. We'll have to wait and see what happens."

"I miss Daddy."

"I know you do, sweetheart. I do, too."

He wrapped his arms around her neck. "Mom."

"Yes, dear?" she said, pulling him closer.

"Thanks for being a good mom. Tori doesn't like her mom very much. I think she must not be very nice to go off and leave Tori."

Dana chose not to comment.

"I think Josh is a good dad," Patrick said. "Don't you?"

"Yes, I do."

"I like him, Mom."

"I like him, too, son."

"Thanks for talking to me. I love you, Mommy." He kissed her cheek.

Dana returned his kiss and rubbed her nose against his. "I love you, too. You're the best boy in the world."

Except for the encounter with his former mother-in-law, the week went smoothly. Josh ate lunch with Dana in the parking lot on the days she worked, and they continued walking together. So that he could be with them as much as possible before his trip, Josh drove the kids to school and picked them up every day except Dana's library day. The four of them spent every afternoon and evening together, working on school assignments, fixing and cleaning up dinners, and playing baseball in the yard.

No more was said about Monica or the incident with Camille. Josh didn't try to tell Dana again that he loved her. He chose to bide his time and wait for the right moment.

Sunday, Josh and Tori went to church with Dana and Patrick again. Josh had no desire to see Camille. Avoiding her at his church would be impossible.

After the service, Josh packed for his trip and then helped Tori gather the things she wanted to take to Dana's house. He put his larger bag and his laptop in his truck and placed his carry-on bag in Dana's guest room.

He was sure it hadn't been easy for Dana to let him stay the night. The fact that he had to leave so early Monday was probably what made her give in. Whatever the reason, Josh was glad. It was hard living so close to her and parting from her at night when all he wanted was to spend more time with her.

They let the kids stay up later than usual, and Josh spent extra time telling them both goodnight and good-bye. He could tell they were excited about their break but disappointed that he had to be gone.

He and Dana talked in the living room for a long time after they tucked the kids in. She was careful to keep their conversation on neutral ground. He ached to tell her how much he loved her, but her reserve made him keep it in.

After a while, he pulled her onto his lap and kissed her. It felt so good to hold her, to feel her arms around him and her hands caressing him. He longed for her to be his. He didn't ever want to let her go.

"Will it bother you if I call you constantly while I'm gone?"

She laughed and pulled away from him. "I'll have your child with me. Of course you should call whenever you want."

"I'm serious," he said.

She laughed harder.

"What if I want to call you right before I go to sleep?"

Her laughter stopped.

"What if I want your voice to be the first thing I hear when I wake up? What if I'm eating lunch, and I need to hear your laughter? What if it's two in the morning and I can't sleep because all I want is to be with you?"

"Call me whenever you need to, whenever you want to."

"Are you going to call me?" Josh asked.

"You might be busy. With meetings or . . ." She looked away, and her voice trailed off.

"I am going to see Monica and talk to her. I plan to do that early in the week to get it out of the way. I am not going to be with Monica." He touched her chest with his index finger. "You are the only one I want to be with."

He let his words hang between them while he traced small circles over her breastbone. "I'll keep my phone with me. If I'm tied up with business, leave me a voice mail, and I'll call you back as soon as I can. If it's an emergency or you need me right away for any reason, use the number I gave you for Atlanta Architecture. The secretary will be able to pull me out of whatever meeting I'm in. If you need me for anything, you call me." He gave her a grin. "I hope you'll miss me and call just to hear my voice."

"I barely know you. I can't imagine that I will miss you."

Other than the teasing spark in her eyes, she wore a deadpan expression. Josh tickled her in the hopes of breaking her composure. She wiggled out of his grasp and rolled off the sofa. He followed her.

For several minutes, they wrestled until Josh had Dana pinned beneath him. They were laughing and breathless. Josh held her arms against the floor, his hands gripping her wrists. One of his knees was on either side of her hips. She bucked against him, and the laughter stopped. Sexual tension thrummed between them.

Dana's eyes shifted to the point where their bodies met and darted back to his face. "I didn't mean to do that," she whispered.

Josh took in every detail of her. Her hair fanned out around her, framing her face. She was beautiful. Without taking his eyes off hers, he bent and kissed her, caressing her lips with his.

"Oh, Dana—

She turned her face away. "I think we better get some sleep. It's getting late. It'll be an early morning and a long day, especially for you."

When he stood and pulled Dana to her feet, he wondered why she wouldn't let him say what he so desperately wanted to say. It was clear she cared for him on some level. She wouldn't be so good to Tori or spend so much time with him, not to mention how her body responded to his, if she didn't feel something for him.

He followed Dana to her spare room. She flipped on the overheard light after she went through the door. She said something about extra blankets and pillows. Then she walked to the bedside table. She turned on the light by the bed and turned back the covers. Josh wasn't really listening to her; he was too interested in watching her move round the room. He remained in the same spot, only shifting enough to follow her movements. When she returned to the doorway, the comment she made right before turning out the light on the ceiling caught his attention.

"What was that last part? I didn't quite catch it all."

"I said if you need anything, you know where to find me."

He smiled.

After she kissed his cheek and murmured a goodnight, she left, closing the door behind her. He waited until the sound of her footsteps faded before he flipped the wall switch back on. He changed into pajama pants and no shirt, put the bed covers back into place, turned out the lamp, and took his toiletry bag across the hall to the bathroom. When he finished and put away his toothbrush and toothpaste, he quietly walked to Patrick's room. He could see by the glow of a nightlight that both children were asleep. Not even Zoe, who was curled beside Tori on the bottom bunk, stirred.

He padded back across the dark house. Taking his bags with him, he went to Dana's door. For a moment, he stood still, taking slow, deep breaths. When he eased the door open a crack, he saw her on the far side of her bed, reading. The lower half of her body was under the covers, but he could tell she wore a pair of pajamas. Ducks in flannel never looked so good. He calmly and purposefully entered the room, shut the door behind him, and locked it. Without a glance in Dana's direction, he carried his bags into the master bath and laid out what he would need in the morning. Even though she hadn't spoken, Josh knew she watched him through the open doorway. It made him smile.

Josh avoided her gaze and lifted the covers to climb into bed beside her. He pulled the covers up to his waist and leaned back against the pillows with his hands clasped behind his head.

He finally met her eyes and flashed her one of his best smiles. She didn't return it. "What are you reading?" he asked.

She sat, unmoving and silent, eyes locked on him, her face expressionless. She stared and he made a point of making himself more comfortable.

"What in the world are you doing?" she asked.

He continued to be deliberate in settling himself into the bed. He eased closer to her before turning to face her with an easy smile. He felt her inching away and threw his arm across her hips to keep her from leaping from the bed.

"You told me if I needed anything that I knew where to find you. I've found you, and what I need is you."

"I am not having sex with you."

Josh almost laughed. "I bet I can make you want to."

She turned her eyes to her book, but Josh could tell she wasn't reading. "I didn't say I didn't want to. I said I'm not going to. There's a big difference."

"Are you saying you want to have sex with me?"

She turned a page. "I don't think this is an appropriate conversation. Neither do I think it appropriate for you to be in my bed, especially with two young children in the next room. If they find us in bed together, it would send them the wrong message."

"I checked on them. They're fast asleep. I'll be up and gone long before they wake up." He eased the book out of her fingers and shifted so that his body rested on her legs. He placed the book on the nightstand. She followed the movement with her eyes. He turned her face toward his. "Let me sleep with you tonight, Dana. I only want to hold you and be close to you. Besides, I think we should wait until we're married before we have sex."

He watched her eyes widen.

"Dana Bradley, I'm in love with you. I want you to be my wife."

When Dana's alarm went off Monday morning, the first sensation that hit her was how good it felt to wake up in Josh's arms. He reached over her and fumbled with the clock. After turning it off, he settled next to her and nuzzled her neck. She turned to face him, slid her arms around him, and kissed his lips. She knew she was crazy to be doing this, but it felt so good.

"Shower with me?" he whispered in her ear.

"You cannot be serious!" She attempted to slip away from him, but instead of releasing her, he pulled her more snuggly against the warmth of his chest.

"No, I guess I'm not." He sighed. "I know better, but I would like to be naked with you." He nibbled at her earlobe.

"That is never going to happen."

He stopped what he was doing to her ear. "Why do you say that?"

"There is no way I'm letting you see this body unclothed."

"You're telling me we'll always make love in the dark?"

"Are you ever serious, Josh?"

"What makes you think I'm not serious about making love to you? Why can't you understand that I love you? I think you're beautiful, and I can't wait to see you without clothes." He nibbled her ear again. Then he trailed kisses across her cheek to her lips. He kissed her hard and deep. "Will you marry me?" he asked against her mouth.

"No," she said, but her voice lacked conviction.

"Why not?" he asked in an unconcerned tone before he kissed her again.

"Because I think you'll change your mind in the next few days."

"I'm sure about this, more so than I've ever been about anything else." He kissed her again. "Do you love me?"

"I refuse to answer that question."

"Ah." He sounded smug.

When Josh backed out of her driveway, waving goodbye and blowing her kisses, Dana was hit with the second sensation of the morning. It was really going to hurt when this was over.

Josh settled into his seat for the one-and-a-half-hour flight from Standiford Field to Atlanta and was struck with inspiration. He pulled out a pad of drafting paper and the set of colored pencils that he carried with him when he traveled. He started by sketching several rough renditions of what he had in mind, making subtle changes from one rendering to the next.

Grudgingly, he folded his tray table up for takeoff. He clutched his supplies in one hand while tapping his finger on the armrest with the other the entire time the plane taxied and sped down the runway. When the captain okayed it, he immediately lowered his tray table and started drawing. He worked intently during the flight, pausing only when he accepted a cup of coffee and sugar packets from the flight attendant. He had completed each rendering to his satisfaction with colored details by the time the announcement was made to prepare for landing.

He smiled to himself and returned his drafting supplies to his duffle. Now he only needed to find a craftsman to make it happen. Surely someone in Atlanta could pull this off. Jordon or Abby would probably know someone.

"Are you some sort of designer?" the person in the seat next to him said in a soft Georgian drawl.

He turned to face the attractive woman beside him. "Not exactly, ma'am. I'm an architect."

"That's interesting. Were your sketches done with someone particular in mind?" Her eyes focused on his left hand for a split second.

"Yes, they were," he answered with a wide smile. "They certainly were."

"Do you live in Atlanta?"

"No. I'm only in town for a few days on business."

She held out a business card. "If you have time while you're in town, I would love to see more of your drawings. I may be able to help you with your project. My name's Mallory. Mallory Vincent."

Josh tucked the card into his bag and shook her hand. "Josh Peters."

"It's a pleasure meeting you, Mr. Peters. I hope you enjoy your stay in Atlanta."

"Thank you."

Josh grabbed his bags, exited the plane, and headed down the concourse toward the baggage claim area. He pulled out his phone and turned it on. He had two missed calls and two new voice mails. He checked the missed-call log. The first number was Abe. The second number he didn't recognize. It wasn't Dana, so whoever it was could wait. He dialed his brother. He was eager to find out if Jordon could help him with his project.

"Josh!"

"Jordon, hey, I'm in Atlanta."

"Just get here?"

"Yeah. I'm on my way to baggage claim now."

"Do you know what your schedule is for the week? Abby's planning to fix you dinner at least once while you're here."

"I'm not sure yet. I have a meeting at Atlanta Architecture this afternoon. I should know more after I talk with Abe. I'll give you a call sometime this afternoon or early evening for us to schedule something. Is Abby up to cooking?"

"Yeah. She's been feeling great. Now that she's made it through her first trimester, she says she feels human again. She's not throwing up all the time any-more. She seems to have more energy, and she's started to feel the baby move, too. I even felt him the other night. It was the most awesome thing!"

Josh smiled. "Do you know for sure you're having a boy?"

"No. It's not quite time for that yet. We haven't de-cided if we want to know before we see him or not. I think he's a boy, but Abby's convinced it's a girl."

"We found out with Tori because I didn't like call-ing the baby *it*, and I didn't want to refer to her as the wrong sex. I don't know. Knowing she was a she made it more real for me."

"How is my niece? Mom said she's staying with a neighbor. Mom talked like you and this woman are get-ting close."

Josh told his brother how Tori was doing and about their new house. He quickly described Dana and Patrick, assuring him he would give him more details when he saw him in person. He also asked his brother for help on his project. Jordon knew the perfect place and promised to take him there.

By the time Josh was done talking to his brother, he'd pulled his bag off the luggage carousel and was headed to the car rental counter. While he stood in line, he called Dana. He couldn't believe how good her voice sounded. She and the kids were packing a picnic lunch and had plans to make a day of it at the zoo.

He talked to Victoria for a while. He could tell she was excited. Patrick didn't want to talk on the phone but did yell hello from the background.

When Tori passed the phone back to Dana, Josh could hear the kids clamoring to leave. Dana told him they would call when they got home from Louisville that evening.

"Please be careful, Josh."

"Don't worry; I will be. I promise." He wanted to tell her again that he loved her, but decided he may have been pushing too hard.

Josh waited until he finished at the rental counter and settled in the car before checking his voice mail. Abe's message said he was checking to be sure there'd been no delays and to confirm the one o'clock meeting. The second message was from Monica. She sounded enticing and sultry even on voice mail. She wanted to meet for breakfast and was dying to see him. He rolled his eyes before he deleted her message.

Josh called Abe to tell him all was set for one. After that, he called Monica. He wasn't ready to see her yet and planned to bow out of breakfast. She answered her phone on the first ring and immediately began talking. He told her he was checking into his hotel and would call her later to set up a time to meet.

"Where are you staying?"

Without thinking, he told her. Before he could stop her, she told him she would meet him in the lobby and hung up. Josh slapped his phone down on the passenger seat. How in the world was it possible for that woman to always get her way?

Josh pulled into the garage near his hotel and parked his car. He went to the lobby, watching for any sign of his ex-wife. With any luck, he could avoid her by getting to his room before she arrived. He was getting ready to ask the staff not give out his room number without calling him first when the familiar scent of Chanel No. 5 reached his nose.

"Hello, Monica," he said without so much as a glance in her direction.

"I've been looking for you, dear. I'm so glad I found you. Let's get a bellhop and get these things to the room."

The man at the desk lifted the phone.

"No thank you," Josh said. "I'll take care of the luggage myself."

Monica flashed the man at the desk a smile. "He is so independent." She squeezed Josh's arm.

He wanted to shake her off, but knew he'd have to cause a scene to do it. He sensed she knew his thoughts, but she also knew he was not the kind of person who caused scenes. She was definitely up to something, and it wasn't going to be anything good.

Josh made his way to the room without speaking. Monica talked the entire time. Josh ignored her. He considered being rude and shutting the door in her face after he was inside, but she ducked in when he opened the door.

He set his bags near the entry. By the time he shut the door, she had removed her suit jacket and stood looking at him. She wore a form-fitting, sleeveless sweater. She looked good, very good.

"What are you doing here, Monica?"

"I wanted to see you."

"What do you want?"

She licked her lips and glided toward him. "Is it too much to believe that I missed you?"

"Not for one minute do I believe you've been down here pining away for me. If you cared so much about me, you wouldn't have left in the first place."

She placed her hands on his chest and locked her eyes with his. "What if I've realized I made a mistake?"

She was taller than Dana, and the heels she wore brought her head even with his nose. She was close, very close. Her finely formed body pressed against him.

Her perfume filled his nostrils. How many times had he longed for this moment? Prayed for this moment?

"I don't believe you."

She ran her hands down his torso. "Come on, Josh. We were always good together. Let's forget the past and start over."

Josh couldn't believe it. He gripped her wrists and pushed her away.

"I'm not going to play games with you, Monica. Tell me what you want. Tell me now or get out."

"I want you and Victoria to come back to Atlanta," she gushed. "We can move out of the city. You could design us a house. We could live in Alpharetta near Jordon and Abby. That's a great place to raise a family. You'd be close to your brother, and I'm sure Victoria would love the baby."

"It won't work, Monica. There's someone else in my life now."

She pulled herself free of his grasp and waved a hand. "Mama told me about Dana Bradley." She rolled her eyes. "Please, Josh. I know you've always been one for hopeless causes, but really."

She walked away from him and sat on the edge of the bed. Slowly she crossed her legs and examined her nails. "As I remember, her husband's death devastated her. I would imagine she still loves him. You can hardly compete with a dead man. Do you honestly think she could love him and you at the same time?"

Josh stared at her. The muscles in his jaw flexed, relaxed, and flexed again.

"Think about it," Monica murmured. "She's convenient. She's helping you with our daughter. She's hurting, and you pity her. You and I have known each other for years. We shared dreams. We have a child together. Which relationship makes more sense?"

Was Dana still so consumed with her love for Brandon that there was no room in her heart for him?

He heard Monica softly clear her throat. When he looked at her, she was giving him a small, concerned smile. She stood and bent to retrieve her jacket. Josh shook his head to keep from staring at her shapely backside.

She slipped into her jacket. "Come on. Let's grab some breakfast, and you can tell me all about Victoria."

Those last words brought him back to reality.

"If you were interested in Tori, you would've wanted her to come with me to Atlanta. You would have taken time off work to be with her."

"We need to work things out between us first," she said. "Breakfast?"

"No, thank you."

"Suit yourself. I'll go, but I'll see you later."

She breezed past him to the door. Automatically, he moved to open it.

She paused inside the open door and kissed him on the mouth. "I always get what I want, Josh."

Chapter 14

Dana, Victoria, and Patrick heard the lions roar, fed the giraffes, rode an elephant, did the Sky Trail twice, the zip line three times, and saw every animal in the Louisville Zoo. Their last stop was the gift shop. The staff locked the doors after the three of them left with their purchases. Both children were silent while they trudged to the car and got in. Dana smiled when she looked in the mirror and saw both of them asleep in their seats. She hadn't even driven out of the parking lot.

Staying busy all day kept her from missing Josh as much. Now that the car was quiet, it was much harder not to miss him. She was tempted to call him, but didn't. Talking on a phone while driving wasn't worth the risk.

After an hour-long drive, she parked in her garage and woke the kids. She got Patrick settled in his bathtub and Victoria in the guest tub before going to the kitchen to fix supper. When she tapped Josh's picture on her phone's favorites list, she could hear Tori singing.

"I thought the lions had eaten you or something," Josh said when he answered.

Dana laughed. "They wanted to stay until the zoo closed, and they were having such a great time that I let them. They're worn out; both of them fell asleep on the way home. Right now they're taking baths." She moved down the hall. "Can you hear that?"

"I hear her," Josh said affectionately. "She always does that."

Dana walked back to the kitchen. "That is the sweetest thing." She sighed. "They've both been so good today. I was afraid they might fight once they were together all night and all day, but so far it hasn't happened."

"They're good kids. They may never fight. Jordon and I always got along. We had occasional spats, but they were never anything serious."

She spread butter on three slices of bread and remained quiet.

"I miss you, Dana."

"I miss you, too. How is everything going? Do you know when you're coming back?"

"I'm flying out of here first thing Friday morning. I should be home by lunchtime. At least we'll have the weekend together.

"I met with Abe and the higher-ups at Atlanta Architecture. They want me to do more than head up this project."

Dana gripped her phone and held her breath.

"They've offered me a senior partnership," he said.

"That sounds like a big deal."

"It is. A very big deal. I get the impression they think I'm some kind of well-connected public relations guru. It all comes down to Marcus Taylor requesting me. And, somehow, that was Monica's doing. I'd have to move to Atlanta if I accept the partnership. It would be more money and more job security, I suppose, but I'd lose the flexibility I have now.

"Any thoughts on that?" he asked after a minute of silence.

"Sounds like she's trying to make it easy for you to come back to her," Dana muttered before going a little nuts with her spatula and flipping a grilled cheese sandwich onto the stovetop instead of in the pan. She bit back a groan and cleaned up her mess.

She started a new sandwich. "Do you know what you're going to do?"

"What do you think I should do?"

"I think you should do what's best for you and Victoria. And what makes you happy."

"I agree. That's exactly what I plan to do."

Dana wanted to know what that meant but told herself it wasn't any of her business.

Patrick and then Tori wandered into the kitchen. Dana fixed their plates and got them settled at the table. She kissed each of them on the head, gave them a reassuring smile, and left the room to finish her conversation.

"I saw Monica today," Josh said.

Dana closed her eyes and braced herself.

"She tricked me into seeing her," Josh said. "You were right. She wants me back. Well, she wants me in Atlanta anyway. She's trying to manipulate me, Dana. Is that the kind of woman you think I want to be with?"

"No. I think she's come to her senses. Maybe she's not intentionally trying to manipulate you. Maybe she's acting out of desperation to be back in your life."

"Your heart is too good to conceive the kind of thoughts Monica is capable of," he said. "It has certainly taken me too long to figure it out.

"I don't want to talk about my ex-wife," he said after a minute. "I don't want to think about my ex-wife, and I definitely don't want you thinking about her."

Dana heard him take a breath and let it out. "I'm going to have dinner with Jordon and Abby tomorrow," he said in a happier voice.

Dana was relieved by the change in topic. She laughed when he told her what Jordon said about the baby moving and the boy-versus-girl opinions Jordon and Abby had.

"That's better," Josh said. "That's the way I want you to be, laughing and happy."

"You make me happy," she said without thinking. She went to the kitchen. Thankfully, the children were finishing their meal. "Tori's ready to talk to you." She gave the phone to Victoria before she said anything else she would later regret.

She was surprised that Victoria found the energy to give her dad all the details about their day.

"Twins, Daddy," Victoria said after listening for a minute. "Tell them I want them to have twins, a boy and a girl. They'll be Patrick's cousins, too. He doesn't have any cousins at all. I'm sure he'd like a boy cousin . . ." Patrick nodded his head. ". . . and I'd like a girl cousin. Tell Uncle Jordon for me, Daddy. Tell him we need both."

Tori was quiet and listened.

"You're right," Victoria said into the phone. "I'll have Patrick pray for twins, too." Patrick nodded again.

"Hey, Josh!" Patrick called. "I wish you were here. We miss you."

Tori told her dad goodbye before holding the phone out to Patrick.

He stared at it for a few moments until Tori persuaded him to talk.

"Hi," Patrick said.

Patrick was quiet, and she could hear Josh asking him about the zoo. At first, Patrick made short, simple comments, but the longer he was on the phone with Josh, the more vocal he became. It amazed Dana that Josh was able to coax him into talking on the phone. Before long, both children were yawning.

"I better let you go," she said after Patrick passed her the phone. "I need to get these two in bed."

"Will you call me back after they're tucked in? I want to hear your voice again before I go to sleep. In fact, call me from bed. I'll pretend I'm there with you."

"Josh!"

He gave her a throaty chuckle. "I meant what I told you. I have every intention of seeing you naked. You better get yourself prepared."

She couldn't hold in a soft laugh.

"Oh, and Dana."

"Yes?"

"The only way I would take the job here is if you want to move to Atlanta."

*

Right before leaving his room Tuesday morning, Josh received a call from Tom Farris. He was missing one of the detail drawings from the plans Josh had delivered the previous week.

"I hate to bother you while you're out of town," Tom said. "I know you brought the plans over last week to avoid this. I checked everything but didn't realize it was missing until we needed it."

"It's not your fault it's not there," Josh said on his way to the parking garage. "I remember printing it. It must be in my office at the house. Dana has a key. I'm sure she won't mind letting you in. She's taking the kids to the aquarium up by Cincinnati today, though." Josh looked at his watch. "She's probably already left."

"No problem," Tom replied. "Steve knows how to get in touch with Dana."

Josh told himself that Dana was nothing like Monica. He kept repeating it over and over in his head. Then he realized Tom was talking. "Wait a minute, Tom. What was that last part?"

"I said I'd have Steve run over there and pick it up. He'll know what he's looking for. Thanks. Have a safe trip home."

After he finished work Tuesday, Josh drove out to Jordon's. His brother took him to a small shop not far from his and Abby's neighborhood. Josh was surprised to see the woman who sat next to him on the plane walk toward them. She and her husband owned the shop and specialized in custom-made pieces. A little more than an hour later, after talking with Mallory Vincent and her husband, Josh had picked one of his designs, had chosen the stones to be used, and had paid a deposit so that the Vincents could create it for him.

Over dinner, he, Jordon, and Abby talked about Victoria, Patrick, Dana, and the baby. When he told his brother and sister-in-law about Tori's twin request, they both laughed. Abby rubbed her belly and studied the swell of it. The three of them visited for a long time. Josh hadn't realized how much he'd missed his brother and sister-in-law.

"I haven't seen you smile this much in a long time," Jordon told him when they walked to the door. "Dana must be something else. I can't wait to meet her."

On the way downtown, Josh called Dana but got her voice mail. He checked the time. She and the children were probably making their way back to E-town. He left a message for her to call when they got home and settled. Even though he'd talked with her first thing that morning and again around lunch, he was eager to hear her voice.

When he reached his hotel, he hurried to his room and changed before returning to the lobby to meet Abe. Josh waited only a few minutes before he saw his friend walk in the front doors. They rode in Abe's sedan to the meeting between Atlanta Architecture and the board of directors from Southern Finance. Most of the talk on the way was Abe touting the benefits of Josh taking the position that had been offered to him.

The meeting place was an upscale bar and grill in downtown Atlanta. The patrons were dressed in suits and business casual attire. Sounds of conversations and televisions tuned to ESPN, CNBC, or CSPAN created a constant hum in the background.

Josh was not surprised, nor was he thrilled, to see his ex-wife coming toward him.

"Is that who I think it is?" Abe asked.

"It's her."

"Man, she looks good."

"Looks can be deceiving," Josh muttered.

"Abe," she said with what sounded like sincere pleasure. "How long has it been?"

"Too long, Monica." Abe returned her quick embrace. "I'd heard you were back in Atlanta."

She moved to Josh's side and looped her arm through his. "I do love this town, but it's not the same without Josh here with me."

Abe looked at him with raised brows. Josh shook his head and rolled his eyes, all the while biting his tongue to keep from saying something nasty to Monica in public. He maneuvered himself free of her grasp.

"Come with me, gentlemen. I'll take you to Marcus Taylor and the rest of the board."

Monica guided them to the back of the bar, up a set of wrought iron stairs, and into a private room. Monica led Abe and Josh around the room and stopped periodically to speak to someone or introduce them. Josh couldn't help but notice the looks most of the men gave her. He could tell she was aware of the attention. He wondered how many of the men in this room she'd slept with. Watching her now, it wouldn't surprise Josh to know that Ross Franklin hadn't been the only man she'd been with while they were married.

After he slipped away from Monica and ordered a drink, Josh checked his watch. Dana should be home by now. He checked his phone. No missed calls. He made sure it was set on vibrate and slid it back into his pocket.

"Expecting a call, dear?" Monica whispered in his ear.

Josh jerked in surprise. She wrapped herself around his arm before he could put space between them.

"Dana took Victoria and Patrick to Newport Aquarium today. She told me she would call when they were home and settled for the evening. She should be home by now."

Monica gave him a fake pout. "Let's not talk about her tonight. Think about being here with me." She squeezed closer to his side and rubbed her breast against his arm.

Josh managed to rein in his temper and pull away from her at the same time. He looked around. Thankfully, Abe had moved off to talk with a group from Southern Finance, and no one else seemed to be paying the two of them any attention. He turned back to his ex-wife.

"I love her, Monica."

Monica's normally cool blue eyes turned arctic. Just as quickly, her countenance changed. The anger and tension melted into a look of adoring interest.

"This must be the architect we've been hearing so much about," a voice said from behind Josh.

"Marcus," Monica said with a warm smile. "This is Josh Peters. Josh, Marcus Taylor."

Josh shifted to face the man and extended his hand in greeting.

Taylor shook his hand. "I'm excited to see what you've drawn up so far on this plan."

"Several of us have been working rather intensely, Mr. Taylor. I know the board won't be disappointed."

Taylor waved a hand. "Of course we won't be. But please, call me Marcus. With all Monica has told me, I feel as if I already know you."

Josh glanced at his ex-wife. She looked quite satisfied with herself.

"That's a fine woman you have there, Josh. May I call you Josh?"

Struck speechless, Josh merely nodded.

"I'm happy to see you two so well suited. I like having employees with happy, stable home lives. Happy at home means happy at work."

Josh watched Monica's smile grow. She stepped closer and slipped her arm under his jacket. What she was up to finally hit him. The irony was staggering.

"Actually—" Monica's nails dug into Josh's flesh. It took a great deal of restraint to keep from yelping in pain. He cleared his throat and held his tongue. He had no desire to take part in a scene that would reflect negatively on him, Abe, or the others from Atlanta Architecture.

Taylor seemed unaware of the exchange taking place. Josh pulled Monica's arm from around him and gripped her hand hard enough to cause her pain. She smiled at him, conceding a momentary truce with her eyes.

"Actually," Josh began again, giving her hand another squeeze. "I've told Monica for years that a good home environment is the key to a happy and successful life in every aspect."

With relief, Josh accepted his drink from the server a few minutes later. Monica hovered while he continued to speak with Taylor. When Josh finished his drink, he excused himself and found a men's room. Surely even Monica wouldn't follow him there.

Josh removed his sport coat and was not surprised to find blood on his shirt when he checked himself in the mirror. He pulled his shirttail farther out of his waistband and could see that the area was already swollen. He cleaned off the blood and asked himself how he had ever shared his life with someone so ruthless.

He was slipping his arms into his coat when his phone vibrated in his pocket. He pulled it from his slacks and thanked God it was Dana. "Are you okay?"

"Yes, we're all right." Her voice sounded strained and tired.

Josh left the men's room and walked until he found a door leading out onto an outdoor balcony. It was empty, and he stepped out and closed the door. "Honey, what happened? You sound upset. Are you sure you're okay?"

"There was an accident on the interstate. Don't worry. We weren't hurt or anything. It was just seeing . . ." He heard her take a shaky breath. "I came upon it after it happened. The ambulances were already on the scene and everything, but I watched them pull people from the wreckage."

Josh could hear her crying. More than anything, he wanted to be with her, to hold her. He prayed for her not to be sick.

"Dana, I love you. It's going to be all right. Are the kids okay? Did they see any of the accident?"

Dana took another deep breath. "No, I'm sure they couldn't see much from the back. They were watching a movie, too, so they were distracted from what was going on outside. I didn't break down until I got them into bed. I think I held it together well enough not to freak them out. I hope I did."

"I'm sure you did, sweetheart. Dana, you are so brave. You can't imagine how proud I am of you."

"I don't feel brave."

Josh told her how much he admired her strength and how great it was that she was so caring and loving when she had so many reasons not to be. She finally cut him off, but instead of crying she was laughing.

"Josh Peters, what am I going to do with you?"

"Keep me close to your heart, I hope."

Dana sighed. "How is it that you know exactly what to say to make me feel better?"

"I have a gift," he teased. "I don't want you to be anything but happy," he added in a more serious tone.

"You make me happier than you'll ever know."

Josh smiled. Man, he wanted to go home.

"I better let you get back to your party," Dana said after they talked for a while about the children and the aquarium.

"Are you sure?" Josh asked. "You'll be all right? You don't feel sick?"

"No, I'm not sick. I think you've taken care of that problem for me." She let out a relieved sigh. "I plan to soak in a warm bubble bath when I get off the phone."

"How can you do that to me?"

"Do what?" she asked.

"Leave me hanging with the thought of you in a bathtub while I'm stuck two states away."

"Oh. I didn't think about it that way."

"Well, I won't be thinking about anything else for a long time."

Dana wasn't sure where she was but had the feeling she'd been in the place before. The hall was long; the sterile white walls gleamed. For what seemed like a long time, she moved forward without getting any closer to the door at the end of the corridor. Then, suddenly, she stood at the door. She didn't want to open it, but knew she didn't have a choice. She watched her own hand reach out. An icy pain shot through her arm when her skin met the cold metal. She tried to pull her hand back but couldn't. No matter how hard she tried, she was unable to release it.

The door opened, and Dana felt herself forced into the room. Frigid air penetrated her lungs. Each breath hurt. Warmth was forced from her; her legs, arms, and fingers grew stiff. She was unable to turn back. She couldn't remember ever being so cold.

The room was dark except for the center where the light was excruciatingly bright. It made her squint. She wanted to run away, but all she could do was trudge forward.

After a while, she felt cold metal against her hip. She looked down to see a table. When her eyes adjusted to the brightness, she realized someone was lying on it. Looking to her right, she saw a familiar pair of men's shoes. Her eyes moved slowly up long legs, past a belt. She wouldn't allow her gaze to travel past the buttons on the shirt. The clothing was torn and soiled.

Blood was everywhere.

Almost as if someone gripped her, she felt herself turn to the left. The man's face was away from her; his upper body was strangely twisted. Against her will, Dana watched again while her own hand, now trembling, reached and turned the ice-cold face. Instead of what she expected—Brandon's dark brown eyes—a pair of piercing blue eyes stared blankly at her.

She opened her mouth to scream, but no sound came out. She felt herself falling. Right before her head struck the concrete floor, she woke with a jerk.

Rigid and numb, Dana lay in her bed. Her breaths were short and rapid. Darkness surrounded her. She touched her face. Her cheeks were wet, and her hands felt frozen. She made an effort to breathe deeply, trying to bring herself under control.

With stiff fingers, she grabbed her phone.

"Dana?" Josh said hoarsely after the phone rang several times. "What's wrong?"

Dana couldn't make her voice work. She looked at her clock. It was a little after two in the morning.

"Are you there?" Josh asked.

"I . . ." she said in a raspy voice. "I had a nightmare, and I called before I realized what time it was. I needed to make sure you were all right."

"It's okay." She heard the sound of him moving in bed. "Tell me about the nightmare. It'll make you feel better."

She took a deep breath and told him every detail. Believing it had happened seemed ridiculous after talking about it. She rubbed her face with her free hand.

"It seemed so real. I was afraid something happened to you."

"If I have to be down here again, I want you and the kids to come with me."

"Okay."

"You gonna be all right? Can you go back to sleep?"

"I think so."

"Have sweet dreams about me. Got it?"

"Got it," she replied. "I'll be glad when you get home."

"Me, too, sweetheart, me too."

Wednesday morning Monica stood in the alcove near the elevators watching the activity in the hotel lobby. She checked her watch. It wasn't quite nine o'clock. She knew Josh wasn't meeting with the board until eleven. She also knew he'd been out until early this morning. She assumed he'd be sleeping in.

Wearing her most seductive smile, she made her way to the concierge's desk. After talking with him a few moments, the man hurried to retrieve a master key and then escorted her upstairs. When the concierge opened the door, Monica could hear the shower running. She thanked the concierge profusely, closed and locked the door, and made herself comfortable in Josh's room.

While she sipped one of the cups of coffee she'd brought with her, she scanned the pages of Josh's Bible lying open on the desk. She read the marked verses.

Love is patient and kind. Love is not jealous or boastful or proud or rude. Love does not demand its own way. Love is not irritable, and it keeps no record of when it has been wronged. Yadda, yadda, yadda.

. . . the greatest of these is love.

She'd forgotten how Josh read his Bible every day, how sentimental he was. She wondered how the two of them ended up together. When he walked out of the bathroom with only a towel wrapped around his hips, she remembered.

He moved around the room as if he didn't realize she was there. Her gaze lingered over his body. His skin and hair were damp. She could tell he still ran every day. When his eyes met hers, he stared in surprise for a few seconds. Then his eyes clouded, and his face tensed.

"What the hell are you doing in my room?"

His reaction startled Monica, but she recovered and gave him a warm smile. "I brought you coffee. Hazelnut, black with extra sugar, exactly the way you love it." She lifted his cup from the carrier and offered it to him.

"I'm afraid you'd try to poison me," he muttered. He backed into the bathroom and returned wearing one of the hotel's robes.

"I want you out and I want you out now. I swear, Monica, I have a mind to call the police. Have you gone completely crazy? It's like you've become some obsessed stalker or something."

As he talked, he took the coffee from her hands and walked into the bathroom. Monica heard the sound of liquid running down the drain and a cup hitting the bottom of a trash can.

"That was a seven-dollar cup of coffee, Josh!"

"Good! Maybe you'll leave me alone and not buy me anymore. I would especially appreciate your not breaking into my room to bring it to me. How did you get in here anyway?" He walked back into the room and glared at her. If Monica hadn't known him so well, she might've been frightened.

"Oh, that was easy," she said. "I told the concierge that I'd gone out for coffee without my key and my husband was in the shower."

"Lying doesn't bother you?"

"I wasn't lying. You are my husband."

"I was your husband. Past tense. As in since the divorce you wanted."

"I told you I changed my mind."

"Oh, please! You think I don't know what you're doing? The only reason you're doing any of this is to earn points with Taylor. Forget it. You're not using me that way."

She walked slowly toward him. "I don't want to use you. Right now, I want to make love to you. It was always good between us."

"It's not going to work, Monica."

She moved closer and slipped her fingers into the chest hair left visible where the robe came together.

"Does she satisfy you, Josh? Is it as good with her as it was with me?"

He backed away and pulled the robe more tightly over his chest. "That's none of your business."

She slid the buttons on her blouse free. "How long has it been, Josh, since you've been with a woman? It's only been me, hasn't it? You've never been with anyone else, have you? Not before or since."

He didn't say a word, but Monica could tell by his expression that she was right. She moved closer to him, slipping her arms out of the sleeves of her blouse.

Josh's phone rang. The tone was a sweet, upbeat song. It had to be Dana. Monica watched Josh's nervous glance dart to the phone.

"Aren't you going to answer it, darling? Would you like me to answer and tell her that you're indisposed at the moment?"

He snatched up his phone. "I want you out, and I want you out now," he growled.

Monica, very slowly, very deliberately, dressed herself. She moved to the door. "I'll see you at Southern later on today, Josh. I look forward to it."

Running a hand through his hair, Josh listened to the voice mail Dana left. "I'm sorry I missed you. I guess you've already gone to work. Give me a call when you can. Oh, Steven is coming by later this morning to get those plans. The kids and I are going on a picnic by the lake, then to a movie this afternoon. If you call and don't get me, we're probably at the theater. I hope you aren't too tired today because of me. Miss you. Bye."

He paced around the room for a while before he dressed. Feeling a little calmer, he called Dana. When the call went through, Victoria greeted him instead of Dana.

"Hey, sweetheart. How are you this morning?" he said.

"I'm good, Daddy. How are you?"

"I'm fine."

"You sound kinda tired. Are you tired?"

"I'm a little tired. I didn't get much sleep last night."

"That's too bad," she said. "Dana's taking us on a picnic and to a movie today," she said more brightly. "We're gonna take Steve with us. He's on break from school, too. He told Patrick and me that he was going to be lonely today so we invited him to go with us. I think that was nice of us. Don't you think that was nice of us, Daddy?"

"Yes, honey that was very nice of you," he said, trying hard not to sound sarcastic.

"Daddy, do you want to talk to Dana? She's coming in the door right now."

"Where has she been?"

"She took Steve over to our house to get some papers or something. I gotta go. It's my turn to feed Zoe. I love you, Daddy! Take a nap later so you won't be so grumpy."

With that, Tori was gone. Josh heard some muffled sounds. Between Monica's antics and Dana's nightmare, he'd had next to no sleep, he'd already had an exasperating day without leaving his room, and now Dana was spending the day with Steve.

"You've got quite a full day planned," he said when Dana's hello came through the line.

"What do you . . . oh, you mean Steven," she said in an understanding tone that made Josh even angrier. "Josh, you have no reason to be jealous, if that's the problem. Steven is a friend, a dear friend, but if it makes you feel any better, it wasn't my idea. I could hardly tell him he couldn't come when the kids asked right in front of him. What was I supposed to do?"

"I don't know, Dana," he said, his voice growing louder. "If you would listen to me, you would know that to him you are more than a friend. Are you going to kiss him when he tries so you don't hurt his feelings then either?"

"Josh, don't do this."

"Do what?"

"I'm not sure. You're obviously upset about something—something more than Steven going with us on a picnic. I've never heard you talk like this. Is it because I called in the middle of the night? Or has something else happened? Do you want to talk about it?"

"No, I do not want to talk about it!" he yelled.

Long, silent seconds passed. "I think we should discuss this later after we both have time to calm down. Goodbye, Josh."

He was left with the sound of dead space. *Way to go, Peters! You handled that well.*

Josh glanced at his watch. He growled in frustration, gathered his supplies and laptop, and headed out of his room. When he walked down the hall toward the elevators, he couldn't help but wonder what else would go wrong today.

Chapter 15

Monica stopped working when she heard voices. She moved closer to the slightly open door that connected her office to the conference room. Josh and Abe were alone in the room.

"Are you all right this morning? You look tired," Abe said.

Monica smiled. She knew why he looked tired.

"I'm fine."

"What you do at night with your ex-wife is none of my business," Abe teased, "but you need to be at your best for this presentation."

"You're right. It isn't any of your business. It also isn't what you think."

"Sure, Josh, whatever you say. I saw the way she treated you last night. No one would find fault with you for exercising marital rights. If I had an ex-wife and she looked like Monica, I—"

"It isn't that way."

"Everyone saw you leave with her."

Josh said something in response, but Monica couldn't make it out. His voice sounded farther away. He was probably pacing.

". . . is the main reason I'm tired this morning," Josh said. "It was difficult for me to get back to sleep after that."

"Was something wrong with Victoria?"

Monica couldn't understand why something being wrong with Victoria would have anything to do with her. She eased closer to the gap in the door but didn't hear Josh's answer.

"What in the world made her call you at two o'clock in the morning?" Abe asked.

Monica strained to hear but couldn't.

"She's a grown woman and she had to call you in the middle of the night because of a bad dream?" Abe said in disbelief.

"It was more than a bad dream. Her husband was killed in an automobile accident, and yesterday . . ." Josh's voice trailed off again. ". . . worried about her."

"I can see why you'd feel that way," Abe said after few moments. "Well, have another cup of coffee. I'm sure you'll do fine this morning."

The two men conversed more, but Monica couldn't hear well what either of them said. She got the impression that Abe was trying to talk Josh into or out of doing something. It wasn't clear what it was, but she assumed they were discussing Josh's promotion.

Monica was confident Josh would take the job, especially when she finished with her plans. She had no concerns about Josh exposing her to Taylor. Last night would have been his chance to say something, and she had taken care of that. Josh wouldn't say anything now for fear of losing the contract.

Monica walked back to her desk to resume her work once the group was gathered for the meeting. She heard

Josh's voice when he began his presentation. He sounded confident and positive. The earlier strain and tiredness were gone. She'd known he would be able to throw himself into his design. All this would work out. He'd probably thank her someday, even though he wasn't happy with her now. She knew he was going to be a lot less thrilled with her before it was finished. She would do whatever needed to be done to have what she wanted. Dana Bradley wouldn't make him happy. That was obvious. Josh would eventually understand.

After Josh finished his presentation, she heard the group move out of the conference room. Monica slipped into the room and spotted Josh's phone on the table. She could hear the architects and members of the board talking outside the main doors in the corridor. As she kept watch for anyone reentering the room, she easily found what she was looking for, jotted down the number, and returned to her office.

Steven and Dana were pushing the children in swings at the park when Dana's phone rang. She excused herself and walked away from the playground toward the lake.

"Hello?" Steven heard her say. "Yes, this is Dana. Who is this?"

Steven had the feeling that something wasn't right. He could no longer hear Dana, but the way her body stiffened told him something was going on.

This morning when he went by her house to pick up the plans Josh forgot to leave with his dad, Dana was fine, but when he met up with her for the picnic, her mood had changed. She hadn't said anything out of the ordinary, but Steven could tell she was upset about something. Now whoever she was talking to was making that worse. She was on the phone for several minutes with her back to him. Her shoulders slumped more the longer the phone conversation went on.

Steven caught Dana's gaze when she looked over at him and the children. He'd spent enough time studying her from a distance to know that something was wrong. He watched her slide her phone into her pocket, drop onto a bench, and stare out over the lake.

He gave each of the kids one more push. "You two keep playing over here. I'll be right back."

"Okay, Steven!" they yelled.

He walked toward Dana. When he placed a hand on her shoulder, she jerked with a start. She wiped at her eyes. "Steven," she said without looking at him. She sniffed and continued to rub at her face. "I don't want the kids to see me cry."

Steven glanced over at the children who were competing to see who could go higher. Neither seemed aware of any problem. "They're fine," he said before he slipped onto the bench next to her. He placed his arm on the back of the seat around her shoulders, positioning himself to see both Dana and the children. "I'll keep an eye on them. Tell me what's wrong."

She said nothing.

Steven gave her shoulder the slightest squeeze. "We're old friends, Dana. Come on. You can talk to me."

She turned to look at him but still didn't say anything.

"Has something happened to Josh?" he asked.

Her expression changed ever so slightly.

"Did he have an accident?" Steven asked.

She looked at the water. "I don't think this was any accident."

Steven waited a few seconds, but Dana said nothing more.

"Do you have feelings for him? Feelings beyond friendship?"

Not one word came out of her mouth and her gaze remained locked on the water, but Steven knew from the way she pressed her lips together that he'd hit a sore spot.

"I don't think the way I feel will have much bearing on the situation at this point," she said after a minute.

He gave Dana's shoulder another, firmer squeeze and kissed her temple. "You don't want the kids to know you're upset, do you?"

She pasted a smile on her face. "I'm not upset."

Steven studied her. No one who didn't know her well would be able to tell once the tears were wiped from her face. He squeezed her knee, told her he'd be right back, and went to the table where the remains of their lunch sat to grab some napkins. He gave the kids a wave and a smile. He should be able to keep Patrick distracted enough for the rest of the day so he wouldn't notice that something had upset his mom.

"They won't be able to tell you were crying," Steven told her after she dabbed at her eyes and cheeks with the napkins. "Are you sure you don't want to talk about it?"

She smiled and shook her head. Boy, she was an expert at hiding emotions.

"Well, try not to think about it," he said. "Let's enjoy our day. I promise; it'll all work out—one way or another." Steven sat inches from her; his hands enveloped her upper arms. He longed to pull her against him and kiss her.

"You're a great guy. You know that, Steven?"

Josh hadn't had a private moment all day, and he desperately needed to apologize to Dana for being a total jerk that morning. He checked his phone throughout the day, hoping she'd left him a message. He would be happy just to know she'd called, but the only missed calls were from Steve. There were at least a half dozen of those. Josh couldn't imagine why he had called so many times. Surely if something were wrong with the plans he picked up this morning, he would have left a message and been done with it.

He called Dana when he walked from the Southern Finance building. He was disappointed when he heard her recorded voice requesting that the caller leave a message. He looked at his watch. They must still be at the theater.

"Dana, it's me," he said into his phone. "Honey, I want to apologize for losing it this morning. Please forgive me. Call me as soon as you can. I love you."

Once he reached his rental car, he loaded everything, including himself, before pulling up Steve's number. Too late, Josh remembered that Steve was spending the day with Dana and the children. If they were at the theater, he was at the theater.

"Steve, this is Josh. I saw that you called several times today. I haven't received any messages from you, though. I hope everything's okay with the plans. Call me if there's a problem. I didn't mean to cause you any inconvenience. Bye."

Josh drove out of the parking garage and reflected on his day, which, thankfully, hadn't been a complete disaster. The presentation to the board went well. They loved the preliminary plans he and the other architects had drawn up, and they had given Atlanta Architecture the go-ahead to do the final blueprints. His private talk with Marcus Taylor had also gone well, much better than he had anticipated. Marcus had been disappointed but not angry when Josh explained that he and Monica were no longer married. If he could make things right with Dana, all would be right in his world.

Later Wednesday evening when Josh heard Dana's ringtone, he snatched up his phone. "I didn't think you were ever going to call. Dana, I am so, so sorry. I—"

Josh heard little girl giggles. "Tori, is that you?"

"Yep." She laughed some more, then suddenly stopped. "Why are you apologizin' to Dana? Did you do something bad to her?"

"I lost my temper this morning, and I said some things I didn't mean. Is she where you can give her the phone?"

He could hear the sound of Tori walking. "I can't find her. She was right beside me a minute ago. She showed me how to call you on her phone and everything."

He heard more movement. "Patrick, where's Mom? Dad wants to talk to her." Josh heard Patrick's muffled response but was unable to distinguish the words.

"Patrick says, 'Hi, Dad.' We've started calling Dana Mom and you Dad in secret," she said in a loud whisper. "Isn't that cool? I can't wait until we can do it for real."

Josh laughed. "I can't wait, either, sweetheart. While you look for Dana, tell me about your day."

They'd had a picnic at the park, played on the playground, and fed the ducks. She gave a detailed summary of the movie they saw that seemed to include every scene. He also learned that Steven, as his daughter was now calling him, helped prepare dinner and ate with them.

"I found Dana. She's in the bathroom."

"Is she sick?"

Tori was quiet for a moment. "It doesn't sound like it. I've been watching since you've been gone. I don't think she's been sick at all, and she's been eating lots more than she used to. I think we're helping her, Daddy."

"I hope so." Josh heard the tone indicting another call. "Honey, I've got another call. Can you hold on a minute? Don't put down the phone; hold it to your ear for a minute. I'll come back on the line."

"Okay."

Josh checked his display. "Steve?" he said after switching lines.

"Yeah, Josh. It's Steve."

"Could you hold on for a sec? I've got Victoria on the other line. Let me tell her goodbye, and I'll be right back with you."

"Sure. That's fine. Take your time."

Josh switched back to his daughter. "Tori, Daddy needs to take this other call. I'll call you back in a little bit. Will you do me a favor?"

"Absolutely. What is it?"

"I want you to tell Dana a secret."

"Okay. What?" she asked in a low voice.

"Tell her I love her. You got it?"

"Got it," she replied confidently after a little giggle.

"I love you, honey."

"Love you, too, Daddy. Bye."

"Steve, I'm back. Is there something wrong with the plans you picked up this morning?"

"No, the plans are fine."

Josh waited, but Steve didn't say anything more. "But there is a problem?" Josh asked.

"Yes, there's a problem. It has nothing to do with house plans."

Josh paced back and forth in his hotel room and waited for Steve to explain. He paused when he heard Steve inhale and blow out a long breath.

"Josh, did you call Dana today around lunchtime?"

"No, I haven't talked to Dana since this morning. She had just been with you at my house, giving you the missing plans, when we spoke last."

"You said something then to upset her, didn't you?"

Josh started walking again and ran a hand through his hair. "Yes, unfortunately I did."

"She deserves better than that. I expected better from you."

"You're right," Josh said. He cleared his throat. "I left her a message apologizing, but she hasn't returned my call. Apparently, Dana's not ready to forgive me. She had Victoria call me."

"You're not the only one who called and upset her today."

Josh stopped pacing. "What are you talking about?"

"Someone called her while we were at the lake. Whoever it was had Dana so upset she was crying."

"Crying? Is she all right? What happened?"

"Yes, she's all right, as far as I could tell anyway. I have no idea who the caller was or what they said, but I think it must have had something to do with you. The number was from Atlanta. I checked it on the White Pages website. It's a cell number."

"Dana talked to you about the call?" Josh asked.

"Not exactly."

"How did you get the number?"

Steve cleared his throat. "When she took Tori to the restroom before the movie, I slipped her phone from her purse and checked the call log. She doesn't know I did that or that I'm calling you."

"I don't understand any of this," Josh said in exasperation. He stood motionless, thinking before he spoke again. "What's your part in it, anyway?"

"I care about Dana. I'm trying to find out who upset her and why."

"Care about her, how?" Josh asked.

"That's not the issue," Steve said after a long pause. "You're the one she cares about."

"She told you that?"

"Not in so many words, but right now I think we should focus on figuring out who called Dana, why they called, and what the person said to upset her."

Josh walked to the desk by the window and picked up a pen. "Do you have that number with you?"

"Yeah."

Josh stared at the numbers he'd written down. It couldn't be. Knowing the numbers would match, he checked what he'd written down against the directory on his phone.

"I think I know what's going on," Josh said. "I doubt if Dana will talk to me. If you see her, please tell her not to believe whatever the caller said."

❧

When Dana reached the door after tucking the kids into bed for the night, Tori whispered for her to come back. Dana walked to the edge of the bottom bunk. She glanced first at Patrick who was already asleep and then looked at Victoria. Tori patted the mattress beside her.

"What is it, honey?" Dana whispered after she sat down.

"Daddy wanted me to tell you a secret."

Dana tensed at the mention of Josh but was careful not to let Victoria know there was a problem. She brushed a strand of hair from Tori's face. "What's the secret, sweetheart?"

Victoria used her hand to motion Dana to come closer. Dana leaned over until her ear was directly above Tori's lips. "Daddy wanted me to tell you that he loves you." She giggled. "You know what else?"

Forcing herself to smile, Dana looked at Victoria. "What else?" Dana whispered.

"I love you, too, Dana, and I can't wait for you to be my mom."

Dana patted Tori's cheek. "I love you, too, sweetheart." She kissed Tori and left the room.

As she walked across the house to her bedroom, she refused to let herself cry. She'd known all along this would happen. It was foolish for her to believe for a second that she and Josh Peters would fall in love with each other. She had told herself that if he and Monica reconciled, she wouldn't stand in their way.

Dana was ready for him to be back so they could go on like nothing had happened between them. She hoped she was up to it. What if he and Monica decided to live here, next door? That would be awful. She could let go —after all, there wasn't much to let go—but she didn't want to watch Josh and Monica together day in and day out.

When she turned down the blankets on her bed, her phone rang. It was Josh. Instead of answering it, she crawled into bed and pulled the blankets up to her chest. She was hurt and angry, and talking to him would only make that worse. She didn't understand how he had the audacity to say the things he did this morning after what he'd done last night. If he'd rather be with Monica, that was fine, but he didn't need to pretend to care about her. Dana knew he felt guilty. It was the whole pity thing, just as she suspected from the beginning.

Her phone buzzed with a voice mail message. She picked up her book and began to read. Her phone rang again. It was Josh. He left another message. When he called the third time, she turned off her phone.

Thursday morning, after a restless night, Josh left his hotel and headed for Southern Finance. After checking the directory, he headed for the elevator. Even though it was early and there weren't many people around, he was sure she would already be at work. The desk in front of her office was occupied. The young man had his head bent over his desk, studying an appointment calendar.

"Is she in?" Josh asked when he went by.

In reply, the assistant leaped to his feet. "You can't go in there! She won't see you without an appointment, and I know you don't have an appointment."

"Oh, she'll see me." Josh pushed through the door.

Josh almost felt sorry for the guy trailing behind him when Monica looked up from her work and glared at him. A sharp reprimand was on her lips until she realized who caused the disturbance.

"I tried to stop him, Ms. Simpson-Peters. Do you want me to call security?"

"No, Scott. We don't need security. This is my husband."

The young man gave Josh a sympathetic look.

"Ex-husband," Josh said. "She's having trouble remembering that part for some reason. You'd think it would be easy for her since the divorce was her idea."

"That's all, Scott," Monica said. "Be sure we're not disturbed."

"Yes, Ms. Simpson-Peters." The assistant scurried out the door and clicked it shut behind him.

With smug confidence, Monica came around her desk and leaned on the front of it. "To what do I owe this pleasant surprise? Have you come to finish what we started in your room yesterday?"

Josh positioned himself so that he towered over her. She nearly lost her balance when she looked up at him. "I want to know what you told Dana when you called her yesterday."

She looked surprised for a second, but her expression quickly became neutral. "Why don't you ask her?"

"She won't speak to me. I want to know what you told her."

Monica slipped away from him and moved behind her desk. "I didn't tell her anything that wasn't true."

Josh slammed a fist down on the desk. Wide eyed, Monica moved farther back and fell into her chair. "I am not going to play games with you, Monica. I want to know what you said to her."

Josh let out a frustrated growl when she shook her head. "I am finished with you, Monica. Do you understand that? I am not taking the partnership here; I am not moving to Atlanta. You gave up our marriage. You gave up our daughter. It's over. I don't want to hear from you or see you again. I've taken a lot off of you over the years, not to mention the abuse you've dished out to me this week, but I refuse to stand by and let you mess with the people I love. Is that clear to you?"

She sat motionless, looking at him in stunned silence. He turned and stalked toward the door.

"I know you still care for me."

He stopped, turned, and looked at her. "What on earth would make you think that?"

"I heard what you said to Marcus yesterday. You could have told him I lied, but you smoothed it over with him. I know you did that for me. If you hated me, you would have used that against me."

"I don't hate you. I have never hated you, but I don't love you, not anymore. Don't confuse decency with caring. There are still people in the world who try to treat others the way they would like to be treated. I happen to be one of them. You might try it sometime."

"She won't make you happy."

"You don't know what happiness is, Monica." He extended his arm and swept it through the air indicating her office. "You think this is happiness? One day you're going to wake up. Your beauty will have faded, the work won't mean anything, and you're going to be alone. All the money in the world is meaningless without someone to share it with."

He walked away from her. When he reached the door, he stopped and turned back. "And you're wrong about Dana. She already makes me happy."

Chapter 16

When Josh got home Friday, the reception he received from Victoria, Patrick, and Zoe was exuberant. The reception Dana gave him was cool. She was courteous and certainly didn't act angry. She gave him a quick hug but ducked away from him before he could embrace her. He didn't come close to getting a kiss. She invited him in for lunch but maintained her distance. The children talked almost constantly while the four of them ate together, telling him about their week and asking questions about his trip. Dana spoke little, only answering questions from the kids or encouraging them to tell about an aspect of their week's activities. Dana smiled and was pleasant, but not once did she make eye contact with him.

After the four of them cleared the table, Dana announced that she and Patrick needed to run some errands.

"Ah, Mom! Do I have to go? Josh just got home. Can't I stay here with him and Tori?"

"We could all go," Josh said.

"No!" Dana said. "I mean, you're probably tired. It's okay with me if Patrick stays with you, if you don't mind."

"I don't mind," Josh said.

The children whispered to each other.

"Is it okay if we look through the stuff you brought us?" Tori asked.

Josh gave them a smile. "It's okay, but don't open anything yet. Not all of it is for you two. Some of it's for your mom."

Dana walked toward her garage. "I've got to go."

While the children went through what he'd brought, Josh followed Dana into her laundry room. She was struggling to pull her keys from her purse.

"Dana, we need to talk."

She stopped working to free her keys, sighed, and dropped her head. Her back was to him. "There isn't anything to talk about," she said. "I understand. I knew this would happen. You don't need to explain anything to me."

He reached out and placed a hand on her shoulder and felt a slight shudder pass through her. He turned her to face him. "Then maybe you need to explain some things to me because I don't know what you're talking about."

He lifted her chin with his fingers. For several moments, she kept her eyes closed. When she opened them, her expression was devoid of any emotion. "I spoke with Monica while you were gone," she said with no hint of anger or hurt. "You don't have to explain anything to me or continue to pretend there's something between us."

"Dana—"

She stepped away from him and held up a hand, palm toward him. "I have to go. I have a ton of things I need to do." She smiled and walked out the door into the garage.

❦

Later Friday night, Dana stepped from the tub and wrapped herself in a large towel. She sighed. The bath hadn't helped much.

She ran her brush through her damp hair and realized the house was too quiet. She'd left Patrick in the living room watching television, but she couldn't hear it.

She walked through her dimly lit bedroom and stuck her head out into the hall. The TV was off; the house was silent. Even if he'd gone to the basement, she should hear him. From her bedroom, she could see that the basement door was open. She called his name. Neither Patrick nor Zoe responded. Zoe would be wherever Patrick was and would come even if Patrick hadn't heard her call. She called again, this time more loudly. She opened the door wider.

"He's at my house, with Grammy and Gramps," Josh said from behind her.

She spun around. "What are you—"

"I want to talk to you. I didn't want you to have time to put up the emotional barriers you're an expert at erecting. I thought surprise might work in my favor. I see that it has, in more ways than one."

He looked from her face to the towel and back again while he walked toward her. Then he smiled. It was so unfair! He belonged with Monica. Apparently, he enjoyed the time he'd spent with Monica. He wasn't supposed to make her feel this way; she didn't want him to be able to make her feel this way. She swallowed, trying to get a grasp on her runaway emotions.

She clutched the towel to her chest. "This is completely inappropriate. You shouldn't be here."

He moved closer and pulled her away from the door at the same time. Quietly he closed it and positioned himself so that she couldn't move around him. His eyes bore into hers. "I need to talk to you. If catching you in a towel is what it takes to get you to listen to me, so be it." He penetrated through the barrier of her fingers and gripped the top edge of the towel. Dana felt his knuckles on her chest. He surely could feel her heart pounding. "If you promise to hear me out and talk to me without shutting me out, I'll let you get dressed."

She glared at him. "You'll let me? Let me?" She hugged the towel tightly and wrenched it out of his grasp. "Josh Peters, I don't know who you think you are, invading my privacy in my home, taking my son out of my house without my knowledge, and telling me you're going to allow me to do something, but you can forget it. After yelling at me for spending time with a friend I've known for ten years, especially after you . . . with . . ." She finally groaned out some unintelligible sound. "Get out of my house."

"If you had bothered to listen to any of the dozens of messages I left you or returned even one of my phone calls, you would have heard several apologies for the way I spoke to you Wednesday morning. If you had bothered to take my calls after I learned Monica spoke to you, you would have known that everything she told you was a lie."

"Really? She lied? Hah! She told me you'd be this way. She said you felt 'obligated' to me, that you told her you still loved her, but you didn't want to hurt me because I was 'needy and pitiful.' She told me that you want to take the job in Atlanta, that I'm holding you back."

"None of that is true. If you would calm down, I could explai—"

"Calm down? Now you're telling me to calm down." She repositioned her towel higher on her chest. "Do you deny being with her at that cocktail party? Do you deny spending the entire evening with her?"

"Dana, it wasn't—"

"Do you deny going with her that night to her con-do?"

"Would you—"

"Do you deny not being able to answer the phone when I called you Wednesday morning because the two of you were too busy showering together?"

"Now, hold on a—"

"And finally—and I'm really interested in how you're going to try to talk your way out of this one—do you deny lying next to her in bed when I called and talked to you after my nightmare?"

His jaw dropped.

"Monica knew all about my call in the middle of the night. How would she know I called if she wasn't with you, not to mention the fact that she knew I had a nightmare? What did the two of you do? Laugh at me after you talked to me and told me to have sweet dreams? Or did you talk about how needy and pitiful I was?" She reached up to wipe tears from her face. Why was it so easy for him to make her come unglued?

"Oh, Dana, please listen to me, honey." He put his hands on her upper arms and squeezed.

She pulled away. "Please don't touch me. It's okay. I do not need your pity. You are in no way obligated to me. If Monica makes you happy, then . . . you don't owe me anything."

"You don't understand. I need you, Dana."

She let out a bitter laugh.

"Do you have any idea what my night was like Tuesday?" Josh asked.

Dana couldn't help rolling her eyes. "I can imagine, but please spare me the details. You know what? I've had enough of this conversation. I'm going to get dressed. You know the way out."

She turned away with the intention of escaping to her bathroom where she could lock the door. She sensed his movement behind her and hoped he was leaving. Right before she made it through the door, he caught her arm and spun her to face him. The towel nearly fell from her body. She grasped it and then noticed he had taken off his shirt.

"What do you think you're doing?"

"I'm showing you what Monica did to me at the party when I started to tell her boss we were no longer married. Maybe then you'll believe me."

He turned his back to her. Low on Josh's left side was a set of five ugly marks. The area was badly bruised. "It looks awful! What happened?"

"Monica clawed me to stop me from exposing her lies."

"Oh," Dana said when he turned around. She had a hard time taking her eyes off his chest. She pulled her towel tighter again.

"Are you cold?"

"No." She cleared her throat. "But I think I should get dressed, and you should put on your shirt."

"Do you believe me now?" he asked.

She didn't want to, but his eyes told her he was telling the truth. She nodded.

He smiled and caught her in a loose embrace. "Would you do me a favor before you get dressed?"

She used her arms to squeeze the towel against herself. "A favor?"

He nodded and he bent his face toward hers. "Let me kiss you."

"I don't think—"

"You think too much," he said against her ear.

"Okay."

The kiss began slowly, tentatively but then deepened, and Dana gave herself over to him. His arms held her against his body. She could feel the warmth of his chest through the towel and feel his hands moving up and down her back. She wrapped her arms around his neck and ran her fingers through his hair. Nothing about this felt like pity or obligation.

The towel slipped, and Dana tried to tell herself to stop, to pull away. Josh did the stopping. He didn't pull away, which was a good thing. The towel would have fallen to the floor. She reached between them and secured the towel.

She could feel laughter rumble in his chest. "I messed that up, didn't I?"

"I'm glad you did," she said with relief.

He kissed her forehead. "I missed you, Dana. I am so, so sorry all this happened."

Josh waited for Dana in her living room. He snapped the jewelry box closed and stood when he heard her footsteps in the hallway.

"Don't I need to get Patrick? Your mom and dad probably want to go home."

"They're fine," he said. "I told them we would be a while."

Dana looked unsure and glanced toward her back door.

"Honestly," Josh said, "Patrick was happy to see my parents. This is important, Dana. Please, we need to talk."

She rubbed her hands up and down on her pants before she lowered herself onto the sofa. "Okay," she murmured. "I'm listening."

He sat next to her and took a deep breath. "Tuesday night—"

"You don't have to explain that," she said without looking at him. "It's not really any of my business."

"You don't get it, do you? I want it to be your business. I don't want any secrets between us, and I want you to stop blocking me out, pretending you don't feel the things you feel."

"Josh, I—"

"Stop. I love you, Dana. Even if you never care for me the way you did for Brandon, I still want you in my life. I know we haven't known each other long, but I have never known anyone like you. I don't want to live life without you.

"I don't know how Monica found out about your nightmare. I have no way to explain it. I swear I didn't sleep with her, and I need you to know what happened to me in Atlanta. I want you to care about what happened to me."

"I do care."

He stared at her, praying she would say the words he longed to hear. She looked at him, looked away, and looked for a long time at her hands in her lap before meeting his gaze.

"I was afraid to let myself care about you," she said. She took a breath and let it out. "Losing Brandon hurt more than anything I've ever experienced, and I didn't want to open myself up for that kind of agony again."

"I can't promise you nothing will ever happen to me, but you said before that you wouldn't trade the time with Brandon to escape the hurt. Can't you give me that chance?"

Her eyes glistened with unshed tears, but she smiled at him and nodded.

"I know you loved Monica very much," she said after a minute or two. "I didn't want to be in the way if she had changed, truly changed, and wanted to be your wife again. Once I realized how I felt about you . . . well, that's why I didn't tell you."

He shook his head slowly. He wondered if she was ever going to tell him.

"And I was afraid you felt sorry for me and confused that with love."

"I wish you'd get that out of your head," he said. "Pity is one thing I have never felt for you. Yes, I wanted to help you—still want to help you—but not because I felt sorry for you."

She clasped his hands. "Okay. Would you please tell me what happened between you and Monica in Atlanta?"

"From the beginning, even before I decided I would go down there, I told you she was up to something. Well, it turns out that her new boss is a devoted husband, father, and grandfather. Apparently, she thought it would earn her points with him if she pretended to still be married. When I met Marcus Taylor, Monica's boss, he said something that gave me the impression that he thought Monica and I were still together. I tried to explain that we weren't. That's when she stuck her nails in me."

Dana squeezed his hands.

"During the party, she stayed on me like glue except when I slipped away and spoke with you on the phone. I'm sure she was trying to make it appear that we were together. Plus she didn't want me to say something to give her away.

"When you called me after the nightmare, I hadn't been in my room for more than a couple of hours. I fell for it when Monica told me she had a headache. She's been plagued with migraines since we were adolescents, and I believed her. I ended up driving her home in her car. It didn't happen the way she told you. I did not spend the night with her, and we did not shower together the next morning."

"I shouldn't have believed her." Dana looked at the ceiling and then back at him. "Did you want to spend the night with her?"

"No, Dana, the only thing I thought about when I was hiking across downtown Atlanta in the middle of the night was how much I wanted to be home with you and our children."

She was quiet for a few moments and seemed to be letting the information sink in.

"How did you know Monica called me?" she asked.

"Steve. He called and told me someone you spoke to on the phone upset you. Together we figured out that it was Monica."

"But, how did he—"

"That doesn't matter. He was worried about you and wanted to make sure you were all right. I shouldn't have accused you the way I did. I owe Steve a lot. If it hadn't been for him, I would have assumed you were angry because of the way I spoke to you Wednesday morning. I apologize for that. I wasn't angry with you. I hadn't had much sleep, and then the ordeal with Monica when I found her in my room—"

"I thought you said—"

"I didn't let her in. I came out of the bathroom after my shower that morning, and there she was. She admitted to lying to the concierge so that he would unlock the door for her. One thing I've learned from all this is how conniving and manipulative Monica truly is. Her leaving was the best thing that could have happened to Victoria and me. I hope I never see her again."

"Oh, Josh, I'm sorry it ended up this way."

"I'm not. Now that I know you, I know what love is supposed to be." He pulled her onto his lap and kissed her. He placed light kisses over his favorite place on her neck. She pressed herself closer to him. "You never did tell me how you feel about me," he murmured against her skin. "I need to hear you say it."

"I love you," she said before she kissed him.

The kiss lasted a long time. It felt so good to have her in his arms. He didn't want to ever let her go. He cradled her in his lap, held her close. "I want to marry you, Dana. I want to be a father to Patrick, and I want you to be Victoria's mother."

"I want that, too."

He thought he'd have to do more persuading. "Are you sure?"

She looked thoughtful and remained quiet. As he could with Victoria, he could sense the wheels turning in Dana's mind. "Yes, I am," she finally said.

"Are you willing to make it official?"

She sat up. "Official?"

He held the open ring box in front of her. Her gaze dropped from his face to the box.

"Oh, Josh, it's beautiful."

He removed the ring from the box and slipped it on her finger. "I had it made for you. I designed it. See, two emeralds," he pointed out the stones on each side of the center diamond, "for Victoria and Patrick, an amethyst for you, and a sapphire for me."

"When did you do this? Where did you find a jewelry shop to make it?"

"I came up with the idea on the way down to Atlanta."

He told her about Mallory, her husband, and his trip with Jordon to Vincent's.

"Will you marry me, Dana?"

"Yes." She wrapped her arms around his neck. "Yes."

Chapter 17

It took Monica a few weeks to figure out the sensation, but eventually she understood that she was experiencing regret. It didn't set in immediately after Josh burst into her office because she believed he would never sever contact completely. He had spoken out of anger that day. She knew once he went back to Kentucky, he would realize that she was right about Dana Bradley.

But as time went by and she didn't hear from him, she worried that she had finally gone too far. Even the regular phone conversations she had with her mother didn't help. Mama hadn't even seen Josh and Victoria at church. All Margaret would tell Mama was that they were going to a church where Victoria knew other children and that Josh and Victoria were happy there.

She tried to call him using both his cell and home number. Each time she heard a busy signal and then the call would disconnect. It finally occurred to her that Josh had blocked her calls. She tried calling from home, her cell, and her office phone. All gave the same result. She couldn't believe he'd done it.

She tried to push the feeling from her mind, but it kept coming back. She told herself that he didn't mean it. Even after she broke their marriage vows and left him, he'd still been there. Josh had always been there for her. He'd been hers since they were children. No matter what she had ever done, no matter how she had ignored him or mistreated him, he had always been hers. Josh loved her. He had to. He always had, and he always would.

As time passed, Dana, the children, and Josh grew closer. Josh was eager for their marriage to begin, but he could tell Dana needed more time. He gave it to her and let her set the wedding date. He wanted to be sure she completely trusted him. He didn't want any barriers between them.

In all aspects but a few, they were already a family. They shared household chores, ate dinners together, spent practically all of their time together, and treated each other's children as if they were their own. Victoria and Patrick both called him Dad and Dana Mom.

School was out, and baseball was in full swing. After one of their games, Josh was in the dugout with Mark and their boys. The rest of the team had cleared out. Patrick, Alex, and Wesley were helping collect the hats, batting gloves, and trash that littered the dugout while he and Mark gathered the team gear.

"If I'd known you needed a little boy, I could have rented a couple to you cheap."

Josh looked up to see Tammy Windsor smiling at him from the other side of the chain-link fence. He hadn't seen her since their date. Two boys, one about Patrick's age and another a little older, stood beside her.

Josh didn't know her sons played ball. He didn't know much about them at all, not even their names.

"Hello, Tammy."

"I didn't know you coached," she said.

"This is my first year." Patrick walked over and stood beside him. Josh put a hand on his shoulder. "I'm coaching my fiancée's son. This is Patrick." Josh looked down and smiled at him. "Patrick, this is Ms. Windsor and her two sons."

Josh thought she would introduce her boys, but she didn't. Patrick said hello, but she either didn't hear or chose to ignore him. The boys didn't speak either; they stared at Patrick. Patrick looked up at him. Josh shrugged and patted his shoulder.

"No wonder I haven't heard from you. You've been busy," Tammy said.

"Good game, everybody," Victoria called from behind him. Josh turned to see her running across the field toward them. She spoke to Mark, Wesley, and Alex but grew quiet when she realized other people were around. She tucked her body close to Patrick and Josh.

"Where's Mom?" Patrick asked.

Josh looked to where Victoria pointed. Dana stood near the stands talking with a group of people that included his parents, Jennifer, Steve, and Steve's grandmother.

"She's okay," Tori said. "She's over there, talking to everybody."

"Tori," Josh said, "do you remember Ms. Windsor, the lady who helped with the house?"

Tori nodded. "Hello."

Tammy glanced at Victoria, smiled slightly, but didn't speak to her.

Mark slapped Josh on the back. "Good game, coach. We're gonna take off. That is if I can drag my wife out of here." He smiled and nodded in Tammy's direction and gave Tori and Patrick affectionate good-byes.

"How are things in the real estate business?" Josh asked.

She smiled at him and walked around the fence. "It's going well. Summer's a busy time of year. How's your house planning going?"

"I've been busy working on plans for a structure that will be built in Atlanta. It's a fairly large office building. It takes a while to draft something like that."

"I imagine it would."

Josh glanced in Dana's direction and was relieved to see her walking toward them. "Dana," he called with a smile. "I'd like you to meet someone."

Dana held the camera that was strapped across her chest and jogged the remaining distance. When she reached him, she wrapped an arm around his waist. He put his arm around her and squeezed.

"This is Tammy Windsor, the real estate agent who sold my house. Tammy, this is Dana Bradley, my fiancée."

Dana extended a hand to Tammy. "Hello. You have some handsome young men with you."

Tammy shook Dana's hand and glanced back at her sons as if she'd forgotten they were there. "Thank you. Congratulations on your engagement."

"Thanks," Dana said with a smile.

"Well," Josh said after an awkward period of silence. "I guess we better get going. It was good to see you again, Tammy. Goodbye, boys."

The boys mumbled something, and Tammy said the usual nice-to-meet-you business that Josh was sure she didn't mean. After she and her sons turned and walked away, Josh gathered his gear and his family and headed for his truck. Patrick and Victoria ran ahead of him and Dana.

"She's very attractive," Dana said.

He squeezed her hand. "Not as attractive as you."

She grinned at him. "I'm glad you think so."

When Dana awoke the Friday morning that was to be her wedding day, a feeling of nervous anticipation washed over her. In a way, it had taken too long; on the other hand, it was upon her far too soon. She'd hoped to put on more weight before now. Part of the reason she chose June was to have time to do that.

She no longer had trouble with vomiting, and her appetite was healthy. Still, she hadn't gained back much of the weight she'd lost. She'd hoped to have some curves by her wedding night. Maybe the abuse her body had endured for more than two years would keep her from having any curves again.

She rolled out of bed and went to her bathroom. She turned on the shower, removed her clothes, and got a shock. This could not be happening, not today. While she showered, she mentally weighed her options. The wedding would have to be postponed. Josh wouldn't like it, but what else could be done? This may even be a blessing in disguise. She'd have time to gain more weight.

She dressed in shorts and a T-shirt. It was early yet, and Patrick was still asleep. Quietly, she slipped out the back door to go break the news to Josh. She rehearsed in her mind what she would say. They weren't having a big ceremony. Josh's parents and Jennifer's family were the only ones who would be there. A few phone calls would be all that was needed to postpone it.

Josh met her at his back door. He had a huge smile on his face even though he looked as if he'd been awake only a short while. She could see his bare chest where his robe came together and wondered if he wore anything under it. Even straight out of bed he was handsome. His appearance struck her speechless. She felt a sense of relief that he wouldn't be seeing her naked tonight.

"Couldn't wait to see me?" he said and practically carried her into the house. "It's a good thing we're not superstitious, worrying about my seeing you before the wedding and all that."

He kissed her the moment they were inside. He tasted good, like freshly brewed coffee and Josh. It made her regret that they wouldn't become husband and wife today.

He hugged her. "I am so ready for this afternoon. I wish now we'd made it a morning wedding."

She tried to smile, but her rehearsed speech flew from her mind. Unsure of what to say, she looked away.

"What's the matter?" he asked. His lips moved against her neck. The man knew exactly how to drive her crazy.

"We can't get married today."

"Sure we can," he murmured between nibbles. "Everything has been arranged. You're simply a little nervous, but it's going to be fine."

She wiggled away from him. "Josh, I can't."

He pulled her back into his arms. "Sure you can. I love you. You love me. Besides, I can't stand the thought of going to bed another night without you by my side."

She shook her head. "You don't understand."

His smile faded and he studied her. "You're right; I don't. There's no reason for us not to—"

"I started this morning."

He gave her a blank look and blinked. "Started what?"

"My period."

Dana could tell when understanding dawned. "We can't have sex," he said.

"Exactly." She walked a circle, staring at the floor. "I should've planned for this, but I've not been regular since the . . . well, you know, and I didn't need hormones for birth control because you . . . If you give me a few days then we can—"

He grabbed her arm and stopped her. "It's okay. We can go ahead with the wedding. We'll have the rest of our lives to make love." He hugged her close and gave her a slow, lingering kiss while his hands roamed over her body.

"Okay?" he whispered against her lips.

"Okay."

After what seemed forever, Josh and Dana were alone. He picked her up when she stepped from the car, carried her into the house, and made his way to the master bedroom.

"Where are you taking me?"

"To bed."

If she'd been able, she probably would have jumped out of his arms. He tightened his hold.

"Don't worry," he said. "I haven't forgotten. Even if we can't know each other in the biblical sense, we can still work at getting better acquainted."

He laid her on the bed and dropped a quick kiss on her lips. "Don't move. I'll be right back."

He hustled to the kitchen and pulled out the ice bucket and glasses he'd stashed out of sight earlier. He opened the fridge to pull out a hidden bottle of champagne. He plunked the bottle into the ice bucket, surrounded it with ice, and draped a towel around its neck. Cradling the ice bucket in the crook of his left arm and holding the champagne flutes between his fingers, he all but ran back to the bedroom.

When he returned, he found the lights off and the drapes closed but no Dana. He placed the glasses and champagne on the nightstand. He lit the candles arranged around the room and still no Dana. Muffled noises came from the bathroom. He followed the sounds and found his wife in the walk-in closet struggling to undress.

He congratulated himself on the dress he'd picked out for her. In the back, it laced up corset style, making it fit snugly against her slender form. He chose it because she'd be able to continue wearing it after she gained more weight. Right now, she was trying, without success, to untie the laces.

She was standing in her stocking feet with her back to him. Her arms were twisted behind her, and she still couldn't reach far enough to pull the ties loose. When she'd asked him to lace her up before they left for the church, he'd made sure she would need help undressing. He laced the dress tightly enough that undoing the buttons down the front would not free her from the garment, and he knotted the laces.

He leaned against the opening of the closet and chuckled. Dana turned with a start. Her face was flushed, either with frustration or with embarrassment at being caught. Maybe both.

He stepped toward her and placed a hand on her cheek. "I thought I told you to stay on the bed."

She dropped her eyes. "I was only going to change."

"And hide your body from me."

She wrapped her arms around her waist. "You don't understand how bad it is. Can't you please give me time to gain more weight?"

He held her upper arms, loosening the hold she had on herself, and shook her gently until she looked at him. "Dana, I love you just the way you are."

He eased his body against hers. Then he kissed her, coaxing her lips until she responded. After a while, her hands slipped under his jacket. She pushed it off his shoulders, and he shrugged it off. She undid his tie and pulled it from his shirt collar. He let his hands slide over her back and lower.

She suddenly ducked out of his embrace and moved so that she was between him and the door instead of the other way around. She bent over to pick up his jacket and tie, causing her dress to spread enticingly over her backside. They couldn't come together physically as one, but he intended to get close. He ran his hand over her behind and heard a sharp, "Oh!" She jerked upright with jacket and tie in hand. He took his clothing from her, hung up everything, and turned to enclose her in his embrace. He kissed her, deep and long, until he felt her resistance disappear. Picking her up with one arm under her knees and the other supporting her back, he carried her to the bed.

He set her down and began to open the champagne. She turned toward him with her legs dangling over the side of the bed. She watched him open the bottle, catch the bubbles in the towel, and pour two glasses.

She accepted a glass with a smile. "Where did you get this?"

"I have my ways."

"It's been a long time. My tolerance won't be very high."

"Tolerance?"

Dana babbled something about pharmacokinetics and alcohol metabolism. He looked blankly at her while she talked about liver enzymes, steady state, and other things he didn't understand.

He waved a hand to cut off her monologue. "Okay, okay. Speak to me in plain old English."

She smiled. "I'll be a cheap date."

"Good!" he said, returning her smile. "In that case, I'd like to propose a toast." He raised his glass. "To us loving each other for the rest of our lives."

"Hear! Hear!" she answered and tapped her glass against his.

She shivered when she swallowed. "Mmm, that's good."

He took another drink of champagne, encouraged Dana to do the same, and then set the glasses down on the nightstand.

He moved to stand in front of her, pushing her legs apart so that he stood between her thighs. The skirt of her dress spread between them. Her hair was up, and with her hands on his hips, he slipped the pins out of her silky hair one by one. When he removed all the pins, he dropped them beside the ice bucket. Using both hands, he ran his fingers through her hair. She closed her eyes and her head fell back with the gentle force of his fingers.

"Your hair is so soft." He leaned forward and kissed her closed eyelids, her cheeks, and her lips. He drew her to her feet and continued kissing her with slow, deep kisses that came one right after another. He trailed his hands along her waist to her back and began to work on the knot in the laces of her dress. She tensed, and he stopped. He wanted to blow out his breath in frustration. Instead, he picked up her wine glass and handed it to her. "Finish this."

She did, and when the glass was empty, he filled it again. He watched while she continued to sip. He finished off the champagne he had left and refilled his own glass.

By the time her second glass was half-empty, Dana wore a silly grin. He took the glass from her and placed it back on the nightstand. He wanted her to unwind, not pass out. He was surprised when he felt her working at his shirt buttons. She gazed up at him. He wrapped his arms around her and again worked on undoing the knot he had tied earlier. She'd really done a number on it while she was trying to undress herself, pulling the knot tighter instead of loosening it.

Dana pushed his shirt open. She moved her small hands over his chest before she wrapped her arms around him and ran her hands up and down his back. Then she rubbed her cheek against him.

"Josh, you feel so good."

Her voice was husky, and she sounded slightly tipsy. She was killing him.

"Babe," he whispered in her ear, "I need you to turn around."

She sighed as if she hated to let him go before she slowly turned. Josh attacked the knot and, in a few moments, had the dress untied. He loosened the laces and turned Dana back to face him. Immediately, he kissed her to prevent her putting him off again. While they kissed, he unbuttoned the small buttons that went down the front of the dress. Her hands moved all over his body.

When she pushed his shirt off his shoulders, he stopped working on her buttons long enough to pull the cuffs over his hands and let the shirt fall to the floor. They continued kissing as he resumed unbuttoning her dress. Josh ran his hands up her back and slid the dress from her shoulders. Once he had it past the slight swell of her breasts, it fell in a pool around her stocking feet.

Almost instantaneously, she pulled away and fell back onto the bed. She pushed up with her arms, and made an effort to use her feet to push her body across the bed. He grabbed her ankles and tugged.

He laughed. "Oh, no, you don't."

When he got a good look at the length of her, Josh's laughter stopped. Dana clawed at the bed coverings and pillows. He tossed the pillows from her reach. After struggling without freeing the comforter for a few moments, she drew her arms over her face. Josh focused on her body.

His fingers inched their way from her ankles to her thighs. He caressed her legs through silky stockings and toyed with the straps holding them in place.

He ran a finger from one of her hips to the other. "What is this?" he asked in a choked voice.

"A garter belt and stockings," she said with a shiver. "I started wearing these when pantyhose didn't fit right anymore."

Josh traced the lines of the straps on the front of her thighs, around her hips, and down the back until his hands ran behind her knees. He pressed forward and braced his hands on the bed on each side of her waist. He dropped kisses along her arms that covered her face. "Is it uncomfortable?"

"No," she answered. "It's actually quite comfortable. Better than saggy pantyhose."

"Promise me something."

"Okay," she said from inside her protective cocoon.

"Even when you're able to wear regular stockings again, don't stop wearing these."

She unfolded her arms and looked at him. "Why?"

He smiled and positioned himself next to her on the bed. "You're a smart woman. I bet you can figure it out."

Saturday morning Josh woke before Dana. He slipped from the bed and looked down at her. Gently he brushed stray strands of hair from her face. She stirred but didn't wake. From her profile, which was all he could see, she appeared to be in a deep, restful sleep. Her exposed cheek had the slightest hint of pink to it, and even with her eyes closed, she looked happy. After locating his briefs and pajama pants, he dressed, silently left the room, and went to the kitchen.

Breakfast was his favorite meal to prepare. He and Victoria both liked breakfast. Over the years, he'd become a proficient cook, not a gourmet chef or anything, but he knew his way around a kitchen.

While he chopped vegetables and mushrooms for omelets, his mind played over the events of the previous night. Their first night as husband and wife had been even more enjoyable than he imagined. Dana was quite passionate. Even without intercourse, he'd experienced the best night of lovemaking he had ever had.

He hummed while he removed English muffins from the toaster and buttered them. When he shifted and began pouring coffee into two mugs, he sensed movement behind him. He paused when he felt Dana's caress on his shoulders. Smiling, he resumed pouring, and her hands moved down to his waist. He returned the pot to the coffeemaker, turned, and took his wife in his arms.

Her stomach growled.

"Hungry this morning?"

She pressed a cheek against his bare chest. "I worked up an appetite last night."

"You're supposed to be in bed. I'm making breakfast to bring to you. I almost had it ready." He kissed the top of her head.

She looked up and gave him a sleepy smile. "That's all right."

She pulled away and sweetened the coffee he'd poured. She added a splash of skim milk to one cup and handed him the black coffee.

The two of them lingered over breakfast. Josh had never seen her so open, relaxed, and happy. She had a glow about her, and he decided her reservations about his seeing her undressed had weighed more heavily on her than he could have imagined. Dana was thin, and for the sake of her health, he wanted her to gain weight. The error in her mind was thinking that he didn't find her sexy and beautiful. Last night he worked hard to prove her wrong. This morning she looked happier than he'd ever seen her.

"I've never seen you eat this much," he told her after they finished breakfast.

She looked at him with a sensual gleam in her eyes. "I told you I worked up an appetite."

He laughed and covered one of her hands with his.

Chapter 18

After the wedding, Josh and Victoria moved in with Dana and Patrick. They kept the other house so that Josh could continue to use it for work. Patrick and Tori wanted to share a room, and she and Josh agreed to let them with plans to modify the guest room when they were a little older or got tired of each other. Nothing much had changed. Neither of them took time off work; they hit the ground running in the middle of their marriage.

The day they received their copy of the marriage license, Josh went with Dana to the courthouse so she could get a new driver's license. She officially became Dana Bradley-Peters. She'd already filled out forms for a new Social Security card and mailed them off, and called the personnel department at work to change her name and add Josh and Tori to her insurance. Somehow, it still didn't feel real.

On Tuesday, five days after their marriage, consummating it was possible. Dana was excited when she arrived home from work. Then she realized privacy would be next to impossible while the kids were awake.

"We need to make bedtime early tonight," she whispered when Josh kissed her goodbye before baseball practice. He pulled away and looked at her with wide eyes and raised brows. She nodded. "I will be anxiously awaiting your return."

"I think I'll call Mark and let him know we can't make it."

"You can't do that," she whispered. "Besides we'll have to wait until they're in bed anyway."

He glanced at the children. "I guess you're right. This is going to feel like the longest baseball practice known to man."

Dana gave Patrick a hug and told him to have fun. When they went out the door, she heard Josh groan.

After they left, Dana noticed that Tori was a little pale and that her eyes lacked their usual sparkle. She hadn't eaten much dinner either.

Dana knelt beside the sofa where Tori lay. "Are you all right, honey?"

"My belly kinda hurts."

Dana felt Tori's forehead. She was a little warm.

An hour and a half later, Dana met Josh and Patrick at the door. They'd been talking and laughing but stopped when they noticed her index finger over her lips.

"Tori's already asleep," she said. She turned to Patrick. "Run and get your pajamas. I'll get your bath ready for you." When Patrick walked away, she told Josh that she thought Victoria was coming down with something. "She sat with me the whole time you two were gone. I read her a couple of books, we looked through the photo album I started for her, and then we rocked. She didn't even want to talk. It's not like her to be still for long, not when she doesn't have to be. She felt a little warm, too. I gave her some acetaminophen."

"I'll go check on her," he said.

"She's in the guest room. I didn't want Patrick to wake her."

Dana made sure Patrick was settled in the tub before going to the guest room. Zoe was curled up on the comforter with her head resting on Tori's thigh. Josh knelt next to the bed. After brushing Victoria's hair from her face, he lightly touched her forehead and cheek.

"She doesn't feel feverish anymore, but she does look pale," he whispered after he straightened.

"That was the first thing I noticed."

They stood arm in arm and watched her slow, even breathing for a while.

"What you did must have worked," he said.

Zoe followed them from the room, and Josh silently closed the door. In the living room, they found a damp-haired Patrick in pajamas, shuffling a deck of Old Maid cards.

"Is she okay?" he asked.

"She's sleeping, and her fever's gone," Dana said.

"Oh," Patrick said. "That's good, right?"

"Yes," Dana said with a smile.

While the three of them played cards, Dana kept checking her watch. She saw Josh check his several times, too. The whole thing would have been comical if she hadn't felt so desperate and nervous.

Thirty minutes before normal bedtime, Josh told Patrick it was time for him to get ready for bed.

"It's not bedtime yet," Patrick said after he checked the clock.

"Mark and I put you boys through a rough practice tonight. You'll need the rest. Trust me; the extra sleep will help your game."

"Really?" Patrick asked.

Josh gave him a solemn nod. "Come on. I'll help you brush your teeth." Josh pulled him onto his back and toted him toward his bathroom.

After tucking Patrick into bed with Zoe and checking on Victoria again, Dana and Josh finally found themselves in bed alone. Josh had just removed her shirt and had his fingers on the clasp of her bra when she heard a soft knock.

"Mama?" she heard from the other side of the door.

Dana wrenched her shirt back on and jumped from the bed. She found a pitiful looking Victoria gazing up at her when she opened the door. Dana dropped to her knees. "Honey, what's wrong?"

"Tori?" Josh said from behind her. Dana heard him get out of bed.

"I don't feel good," Tori mumbled right before she threw up all over herself and Dana. Immediately, she started crying.

Dana picked her up and carried her to the bathroom. "It's okay, sweetheart. Don't cry. That'll make your tummy feel worse."

She kept crying.

"It's all right," Dana said. "We just need to get you cleaned up and feeling better. Don't worry, honey."

In the bathroom, Dana held Tori's head when she vomited again, this time in the toilet. Once she stopped throwing up, Dana removed Tori's soiled nightgown and put her in a tub of warm water.

Dana stripped off her own vomit-soaked shirt and, wearing her bra and denim shorts, began bathing Tori. She looked up when Josh walked in carrying clean clothes for Victoria.

"Do you feel better, sweetheart?" he asked Victoria.

"A little," she said. She definitely didn't look any better.

He gave Dana an understanding smile before bending down to kiss her on top of the head. "You are amazing," he said.

Dana shook her head. "Is Patrick—"

"He's fine. He's sound asleep." He caressed her head with his fingers. "Let me finish Tori's bath so you can jump in the shower."

She started toward the bedroom with a towel. "I'll go clean up out here first."

"It's already done. I'm glad we don't have carpet."

Dana couldn't help smiling. "Do you think this is funny?"

"Not at all," he said. "But making light of the situation is better than thinking about what I'm missing right now."

Victoria was sick several times. Dana and Josh were both up with her most of the night. By Wednesday morning, her vomiting had stopped, and Victoria was on the road to recovery. When Dana called from work that afternoon to check on Tori, Josh told her that she'd eaten some soup and crackers and was beginning to play.

The only reason Dana worked Wednesday was so Craig wouldn't be short-handed. By the time she got home, she wished she'd stayed home. She barely made it into the house and to the bathroom before she threw up. Like Victoria, she was sick several times during the rest of the day and night. She couldn't even keep down the Zofran she tried to take to stop it. She kept telling Josh—and herself—that this was different from her other sickness. This was a virus. It would run its course, and she'd be fine.

Once the vomiting stopped Thursday, she didn't recover as well as Tori had. The thought and the smell of food made her stomach roil. She drank Pedialyte but could tell she was becoming dehydrated. She was light headed and weak. She tried not to let Josh know; he was worried enough already. She knew she needed IV fluids, but she couldn't stand the thought of going to the hospital. She convinced Josh that she only needed sleep. He took the children to the basement to play so that she could rest more quietly in the bedroom.

After napping a while, Dana tried to make it to the bathroom, hoping she had enough fluid in her to make urine. It took her several seconds to get out of the bed, and she had to use the walls, door frames, and the countertop around their sinks for support. Even with her misfiring thought process, she knew it was time to seek medical care. She was near the tub, thinking that she needed to get to Josh, when everything went black.

Steven had been working since early Thursday morning stripping wallpaper from the walls of one of the bedrooms in his grandmother's house. He had the paper removed, and after lunch, he would clean up the mess and prep the walls for paint.

He sat at Grandma's kitchen table drinking sweet tea while she bustled around, fixing lunch for him. She insisted that he rest while she cooked. She was talking, but Steven was only halfway listening. His mind was on Dana. He'd been depressed since learning of her and Josh's engagement. He'd thought the ordeal with Monica would somehow work in his favor, but apparently not.

He should be happy for them. They were both great people. Josh was obviously good for Dana. Steven couldn't shake the feeling that it may have been different between him and Dana if he'd been brave enough to confess his feelings for her.

"Something wrong, Stevie?" his grandmother asked. "You're awfully quiet."

"Just a little tired, Grandma." He gave her a grin. "I don't know if you realize it or not, but removing wallpaper that's been up longer than I've been alive is not easy work."

She laughed. "No, I guess it isn't. You're such a good boy to help your old grandma like you do."

"You're not old."

She laughed again. "You're sweet to say so, but that paper was on the wall for decades. I put it there when your father was in grade school. That makes me old."

"Well, you don't act old," Steven said.

"Thank you, dear." She brought the food to the table, sat down with him, and said the blessing. "And what about you, Stevie?"

He had a fork suspended between his plate and mouth. "What about me?"

"You seem so serious all the time, especially lately. You'll grow old before your time if you're not careful. You need to find a sweet, pretty girl and enjoy life a little instead of working all the time."

He thought about asking what a guy should do when he found the girl but couldn't have her. "That'd be nice," he said instead.

"Oh, she's out there. You'll find her, and when you do, I bet you'll know she's the one in a very short time."

"Huh, that's funny. Dana told me the same thing."

Grandma winked and tapped her temple. "Great minds think alike. Speaking of Dana, have you seen her lately?"

"I see her all the time, every time I'm in the grocery store, but the last time I spent any time with her was at my graduation party a couple of weeks ago."

"I saw in the paper that she and the Peters boy applied for a marriage license."

Steven's fork clattered to the floor, and his grand-mother gave him an odd look. He hurried to pick it up and walked to the sink. He took his time returning to the table with a clean one.

"He's such a nice boy," Grandma said. "He's a good friend of yours, too, isn't he?"

Steven slowly nodded. "He's hardly a boy."

"Anyone younger than sixty is a boy at my age, dear."

They ate in silence for a few moments.

"It wouldn't surprise me if they were already married," Grandma said.

Steven almost choked. "You mean that they might have eloped. Are you serious?"

"They are a little old for an elopement, but they may have had a small, simple ceremony without all the hoopla of a big wedding. I don't know, but it makes sense. Otherwise we probably would have received an invitation by now."

He wouldn't believe they were married. He couldn't. That would mean all hope was gone.

From the look of fear on Patrick's face, Josh was sure he heard the noise from upstairs the same time he did. Forcing himself to stay calm, Josh told the kids to stay put. He didn't run, but he took three steps at a time up to the main floor of the house and headed toward the sound.

For a second or two, he panicked. Then, realizing Dana was bleeding, he grabbed the first towel within reach, knelt beside her on the floor, and placed it against the wound as well as he could without lifting her head. He was afraid to move her for fear she had injured her neck in the fall. He tried to revive her with no result. Grappling for self-control, he placed his index and middle finger on her neck to check her pulse. He let out his breath. He could feel it. Thank God. It was weak and fast, but it was there. He could see now that she was breathing.

He wet a washcloth with cold water and placed it against her face and then her neck. Nothing. He ran to the kitchen where he met the children. He tried not to look as scared as he was.

"Mom fell and hit her head," he said and filled a cup with ice. "She's asleep and shouldn't be. I might need to call an ambulance. I want you two to put on shoes and sit in the living room in case we need to leave in a hurry. Okay?"

They glanced at each other.

"Don't be frightened. It's going to be all right."

Josh held ice cubes on Dana's face and neck. She didn't move or make a sound. With shaking fingers, he called 911 and requested an ambulance.

Once the EMS arrived, Josh found himself pushed to the side. From the background, he explained what he could about her fall. They worked on Dana, trying to revive her as Josh had. Josh watched one of the technicians break a white capsule-looking object and wave it under Dana's nose. Her eyes fluttered open, and Josh breathed a sigh of relief. The workers talked to her, trying to rouse her further by asking her questions. Most of her answers were incoherent, but Josh did make out his name.

"I'm here," he said.

Her eyes moved in his direction but never seemed to focus on him. The technicians checked her blood pressure, said things to each other that Josh didn't comprehend, transferred her to a board with straps across her forehead, and finally lifted her onto a gurney.

Josh gathered the somber children and, in a daze, tagged along behind the medics when they took Dana out of the house. He saw her loaded into the back of the ambulance, helped the kids into his truck, and got in. Before he followed the ambulance to the emergency room, he called Jennifer. He knew Dana would want her there. Who was he kidding? He was going to need Jennifer there. He left a message on her office voice mail and prayed she'd be able to leave work early.

Josh drove into the hospital parking lot behind the ambulance. While it pulled under the covered emergency room entrance, Josh parked in the closest space. He and the children went through the doors right behind the medics and Dana.

Inside medical personnel swarmed everywhere. Josh was trying to make sense of all the activity, trying to figure out which way to go, when he realized someone was speaking to him.

"Sir," a woman said. "Sir! Those children cannot be here. You will have to take them to the waiting room."

For a second, Josh stared at her. Then he turned and watched the gurney carrying Dana disappear. He glanced down at Tori and Patrick who were huddled close together at his side. They probably didn't need to see what they were seeing. He motioned in the direction the medics had gone. "My wife—"

"There is a waiting room that way." The woman pointed. "You will have to take the children out and come back."

Down a corridor and through two sets of double doors, Josh found the waiting area. It was packed. It was no place to leave children.

"I'm gonna have Grams come get you."

Thankfully, his mother arrived shortly after his call and within fifteen minutes, he was at the ER information desk trying to convince the dispassionate receptionist that he needed to go into the treatment area. "She was brought in by ambulance," Josh told the woman for the third time.

The receptionist typed about a hundred keys on her computer keyboard and still didn't direct him to Dana. He choked back his rising anger and took a deep breath. "You don't understand, ma'am. An ambulance just now, not twenty minutes ago, pulled up in back. They brought my wife in. She's unconscious. She fell and hit her head. She needs me. Please, let go me through those doors."

A few minutes later, he was led to an examination room where Dana lay pale and unmoving. Several nurses hovered around her, one worked on starting an IV, one talked to her in a loud voice and tried to get her to keep her eyes open, and another took her blood pressure. One of them asked what his relationship was to the patient.

"She's my wife. Is she going to be all right?"

Without answering, the nurse set her lips in a taut line, picked up a clipboard, and motioned Josh to take a seat in a hard plastic chair a short distance from the foot of the stretcher. She began questioning him about Dana's medical history.

"Does she have any underlying or chronic medical conditions?" the nurse asked after he'd explained what he could about her current condition.

"She has a weight loss problem, but she'd begun to gain weight. Until she came down with this bug anyway."

"Weight loss problem? You mean anorexia or bulimia?"

"No. Her husband died—"

"You said you were her husband."

"Her first husband died a little over two years ago. In her mourning, she had trouble eating and keeping food down. Overall, she probably lost around thirty or forty pounds. She recently broke out of the cycle and has been able to eat and gain some weight."

"How about previous surgeries and hospitalizations?"

"She had a C-section in May 2000. She suffered from gestational hypertension during her pregnancy."

"How many pregnancies has she had?"

"One, only one."

"Is there any possibility that she could be pregnant now?"

"No," Josh said quickly. The nurse gave him a sharp look. He cleared his throat. "The day before she became ill, she finished her, uh . . ."

"Menstrual cycle?" the nurse asked.

Josh nodded and was glad the information satisfied her. He didn't think he could possibly explain that he had yet to have sex with his wife.

Just then, a bookish looking man with thinning hair came into the room and introduced himself as Dr. Mason. Josh stood and shook his hand. The clipboard nurse handed the doctor the notes she'd taken and left the exam room. The physician looked over the notes, asked Josh a few more questions, and stepped beside Dana's bed.

Josh watched expectantly while Dr. Mason talked to her. She seemed to be attempting to look at the doctor but still didn't focus her eyes. It appeared to Josh that she was having a hard time keeping her eyes open. The physician shined a small light in her eyes several times and tapped various parts of her body with some kind of little hammer thing. With gloved hands, Dr. Mason probed the injury on Dana's scalp. She winced, and Josh stroked her leg through the sheet.

Mason quietly spoke to the one nurse who remained in the room. She stepped over to a wall of cabinets and returned with a small, plastic-wrapped bundle. Josh watched the doctor trim the hair around Dana's injury, clean the wound, apply something Josh hoped would numb the area, and then stitch it up. Josh rubbed her legs throughout the procedure. Her legs felt cold, and he asked for extra blankets once the procedure was finished.

As Dr. Mason tugged off his gloves, he explained to Josh that Dana appeared to be suffering from a concussion. "We're going to do some lab work to find out why she fell to begin with and do a CT scan to check for any further injuries or problems. More than likely she'll need to spend the night in the hospital for observation."

The doctor asked if Josh had any questions. Josh shook his head, and the doctor left the room. The nurse had cleared the used supplies and returned with two warmed blankets. Josh helped her spread them over Dana's supine form. A contented sigh escaped her and her face relaxed a little. He thanked the nurse before she left the room. Josh was alone with his wife.

He bent and kissed her lips. He thought he felt a slight return of pressure but decided it was wishful thinking. Josh whispered to her, trying to reassure himself as much as he was trying to comfort her. He looked over his shoulder when he heard someone behind him clear his throat.

"Excuse me. I'm from X-ray. I've come to take Ms. Peters for a CT scan."

"This is Dana Peters," Josh said.

The technician prepared the stretcher to be rolled from the room. "You her husband?"

"Yes."

"I'll have her back here in thirty minutes or so."

"Could I go with her?"

"I'm afraid not, but I promise I'll take good care of her and won't let her out of my sight."

Josh kissed Dana goodbye and walked with her and Mr. X-ray as far as he was allowed. He watched until she was pushed through double doors that closed behind her, putting her out of his sight. He checked his watch. Deciding a walk would help him kill some time and work out some anxiety, he strode out of the ER and exited the hospital. As he walked, he called his mom, checked on the children, and told her what he knew so far. Then he dialed Jennifer's cell phone and was relieved it didn't kick to voice mail. That meant she'd left the clinic.

"I'm on my way," she said in way of greeting. "I'll be there in a few. I'm driving too fast to talk."

To keep from thinking about Josh, Monica sunk herself further into her work. She put in twelve-hour days at the office and then went to the gym for at least an hour every day. It didn't help. She wondered what Josh was doing and how much time he spent with Dana. She wondered if he was still with Dana or if her interference had done the trick. She even wondered what

Victoria was doing. Monica hadn't realized how much she enjoyed hearing about her daughter until she didn't have news about her anymore. Mama could tell her nothing. She rarely saw Josh or Victoria. They still weren't going to Mama's church, and if she dropped in at Margaret's while Josh was there, he would leave shortly after she arrived.

Her mother called her one day while Monica prepared to leave her office for lunch. She was irate, and it took several minutes for Monica to get her calmed down enough to understand what she was saying.

"He and that skinny little twit have applied for a marriage license," her mother finally said. "It wasn't supposed to be this way. He was coming down there to see you. You two were supposed to get back together."

"When?" Monica asked after she took a few moments to process the information.

Her mother went on ranting as if Monica hadn't spoken. "I cannot believe this! First, he takes my baby, my sweet, innocent baby. He takes her and makes her miserable. Oh, we all thought we knew him, didn't we? The gracious gentleman all those years you two dated. Then he gets his ring on your finger and tries to suffocate you and isolate you away from the rest of the world. Wanting you all for himself. Wanting to keep you home, having his babies, slaving and wasting away with no friends or family to support you. Then when you couldn't stand the oppression any longer, you left. Left your family and your own precious baby girl. He drove you to it, Monica. This was all his fault. I know it."

Hearing her mother carry on, believing what she said was true, made Monica feel guilty. That was a sensation she hadn't experienced in a number of years, if ever. For several minutes, her mother hounded Josh's character.

"Mama," Monica said, trying to stop her mother's verbal barrage.

"Male chauvinist—"

"Mama, that's not quite the way it was."

". . . adulterous, evil, man. Monica, how can you allow him to raise your daughter? We've got to get her away from them!"

"Josh is a great dad."

"See. I knew it. You still defend him. After all he's done to you. Darling, you are a saint."

Monica rolled her eyes. "Mama! Stop! Just stop, and listen to me."

The connection went silent. Monica never raised her voice to her mother.

"Now, Mama," Monica said, hoping her mother would stay calm. "Do you know when the wedding is to be?"

"No, Margaret won't discuss it with me except to say that she's thrilled with what's her name and happy that Josh found someone to love him. Hah! He had a perfectly good someone who loved him until he threw it all away."

"Mama," she said before her mom got going again. "When did they apply for the license?"

"When? Oh, I don't know. Let me get the paper."

What had gotten into Josh? He was in Atlanta not three months ago. He and the Bradley woman weren't even engaged then. And now they were getting married? Josh was a thinker and a planner, not a man who gets married after dating someone for a few months. That Bradley woman must have put him up to it. She probably needed money. She was a widow after all, and most things, in Monica's experience, came down to money one way or another.

For the first time, Monica felt ashamed of herself. This was all her fault. She'd pushed Josh into this. She wasn't going to stand by, though, and let some money-hungry woman take advantage of him. She was going to stop this wedding. Some way, somehow, she would stop it.

"Mama, I'm coming home," Monica said when her mother came back on the line. "I don't know how long I'll stay, but I'm coming as soon as I settle a few things at work and can get a flight."

"Call me with your flight information, and your daddy will pick you up at the airport."

When Josh circled back around to the ER entrance, he heard someone call his name. He turned and saw Jennifer striding from the parking garage. Josh couldn't help but feel relieved.

At Jennifer's urging, he relayed the events leading up to Dana's accident and the events of the day. He explained what had been done to Dana so far and what Dr. Mason had told him. He checked the time after they walked through the door together. "She's having a CT scan done right now. She's supposed to be back to the exam room in about ten minutes."

To Josh's surprise, the same receptionist who had grudgingly helped him greeted Jennifer warmly. Her smile was sympathetic when she asked Jennifer if she had someone in the hospital. Jennifer explained about Dana being brought in by ambulance.

Turning to Josh, she said, "Darlin', is that your wife?"

"Yes, ma'am."

She patted his arm. "Well, sweetie, I hope she's better real soon."

Josh coughed and covered his mouth to disguise his surprise. He got a similar shock when they approached the nurse's desk. Clipboard nurse gave Jennifer a friendly smile.

"How do you know those women?" Josh asked Jennifer.

"I worked here right after I graduated with my advanced degree."

"Both of them acted differently with you than they did with me."

"The emergency room is a challenging area. Sometimes we develop a certain callousness to protect our-

selves. That's part of the reason I don't work here anymore."

Josh nodded, not truly understanding what she
meant.

Josh grew increasingly restless while they waited
for Dana's return. He found himself glancing at his
watch repeatedly. Then he paced and babbled. Jennifer
listened with calm patience, offering reassuring or comforting comments from time to time.

"We didn't even have a honeymoon. I should have
taken her on a honeymoon."

"Dana wouldn't want to leave the kids," Jennifer
said. "She's never been away from Patrick for more
than a couple of nights at most."

"What if she dies?"

"She is not going to die! She'll be confused for a
few hours, maybe a day, and she'll have a major
headache, but she is not going to die from this."

Mr. X-ray returned, and Josh made his way to
Dana's side. Her eyes were open, but she still looked
dazed and disoriented. Josh followed along while the
X-ray tech parked the stretcher and raised the head so
that Dana was more upright. That's when Josh noticed
she was off the board.

"Her neck and everything is okay?" Josh asked the
man.

"Sure enough," Mr. X-ray said. He glanced back at
Dana and winked. "To her surprise, we even found a
brain in there." Dana gave him a weak smile. "You take

care now, Dana. Don't beat your head against the tub anymore. Okay?"

"Okay," she answered in a gravelly voice.

Mr. X-ray said his goodbyes and left the room after telling them that Dr. Mason should be in shortly.

Josh caressed Dana's face. "I was so worried about you. How do you feel?"

She groaned. "Head hurts. Everything's blurry."

Jennifer stood from a bent position after she finished an inspection of the stitching job on Dana's head.

"How?"

"Your husband called me," Jennifer said. "Of course I came."

Dana tried to move her eyes from Jennifer to Josh, but Josh could tell the effort was painful for her. "Close your eyes, babe. It's all right if you don't look at us." He couldn't stand to see her in pain.

"Water? Thirsty. And hungry."

Josh and Jennifer looked at each other from opposite sides of Dana.

"You're hungry?" Josh asked with buoyed spirits.

"Yeah."

Jennifer squeezed her hand. "I don't know if they'll let you have food or not, but I'm sure you can have water. I'll check and see. I'll be right back." Jennifer squeezed her hand again and gave Josh a smile before leaving the room.

Dana closed her eyes and grew quiet. Josh murmured how much he loved her and fingered her hair on the opposite side of her injury. Josh bowed his head and thanked God she was going to be all right. When he heard Dana whisper the word sorry, he raised his head.

"Honey, I'm the one who should apologize," he murmured. "Do you remember what happened?"

"Not really."

"You fell in the bathroom. You were alone. I shouldn't have left you alone." For the first time in his adult life, Josh felt an overwhelming urge to cry.

Dana laid her hand on his hand. "Love you, Josh."

A tear slid down his face, but he smiled. "I love you, too. God, Dana, I love you so much."

Chapter 19

Later that evening, once Dana was in a room and sleeping, Jennifer suggested Josh run home to get the things he'd need for the night while she stayed with Dana.

"Go by your mom's, see the kids, and grab something to eat, too," Jennifer said when he stood to leave.

"You don't mind staying?"

Jennifer's expression answered his question.

"Okay," he said. "I'll be back soon."

"Take your time. When you get back, I'll go home for the night and let you have some time alone with your wife."

"Thanks, Jennifer."

"You're welcome."

He stood at the foot of the bed watching Dana breathe.

"Josh, I promise to take care of her."

"I know. Okay then, I'll be back shortly." He walked to the door and looked back at Dana before he closed the door behind him.

Less than an hour later, after going by his house and eating dinner at his parents', Josh was on his way back to the hospital. Dana was asleep when he got to the room.

"Did she sleep the whole time?" Josh asked.

"Yes, but she's been restless," Jennifer said.

After Jennifer left, Josh unpacked what he had brought back with him. He set the cards Tori and Patrick made for Dana on the window ledge next to the bed and stared out the window, absently watching the traffic move up and down Dixie Highway.

"Missed you," Dana murmured. "Kids okay?"

He turned toward her. "I thought you were asleep. How did you know I was gone? Jennifer said you slept the whole time."

She started to shrug, stopped partway through the motion, moaned quietly, and gave him a small smile. "Just knew. Kids okay?"

"They're fine. Mom is going to bake some cookies with them, and Dad is going to let them paint some things for the train set."

Dana closed her eyes. "Your parents are great."

He moved closer to the bed. "I know." He took her hand and held it in both of his. Her color was much better, and when she opened her eyes to look at him, he could tell she was able to focus on his face even though her eyes lacked their normal sparkle. "Does your head still hurt?"

"A little."

"Only a little?" he teased.

"I'm hungry, though, and this . . ." She pulled at the front of the hospital gown. " This is scratchy."

"Hungry? Great, I'll check at the nurse's station to see if they will bring you something. I brought pajamas for you. I'll help you change when I get back." He squeezed her hand and left the room.

The nurse who returned with Josh temporarily unhooked Dana's IV, and he helped her change into her flannel duck shirt. A tray was brought in and she ate some soup with crackers and Jell-O. When Dana finished eating, she lay back in the bed with her eyes closed. He knew she didn't sleep because she would speak occasionally. Josh sat next to the bed, holding her hand. He had the TV turned on with the sound muted, but his eyes were on Dana more than the program. He watched her breathe, and he watched her face for any sign of distress.

Later in the night when the hospital grew dark and quiet—which wasn't really very dark or quiet—Dana became restless. She groaned in her sleep and shifted constantly. Josh stood over her, checked to see if she was warm enough, adjusted her covers, smoothed her hair, whispered words of comfort, and kissed her brow. None of that seemed to help. He was considering calling for a nurse, when an idea came to him. He eased her over in the bed and placed himself on her good side. She snuggled against him and then stilled. The groaning stopped, and he felt her body relax. Her breathing became even, and Josh knew she was comfortable. Sometime in the night, he dozed, too.

Steven slammed on his brakes in the middle of the street when he saw Josh and Dana through the open garage door late Friday morning. The view he had from across the cul-de-sac was a poor one, but he could tell something was wrong. Josh was practically carrying her. Steven backed up and turned toward Dana's house.

He got out of his car and walked into the garage. Josh's truck was parked on the other side of Dana's car. The doors were open, and he saw a bag in the back seat. He took it out and shut the doors.

He told himself again that they couldn't be married yet. He shook his head. No matter what, something was wrong, and Steven wanted to help her.

Looking exhausted, Josh acknowledged his presence with a lift of his chin. Steven followed them into the house. He set the bag in a kitchen chair and watched Josh help Dana sit on the sofa. Steven couldn't take his eyes off her. Her head was bandaged, and she looked awful. It broke his heart.

"My God, Josh, what happened?" Steven whispered.

"She fell. She'd been sick. She passed out in the bathroom and hit her head on the tub."

"What can I do to help? Does she need someone to stay with her?" Steven continued to stare at Dana who sat unmoving with her eyes closed.

"I'll be with her," Josh said.

"What about the kids and Zoe? Where are they?"

"They spent the night with my parents."

"Is there anything I can do for her?"

"No. I'm going to help her with a bath and put us both to bed. We had a long night at the hospital."

Steven dragged his gaze from Dana and looked at Josh. "I know you're engaged, but—"

"We're married."

"Married? When? How? Why didn't somebody tell me? Why wasn't I invited?" Steven was hurt on more levels than he cared to think about.

Josh ran a hand through his hair. "It was only a few days ago. Dana's friend Jennifer and her family, my mom and dad, and the kids were the only people there. We're having a party sometime. You'll be invited to that." Josh used his other hand to plow through his hair. "Look, Steve, thanks for stopping by, but I need to get Dana to bed."

Steven glanced at her. She hadn't moved; her face was tight with pain. "Oh. Yeah. Sure. But if she needs anything, anything at all, call me. It doesn't matter what or when, I'll be here. Go ahead and take her to the bedroom. I'll shut the garage and lock the back door on my way out."

Josh mumbled something that may have been a thank-you before he picked up Dana off the sofa. She turned her face into his chest and settled against him as if she were right where she belonged. Steven heard Josh murmur to her, but he couldn't make out the words. Steven shut the garage door, locked the back door, shut it, and walked to his car with his head down.

Dana was overwhelmed with pain, exhaustion, and relief at being held in Josh's arms. A tear she didn't have the energy to hold back ran down her cheek.

"Oh, babe," Josh murmured. "It's okay. I'm going to give you a bath and put you to bed. Please don't cry."

He eased her onto the bed and leaned her against some pillows. She kept her eyes closed because her head was throbbing. He left her for a moment, then returned and carried her to the bathroom. He helped her out of her clothes and into the tub of warm water. He placed a folded towel behind her head and urged her to lie back and relax. He washed every part of her body with slow, deliberate strokes. The warmth of the water and the feel of Josh's hands caused her pain to ease and the tension to melt away. Gently he washed her hair. It felt so good to have the dried blood washed away. She let out a sigh and opened her eyes for the first time since leaving the hospital.

He helped her stand and exit the tub before wrapping a towel around her. Using another towel, he dried her hair and checked her stitches.

"The nurse at the hospital told me to do this. Am I hurting you?"

"No, not at all," she said.

He eased a comb through her hair and dried it with the blow dryer. He dressed her in pajamas and tucked her into bed under a thick mountain of blankets. She would have laughed at how ridiculous the two of them must look if she hadn't been afraid of how much it would hurt.

"Thank you," she murmured when he brought the covers to her chin.

He smoothed the hair away from her face. "For what, sweetheart?"

"For taking care of me."

She looked up at him. Even as tired as he had to be, she still thought he was handsome. In the low light spilling from the bathroom, she could see his concern for her in his expression.

Josh knelt and kissed her. It was a soft kiss, a brush of his lips against hers. She put a hand on the back of his neck, begging him for more. The kiss grew deeper and slipped into another kiss and then another until they were in each other's arms. Suddenly Josh stopped and pulled away.

"Dana, we can't. I might hurt you. You need to rest. The doctor said so."

She took a deep breath and let it out. "But I need you."

He kissed her forehead, and she leaned back against the pillows. "I need you, too. And I want you. More than anything, but we can't now. I couldn't stand it if I hurt you." He kissed her forehead again. "It won't be much longer."

He stood and looked down at her for a while. "You rest now. I'm going to shower and lie down."

"Okay," she said and closed her eyes.

Dana heard the sound of the shower and heard the water cut off. She waited for Josh to come to bed. It was impossible for her to get comfortable without him beside her. After coming from the bathroom, instead of joining her in bed, she sensed him moving toward the door.

"Where are you going?" she asked.

"The guest room. I'm afraid I'll hurt you if I stay in here."

"You won't. Please. Stay with me."

The curtains were drawn, and the room was dark. She couldn't see his face, but she hoped he could hear the pleading in her voice. Finally, he crawled into bed beside her. She curled into him and relaxed.

Dana's condition steadily improved. By the second day out of the hospital, her headache was gone and she felt almost normal. She was tired of being waited on and coddled. She grew bored. It still bothered her eyes and her head to watch TV or read, and there was little else to do.

Josh refused to allow her to do anything he considered strenuous until she had the follow-up visit with her physician, had her stitches removed, and was released to regular activity. He cooked the meals, took care of the children, and kept the house picked up. Because he wouldn't leave her by herself for more than a few minutes, Josh let Joseph temporarily take over his coaching responsibilities and take Patrick to and from baseball practice. He brought his work over from the other house and worked at the kitchen table while she sat within sight in the living room. He even accompanied her to the bathroom.

She was able to have company. Craig and Elizabeth came one day, and Jennifer, Mark, and Steven stopped by for at least a few minutes every day. Margaret and Joseph regularly checked on her, too.

Wednesday when Josh, Tori, and Patrick went to the grocery, Steven stayed with her. Josh didn't leave until Steven arrived, and then he and the children kissed her goodbye about a dozen times.

"How about some lemonade?" she asked after Steven settled on the sofa beside her.

He jumped up and started toward the kitchen. "Sure. I'll be right back."

"I was offering to fix you a glass. Are you going to treat me like an invalid, too?"

He grinned. "I'm afraid so. Your husband's orders."

"I see how it is. This is a conspiracy!" She laughed, and Steven smiled, shook his head, and turned toward the kitchen.

"I guess congratulations are in order," Steven said when he returned with two glasses of lemonade.

"Congratulations?" she asked after she took a sip. "Oh, you mean our marriage. Thanks. We're having quite the honeymoon period." She hoped Steven missed her sarcasm.

"I guess so. Not too many newlyweds get to spend a night in the hospital together. Sounds romantic."

"You have no idea."

❧

Monica arrived in Louisville early Wednesday afternoon. She made her way through the throngs of people in the airport and found her father waiting for her near her flight's baggage carousel. The drive to Elizabethtown was calm, and she and her father discussed mundane things like work and the weather. He didn't say anything about the reason for her visit, and neither did she.

Monica spent the rest of the afternoon baring her soul to her mother. She confessed everything—well almost everything. Her mother learned about Josh finding her with another man. When her mother insisted that Josh forced her into it, Monica firmly set her mother straight.

"I was selfish, Mama. Completely selfish. I was a horrible wife and worse as a mother. I never took care of Victoria. I doubt I changed even one diaper. Josh did everything."

When Monica finished, her mother ran to her room in tears, leaving Monica alone.

Feeling bad for doing wrong wasn't something Monica was used to, and telling her mother about it had only made it worse. Whoever said that confession was good for the soul must have been a real fruit loop. Then she thought that maybe that was in the Bible somewhere, which meant God said it. That made her feel worse than ever.

She stood and walked down the hall to the room she'd used when she lived with her parents. When she passed her mother's door, she could hear soft sobs. Monica knew her mother wanted time away from everyone, especially her, to cry it out. That was how she'd always been.

Monica changed into her exercise apparel and running shoes and left the house. She hadn't run in a while. Her trainer had her on a program of aerobics, yoga, and weight lifting. She liked going to the club for workouts. It was a great place for seeing and being seen. Today though, Monica had no desire to see anybody. She ran through her parents' neighborhood, focusing completely on her breathing and the sound of her feet striking pavement.

When she returned to the house, she found her mother, dry-eyed and composed, in the kitchen. "It's Wednesday," her mother said.

Monica smiled at her mother. "What do we do on Wednesdays, Mama?"

Her mom returned her smile. Her tone was brighter when she said, "We have dinner with your sisters and their families and then go to church together."

Monica swallowed but held her smile. She couldn't remember the last time she'd been to church. Not since before moving to Atlanta, she was sure. But, if a person wanted to change her ways, church was probably the best place to start. She moved next to her mother and kissed her cheek. "Let me shower and dress, and I'll help you with dinner."

The smile her mom gave her melted something inside Monica. Her mother loved her. Despite all that Monica told her today, her mama still loved her. Mother love must be a miracle. When she left the kitchen, Monica wondered if she'd be able to do it.

❦

Dana would have been insane by Thursday morning if she hadn't had an appointment to have her stitches removed that day. It had been a week since she'd fallen, and she couldn't tolerate doing nothing a moment longer. Despite Dana's best cajoling, Josh remained steadfast in his determination to protect her—from himself and her—which meant they still hadn't had sex.

To make matters worse, Dana agreed earlier in the week to meet Elizabeth at their favorite salon after her physician's appointment. It must have been the trauma to her brain, because at the time Dana had agreed with Elizabeth's argument that her hair needed help after the ER trim. Now she sat in the passenger side of the car not wanting to get out. She wanted to go home with her husband. To finally be with her husband.

"Elizabeth is on the sidewalk waiting for you," Josh said. "You have to get out. I'll be waiting for you at home, anxiously, very anxiously. Don't worry; we'll still have plenty of time before Mom and Dad bring the kids home." He kissed her until she felt it in her toes. "That's only a taste of what will be waiting for you."

"How about we skip the pedicures?" Elizabeth said when Dana reached her side. "That will cut our time here in half. I'll have you home sooner. I wasn't thinking that you might need time for other things after your recuperation period."

Dana merely nodded her agreement. She was unable to hide her relief or embarrassment.

Elizabeth laughed.

After dropping Dana off, Josh moved his laptop and work materials back over to his office. He went back home and made sure everything was neat, made sure the curtains were drawn in the bedroom, and made sure there were plenty of candles. He looked at his watch and wondered how long spa treatments and haircuts took. He wished he'd had Dana cancel and brought her home. He groaned and went next door to his office, hoping work would get his mind off what he was missing.

He kept himself busy for about forty-five minutes and had stretched the span between checking the time from two minutes to ten when his cell phone rang.

"Is this Peters's Party Planning Service?" he said after checking the display.

"Josh, we have a problem," his mom said. "A huge problem. Are you alone?"

"Yeah," Josh answered, feeling confused. His mother was not one usually given to dramatics. "I'm sure it can't be as bad as all that. It's only a cookout, for heaven sakes."

"If only this were about the party. There may not even be a party, not after the visit I had this morning."

"How could a visit you had affect our party?" Josh asked.

"Monica—"

"Monica! What in the world is she doing coming to see you? Does Tori know she's here?"

"The kids were in the basement with your father. I didn't let Monica know they were here. I haven't said anything to Tori either. I didn't know if Tori should see her or not. I hope I did the right thing."

"You did the right thing, Mom, but why did Monica come to see you? How long has she been here?"

"She arrived in town yesterday and apparently has had a complete change of heart. I even saw her at church. She told me today that she spoke with Pastor Humphries for more than two hours last night after the service. She's a different person, Josh."

"I'm happy for her, but I don't know what that has to do with me."

"That's the problem. She's convinced herself that she can win back your love, yours and Victoria's. She's determined to stop your marriage to Dana. I tried to tell her you were already married, but she didn't listen. She has it in her mind that Dana is after you for your money and nothing else."

"That's ridiculous!"

"She is a widow who works part time, lives in a new home, and drives a nice car."

Josh heard Monica's influence in every word his mother spoke. "Dana is also a saver, who was married to a saver. She and Brandon had emergency funds for every imaginable crisis. They both made good salaries and had a financial plan in place to protect each other and Patrick in the event of one or both of their deaths. Dana doesn't need my money. Money is not an issue for either of us."

He heard his mother let out her breath. "Monica had me a little worried because she was so sure. She's always had financial matters figured out, and you haven't known Dana that long. Anyway, she's convinced herself that Dana is manipulating you into a quick marriage, and that she's got to save you. She feels responsible for your divorce. She told me it was her fault you were being trapped in a relationship with Dana."

"She's right about the divorce, but she's totally off base about Dana and me. I love Dana, Mom. You know that. You've seen what kind of person she is, how great she is with the kids, both of them. She loves Victoria, and she loves me. We're going to be happy together for the rest of our lives. And you know I was the one to push the summer wedding, not Dana."

"Still, Josh, I'm afraid Monica's being here will make trouble for you."

"Why? I don't even think she can find me. She can't call me. This subdivision is so new, she wouldn't be able to find it unless someone told her where it was, and her family's never been here."

His mom made a strange whining sound.

"Mom, you didn't!"

"I didn't mean to. I didn't even realize that I told her until she left. She's probably on her way there now."

The doorbell rang. "I think she just arrived."

"I'm sorry, son."

"Don't worry about it. It's not your fault. I'll talk to you later. Don't worry about the party, either. I promise we'll still have reason to celebrate Saturday."

He ended the call, took a deep breath, and walked to the front door. Sure enough, there stood his ex-wife. He looked at his watch. Now he hoped Dana's appointment would be long enough. He didn't want her to come home and find Monica there.

After much teasing from Elizabeth, Dana was able to relax and enjoy her time at the salon. The stylist took inventory of her hair and suggested a layered cut to blend in the area where her stitches had been. Dana consented, and the woman went to work. When she was done with the cut, she dried and styled it, giving Dana instructions on how to style it on her own at home. The result was a carefree cut that framed her face. Dana couldn't believe how good she looked and smiled at her reflection in the mirror.

For her nails, she chose darker nail enamel than the pale pink she usually opted for. The manicurist suggested that the darker color would draw attention to her rings and hands. Dana had been thoroughly pampered and primped. She felt fabulous. She felt beautiful. She couldn't remember the last time she felt this good.

"I have got to get you home," Elizabeth said when they were finished. "Josh is going to flip! You look fantastic."

Dana was nervous and excited at the same time. She laughed when Elizabeth dropped her off and gave her a double thumbs-up before backing out of the drive.

Some of her enthusiasm left when she was unable to find Josh in the house. Deciding he'd gone next door to work, she walked across the yard to look for him.

Dana opened the back door and was greeted by an excited Zoe. She urged the dog outside and slipped into the house so she could surprise Josh. She heard voices and thought he must be meeting with a client. She hadn't noticed a car parked in the drive, but she hadn't been looking for one either. She turned, planning to go home and wait, when she realized the second voice was female and vaguely familiar. The woman was crying. Her curiosity got the better of her and she tiptoed toward the sound.

". . . only realized last night what horrible mistakes I made," the woman said. "I've been terrible to you and Victoria, and I'm begging you for forgiveness. Please give me a second chance. I want to be the wife you deserve."

Frozen, Dana stared in stunned silence while Josh wrapped his arms around Monica. After a few moments, she forced herself to back away and bolted from the house.

She heard Josh call after her when she reached her back door, but she kept going, praying he wouldn't catch her before she got through the house and grabbed her purse. He was in the yard, yelling and waving for her to stop when she backed from the drive. Her phone started ringing before she made it out of the subdivision. It rang at regular intervals until she finally pulled off at a gas station and turned it off.

Dana didn't know what to do. With no destination in mind, she drove. Eventually, she found herself going through the neighborhood where she and Brandon used to live. After stopping in front of the house that had been their home for most of their marriage, she got out of her car and stood in the street.

The tree they had planted in the front yard when Patrick was born looked larger than it had only a few months ago when she'd moved. The fence that Brandon built to enclose the backyard looked the same. Dana had the urge to go through the gate to the backyard to look at the flowerbeds they'd worked on together and to walk across the deck she'd helped him build. The new owners probably wouldn't appreciate that.

Brandon wasn't there anyway. She wouldn't find him on his mower, cleaning the pool, or fixing something. Brandon was gone, and she missed him. Today she really missed him. He had been more than her lover, more than her friend. They had been part of each other.

She got back in her car and continued down the street. She'd been foolish to think she could have a relationship like that with another man. For a while, she believed that Josh needed her as much as she needed him.

She'd been right all along about Monica coming to her senses. Like she told herself before, she was not going to be in the way of their reconciliation.

Josh was meant to be with Monica. Since there had been no physical union, they could have their marriage annulled. Monica and Josh could pick up where they left off, and she could go back to the way she was before. Only, she wouldn't be like she was before. She wouldn't be sick anymore. She was well, and Josh could heal his relationship with his wife.

Knowing this made what she had to do seem easier. It wasn't going to be any less painful, though. She glanced at the clock on the dash. It was nearly time for the kids to leave Gramps and Grammy's. She pulled into a shopping center parking lot and called Josh to see if he wanted her to pick them up.

"Dana! Thank God you're okay! I've been worried sick, honey. Why did you take off like that? Why didn't you let me explain what was going on?"

"I was upset, but I'm okay now. I've been doing a little soul searching, and I've got it all figured out. Everything's going to be fine."

"I'm so glad to—"

"We can discuss everything later. Do you want me to stop by and pick up Tori and Patrick?"

"Uh, well, I guess."

"I'll be there in a little bit." She ended the call the minute the words were out of her mouth.

Feeling much calmer, she drove to Indian Hills. Thankfully, Margaret was busy in another part of the house. Dana spoke with Joseph for only a few minutes, asking him to tell Margaret hello for her. She didn't want to think about the fact that this would probably be the last time she'd be in their home. She wondered if they knew about Monica, but was too afraid to mention anything, especially in front of the kids.

"I didn't say anything to the children," she whispered to Josh when she arrived home.

"About what?" Josh whispered in return.

"About us."

Josh gave her an odd look, but she ignored it. She worked hard at behaving as if nothing had changed. She hoped Josh would explain the situation to Patrick and Victoria. She wasn't sure she was up to that task.

Josh could barely contain himself until the kids were in bed and he was able to find out what in the world was going on in Dana's head. He followed her into their bedroom, and shut and locked the door behind them.

"Dana, we have to talk. I know you saw Monica with me today."

"She's decided to turn her life around, hasn't she?"

"It would appear she has, but that has nothing to do with you and me."

Dana sat on the bed, and he moved to stand in front of her. The setting was much like their wedding night. Deciding action would be more appropriate than words,

Josh pushed her legs apart and stood between her thighs. Her eyes grew wide, and she looked up at him.

"Josh, I don't understand. What—"

He slipped his hands into her hair, tilted her head back, and leaned over her with his face inches from hers. "I know you don't understand. That's why I've come to explain."

He kissed her. She resisted and tried to pull away from him, but he eased her back on the bed and kept teasing her lips with his. Eventually she returned his kisses. Her hands moved to touch his face and came to rest on his shoulders. He began to nuzzle that place on her neck that made her crazy.

"I like your hair," he murmured against her skin. "You're a beautiful woman, Dana Peters."

She put her palms flat against his chest and applied pressure.

He looked down at her hands. "Your nails look great, too. Your rings look even prettier now." He ran his fingers over the jewelry he'd given her, then lifted her hand to his mouth and kissed the tip of each finger.

"What on earth are you doing?"

"I think that's obvious." He continued kissing the fingers of her other hand. "I'm seducing you."

"Why?"

"Honey, there are certain things that husbands and wives do together."

"What about the annulment?"

He froze. "Annulment? You think I want to have our marriage annulled?"

"Don't you?"

"Absolutely not!" He held her chin in his hand so their eyes locked.

"But when I saw you with Monica today, I thought—"

"I told you before that you think too much. Tell me why you think I want an annulment."

He settled next to her on the bed. She turned onto her side so that they faced each other and explained the conclusions she'd reached. He listened while she stated the facts to back up her conclusions. The entire time, he ran his hand up and down her arm.

"Don't you see?" she asked. "That's the reason it has never worked out for us to have sex."

"What about our wedding night?"

She dropped her gaze. "That was different. We didn't—"

He eased her chin upward until her eyes returned his gaze. "Intercourse or not, that was the best night of sex I've ever had."

She tried to turn away from him, but Josh gripped her denim-clad hip and pulled her lower body toward him. He entwined his legs with hers. Again, their eyes locked. He let his hand glide up to her waist and pulled one side of her blouse free from her jeans.

"What about Patrick and Victoria?" he asked and caressed her skin. "What will an annulment do to them?"

She frowned.

"Families are not grown overnight," he said. "The fact that the four of us have come together as easily and as well as we have is nothing short of a miracle." His hand inched up and he was now tracing over the fabric of her bra. "Don't you think?"

She closed her eyes. Josh smiled to himself as he watched her. He stilled his hand so that his palm rested against her breast. He squeezed lightly. "Don't you think?" he asked again.

Her lids flew open, exposing deep green pools that made Josh want to drown himself. "Think what?" she asked.

"That our family is a miracle," he whispered next to her ear.

"Yes, a miracle." She closed her eyes again. His hand squeezed once more before following the line of her bra to her back. Dana gasped when he undid the clasp.

Her hands moved under the T-shirt he wore and made their way to his chest where they roamed over his skin. His breath caught, and he rolled her to her back so that he was above her, straddling her hips. She pushed his shirt up, exposing his abs. He pulled the shirt over his head and flung it to the floor before pulling her blouse completely free of her pants. His hands shook when he released the buttons down the front of it. With his fingers, Josh traced over the flesh he had exposed on his wife's body. She arched toward him. He lowered himself, bracing his weight on his forearms, and her arms twined around him. They came chest to chest, skin against skin.

Josh could feel her heart beat. She ran her hands over his back and shoulders and then down to the waist of his blue jeans. She wriggled her hands between their bodies and unbuttoned his pants. She worked the zipper down and began to ease her hands inside his clothing.

"Dana."

She stilled her hands. "Yes?" She kissed his neck, shoulder, and chest.

"After tonight—after this—there will be no turning back. I mean to love you for a lifetime, Dana. Is that what you want?"

She looked into his eyes. "Yes. I was wrong before. I shouldn't have run away today. I won't do it again. Please. Make love to me."

Chapter 20

Josh Peters felt more satisfied when he woke Friday morning than he could remember. He didn't hesitate to accept Dana's invitation to join her in the shower.

After they dried each other, she stood at the vanity, clad in bra and panties blow-drying her hair. He came up behind her and pulled her against him. He caught her gaze in the mirror before he ran his hands over her body. She turned off the dryer and leaned into him, smiling a sultry, satisfied smile at their joined reflections. He returned her smile and then kissed her neck. She squirmed and pulled away.

"Stop it!" she said with a laugh. "I'll never make it to work if you keep doing that. It drives me crazy."

He reached for her. "That's why I do it."

She pointed the blow dryer at him like a weapon and took another step away from him. "Hold it right there, Peters. Rein in that libido. Save it for tonight."

He backed away and moved through the open door into their bedroom. He bowed. "As you wish, my lady. Until tonight."

She laughed even harder before turning the blow dryer on again. "And put on some clothes," she called after him.

Humming, he dressed and went to see if the kids were ready for breakfast. He leaned over the lower bed and felt Patrick slide onto his back. He could tell Tori was doing what she and Patrick called fake sleeping. He stood up with a giggling Patrick hanging on him. Josh pretended not to notice and searched the top bunk.

"Tori," Josh said with as much seriousness as he could muster. "Something's happened to Patrick. He's not here."

With that, the two children burst into laughter. Josh dropped onto the lower bunk, and both of them jumped on top of him. He wrestled with them until all three of them were out of breath from laughing.

Josh sighed. "Waffles and bacon for breakfast?"

"Okay!" they both agreed.

"Meet me in the kitchen."

It took Josh and Dana a long time to say goodbye. He followed her out to the laundry room and kissed her several times before he walked with her to the garage.

"I love you," Josh said one more time after she backed out.

"Love you, too," Dana said through the car's open window.

For the rest of the morning, Josh spent the most productive hours, professionally speaking anyway, he ever had. Dana was still on his mind, but the bond forged between the two of them last night gave Josh a sense of completeness.

He'd finished work that placed him well ahead of schedule on the Southern Finance project. He was on his cell, preparing to end a call with Abe, when his phone buzzed, indicating another call coming through.

By the time he disconnected Abe's call, the second caller had hung up. One of the pharmacy numbers was on the missed call log. He dialed into his voice mail and heard Dana's low, rushed voice.

"Josh, a friend has come and invited me to lunch. I'd feel bad if I said no. Sorry to cancel lunch with you and the kids. I'll see you after work. I love you. Bye."

Josh laughed in spite of his disappointment. It had to be Elizabeth. She probably wanted to razz Dana about yesterday.

He tinkered around the house for a while, trying to keep himself and the children occupied. He fixed sandwiches for lunch. While Patrick and Victoria played outside, he unloaded the dishwasher, cleaned the kitchen, and picked up misplaced toys, books, and shoes. Finally, he decided he would run to the grocery store. They didn't need anything, but the three of them could at least talk to Dana for a few minutes while she worked.

Pushing an empty cart, he strolled through the front of the store and found Craig and Elizabeth standing together near the pharmacy waiting area. They exchanged a glance after he greeted them.

"You girls have a good lunch today?" Josh asked Elizabeth.

"Huh?" Elizabeth said. "Oh, you thought I took Dana to lunch."

"You didn't?" Josh asked. "She left me a message that a friend invited her to lunch. I assumed . . ."

Craig and Elizabeth exchanged glances again. A feeling of uneasiness settled over Josh.

"I told her it was a bad idea," Craig said. "I knew you wouldn't want her going anywhere with her."

"Anywhere with whom?" Josh asked, trying not to sound as on edge as he was. He could tell Tori and Patrick were picking up on the tension, and he didn't want to add to it.

"She went to lunch with Monica," Craig said.

Josh couldn't stop the expression of shock that spread over his face.

"I'm sure everything's fine." Craig looked at his watch. "They should be back any time now." He smiled nervously.

The same fear that gripped Josh after Dana's fall nearly consumed him now. He tried to convince himself he was being ridiculous. Then he remembered Monica's behavior at the cocktail party.

"Why is Monica here and why would Mom go to lunch with her?" Victoria asked.

Josh looked down at his daughter. He hadn't mentioned Monica's visit to either of the children. "I'm not exactly sure why she's here, honey." Victoria turned toward Patrick. They whispered to each other, and Josh couldn't make out what either child said.

"Where did they go?" Josh asked.

Craig and Elizabeth both shook their heads.

Josh pulled out his phone and put it back in his pocket when he got nothing but Dana's voice mail. The Avalon was in the parking lot, which meant Monica had driven. He couldn't go looking for them because he had no idea what car Monica was driving. Refusing to give into fear, Josh decided to walk through the store and let the kids pick out some treats. Before he walked away, he asked Craig about Monica's behavior.

"She was acting totally weird." Craig looked at him for a second or two before waving his hands back and forth and shaking his head. "No, no! Not that kind of weird. She was being nice. Way nicer than I ever remember her being. She even asked about Elizabeth and the kids. She couldn't remember their names, but I was surprised she remembered me, much less the fact that I have a family."

Josh took a deep breath, smiled reassuringly at the children and asked Craig to page him when Dana returned. Thanking Craig and telling Elizabeth goodbye, Josh took off to shop.

They were on the far side of the store when Josh heard Dana page him. Both Victoria and Patrick turned toward the pharmacy without any urging from him. When they got closer to the pharmacy, Josh saw Dana walking toward them. He was so relieved that she was all right that he picked her up and hugged her right in the middle of the store. They received several stares, a loud whistle, and a "hey, baby" comment, but Josh didn't care.

"You're not angry with me?" Dana asked.

"No, but I wish you'd told me who you were having lunch with."

"You would have tried to talk me out of it," she said. "She was right here. I could hardly tell her no."

He definitely would have tried to stop her, but he didn't admit it.

Later that evening, Josh watched in utter amazement while his wife paced near the foot of their bed. She was naked, and Josh was enthralled. She was beginning to put on weight, and her body had filled out. He was having an extremely difficult time paying attention to the words she said. And right now words poured from her.

Only moments before, he'd been holding her in his arms after making love to her. They'd been talking, and he'd mentioned how afraid he'd been when he'd learned she was with Monica earlier. Dana sprung out of bed, apparently not thinking about her state of undress, and ranted about the children's safety, which was what she was still doing. She'd come a long way from the woman who had to be coaxed out of her clothes on their wedding night. She was moving around in quite an animated fashion. Josh enjoyed the view, both directly and in the dresser mirror on the other side of Dana. She was upset so Josh made himself listen.

"I had no idea you were worried that she might hurt me."

"Dana."

"What if she tries to kidnap them?"

"Dana."

"What if—"

"Dana!"

She stopped, her mouth still open, and looked at him. He was propped up on pillows to have a good view. She closed her mouth when she saw how he watched her and stood with both hands on her hips. Josh wasn't sure which he wanted to do more—laugh or drag her back to bed.

He nodded toward the mirror and the reflection of her backside. "Do you realize how good you look?"

Dana turned toward the mirror. A second later, she reached for the thick bathrobe draped over the foot of the bed. Josh grabbed it first and held on while she tried to wrestle it away. With his free hand, he captured both of her wrists and then maneuvered himself so that he could haul her onto the bed. The momentum drove him backward into the pillows, and Dana landed on top of him. He laughed, and she slapped at his chest. It wasn't a slap meant to cause injury, but it did get his attention.

"I'm sorry I laughed at you," Josh said, "but you worry too much."

"But I'm the one who talked you into allowing Monica to see them while they're at Gramps and Grammy's, and . . . Hey! What do you mean I worry too much? You were the one who freaked when you found out I'd gone to lunch with the woman."

"That's true, but you know I wouldn't have allowed her to see the kids if I didn't think they were safe. Monica or no Monica, my mom and dad won't let anything happen to those two. They aren't going to let them out of their sight."

His hands rubbed her bare skin along her ribs, hips, and behind. He felt a shiver run through her. She was braced on her arms above him, her hands anchored on each side of his head. They held that position for a few minutes without taking their eyes off each other. After a while, Josh eased her down against him and kissed her.

"I feel sorry for her," she murmured.

"For Monica?" Josh asked with surprise. "Good God, why?"

"She seemed so alone today when we went to lunch. I think she figured out that she made a huge mistake by letting you go."

Josh snuggled Dana against his side. She fit nicely.

"She didn't let me go, Dana. She pushed me away with both hands as hard as she could." He took a deep breath and let it out. He hugged Dana closer and kissed her nose. "What she did hurt me more than anything ever has, but now I know it was all worth it because I have you. You, my dear, are way more than wonderful."

Dana hugged him and rubbed her cheek against his chest. "Do you really think Tori and Patrick will be okay?"

"I'm sure they'll be fine. They were both excited to help Mom get things ready for our party, and Dad was dying to get Patrick over there to help him set up farms or barns or something for his trains. I think seeing Monica was the last thing on their list of exciting things to do, but they'll be okay."

They held each other in silence for a while. Josh thought about how far they'd come together in such a short amount of time. He had no regrets about moving too fast. A second chance wasn't a thing to be ignored.

"No more worries about the kids tonight?" Josh asked. They had an entire night alone, and Josh wanted to take full advantage of it.

"No more worries," she promised.

Monica quietly made her way down the basement stairs in her former in-laws' house. She couldn't help remembering the kisses she and Josh had shared on these steps. She sighed inwardly. That part of her life was over now. Seeing Josh with Dana today made her realize how much she had thrown away. She'd been selfish and cruel, and now loneliness yawned before her. It was what she deserved; she'd done this to herself, after all. Too late, she understood that love was a precious gift to be nurtured and treasured. Josh had loved her; of that she had no doubt, but now his heart belonged to Dana.

She knew Josh and Dana would be happy together. He deserved that. It was obvious, even to Monica, that Dana loved Josh and Victoria. As badly as Monica hated to admit it, Dana was so much better to and for them than she had been or probably could be. While having lunch with her, Monica learned that she liked Dana. Even though she didn't want to, she couldn't help it.

From behind the wall of the stairway, she watched and listened to the children. Victoria and Patrick were painting something. Even though she couldn't see him, she heard Joseph's deep voice when he gave the two children instructions. The three of them were having a good time. She almost hated to interrupt, but she would have to if she was to spend any time with her daughter. Monica stood in the shadows of the stairway and realized she was frightened—afraid to face a couple of eight-year-olds.

She took a deep breath and closed her eyes for a few seconds. She released her breath and stepped into the light. Silence fell. Monica felt three sets of eyes focus on her. She glanced from Victoria to Patrick.

Joseph smiled and carried a chair toward her. "Hello, Monica. Here, have a seat. Make yourself at home." He turned toward the children. "Can you two say hello?"

"Hello," they said in one subdued voice.

Joseph returned to his previous spot at the opposite end of the work table while Monica looked, without really seeing, around the room. She could sense the children's stares. Feeling uncomfortable, she shifted in her chair, swallowed, and forced herself to smile.

"What are y'all working on?" Monica asked.

Victoria and Patrick turned toward each other. It seemed to Monica that they were sharing some sort of nonverbal language that only the two of them understood. In mirrored movement, they turned their heads back to face her.

"We're painting fences," Patrick said.

"They're for the farm," Victoria added.

"Gramps is building barns," said Patrick.

"And we're going to have cows in the fields," Victoria said. "Isn't that right, Gramps?"

Joseph smiled. "That's right. It's for the train sets." He waved an arm toward the miniature trains and buildings behind him.

"Oh," Monica said, vaguely remembering the hobby her used-to-be father-in-law picked up when he retired. She watched the three of them work silently for a while. She didn't remember her daughter being involved with any of Joseph's train projects in the past. Of course, she hadn't accompanied Josh and Victoria often when they came here. With a guilty conscience, it occurred to her that more often than not she was too busy with work or with Ross to go anywhere with her family. She shifted again in her seat and cleared her throat. "Do you like trains, Victoria?"

Victoria stilled the paintbrush she held and stared at Monica. After a couple of seconds, Patrick nudged Victoria with his elbow. Victoria looked at him, and he nodded reassuringly. She turned back toward Monica. "I didn't used to. But Patrick likes them, and I like to be with Patrick."

"Besides," Patrick said, "Tori's a good painter."

Monica leaned forward to get a better look at what they were doing. "I can see that. It looks like you're both doing a good job." That was a lie, but she was trying to be kind. The two of them had black paint everywhere including all over themselves. They both wore what looked like Joseph's old shirts for smocks.

Even as a child, Monica hadn't liked doing anything messy. She'd always hated getting her hands or clothes dirty.

Victoria reached across the table for another piece of fence and bumped a tall bottle of black paint. The bottle fell over, the force knocking the flip top open and sending a blob of black in Monica's direction. Monica jumped up with enough speed and force to knock her chair to the floor. She hadn't been quite fast enough, and the globule of black goo landed with a loud splat on her right foot, covering the crisscross on one of her new sandals. Slime oozed between her toes. Monica yanked the shoe from her foot.

Joseph hustled off and returned with an old towel. Margaret opened the basement door and called down to check that everyone was all right.

"We've had a little spill," Joseph called, "but everything's all right."

With a grim look, he handed Monica the damp rag. Monica got the impression he was waiting for something—probably her explosion. She knew she wasn't recognized for her kindness or patience, especially toward Victoria.

Monica took the towel, murmured thank you, and began to work on the shoe. She didn't look at Victoria; she couldn't. She'd paid nearly $800 for these shoes, and they matched the blue linen pant suit she wore perfectly. Thankfully, no paint splattered on her pants. She dabbed at the paint and was surprised and extremely relieved when all the black came off. She smiled and then looked at the little girl across the table.

Patrick stood protectively near Victoria. His face was solemn. Victoria's expression was one of mortification. Monica felt her heart go out to her. After all, they were only shoes—even if she had paid a small fortune for them—and little girls were more important than shoes. The smile on Monica's face grew wider when she realized she wasn't a complete monster. She held up the shoe for Victoria to see. "Look, no harm done."

Victoria crumpled and leaned into Patrick. The boy put his arm around her shoulders. He reminded Monica of Josh. His coloring was different from Josh's; Patrick had brown hair and hazel eyes. His build was a lot like Josh's, though, and she realized as she looked at the two children that people would assume that Josh and Dana were their biological parents. She pictured the four of them in her mind; they made a handsome family. She sighed silently and used the towel to clean her foot.

While she did, Joseph picked up the paint bottle and moved beside Victoria. Monica watched out of the corner of her eye as he patted Victoria's head and spoke to her in a quiet voice.

When she finished cleaning her foot, Monica surprised herself by asking Joseph if he had an extra smock. For several seconds, he stared at her in silence. Then he left the room. He returned with a smock and laid it across the chair he had righted behind her. He and the children watched with awed expressions as she removed her other shoe, set them both aside, rolled up the legs of her pants, and donned the old shirt. Joseph cleared his throat and urged the children to make room for her.

Monica picked up a paintbrush and painted according to Patrick and Victoria's instructions. They were hesitant at first but loosened up after a few minutes. Monica couldn't believe it; she was enjoying herself.

They painted, played with the train set, and talked for hours. The kids told her about school, their friends, and Patrick's baseball experience so far. Margaret brought down milk, coffee, and a plate of cookies, and joined them.

Later that night, lying in bed at her parents' house, Monica thought back over her afternoon and evening. She enjoyed being with the children. She hadn't understood how fun kids could be. She knew in her heart that she couldn't be maternal, but maybe she could adopt the role of a fun, aunt-like figure. She could see herself taking them shopping, splurging on them, and taking them on fun outings.

She'd talked to Margaret about her idea after the kids went to bed. Margaret told her that Josh had plans for Dana to legally become Victoria's mother. Monica assured her that she didn't want to do anything to challenge the adoption, but that she would like to see both of the children from time to time. She couldn't help but think that maybe, just maybe, she wouldn't be completely alone for the rest of her life.

Saturday, Steven arrived for Josh and Dana's marriage celebration party before any of the other guests. Several times during the evening, Dana noticed Carrie and Steven huddled together in conversation. She made sure to call her husband's attention to the evidence of a budding romance between the two of them. When Steven approached Dana and Josh near the end of the evening, Carrie accompanied him.

He wrapped Dana in a warm embrace. "I am so happy for you and Josh. You two are great for each other." After he released her, he turned and shook Josh's hand. "Congratulations, man, you deserve the best."

Josh and Dana walked with Steven and Carrie to Steven's car. The newlyweds waved goodbye, and the younger couple drove away together. Arm in arm, the two headed back toward their house.

Dana grinned up at her husband. "They seemed to hit it off. Don't you think?"

Josh shrugged.

"I told you he wasn't interested in me that way. He and Carrie are perfect for each other. He can keep her grounded, and she can keep him from being too serious."

Josh laughed. "Just because you're a blissfully happy newlywed doesn't mean you need to take up match making."

"I would never be so interfering, but I don't see anything wrong in encouraging the relationship."

When it grew dark and only the Morgans, Josh's parents, and his brother and sister-in-law remained,

Dana invited everyone inside. The adults talked in the kitchen while the kids played in the basement.

"I think it's safe for you two to share your news now," Margaret said to Abby and Jordon after the group had been talking for a while.

All eyes focused on the soon-to-be parents. Abby's hands rested on her enlarged abdomen. Her husband reached out and placed his palm against her belly.

"Josh, do you remember when you told us Victoria wanted us to have twins?" Jordon said.

"No way!" Josh said. "Really?"

Abby smiled and nodded. "My doctor told me almost from the beginning that I must be wrong about my dates because I was bigger than I should be. They hadn't been able to detect more than one heartbeat, but I knew my dates were right on." She gave Jordon a sideways glance, and they smiled at each other. "Anyway, at my ultrasound, they could see both babies. You're not going to believe this." She took a breath and slowly released it. "We're having a boy and a girl, like Tori wanted."

Josh leaped up from his chair. He hugged Abby, then his brother. "Does Tori know? Have you told her yet?"

"No," Jordon said. "We didn't want to take anything away from you and Dana. That's why we hadn't said anything before now."

Josh went to the top of the basement stairs. "Hey, Victoria, Patrick, come up here. Uncle Jordon and Aunt Abby have some news for you."

All the kids clamored up the stairs. When she got to the kitchen, Victoria asked her dad what the news was. Jordon told Victoria about the twins.

"Oh," she said. "I already knew that."

"How did you know?" Jordon asked. "Did you hear me tell Grammy?"

She shook her head.

"Did you hear us talking just now?" Josh asked her.

"No, Daddy, we were playing a race car game on the Wii." The nods from the other children confirmed what she said.

"Okay, Tori, how did you know about the babies?" Josh finally asked.

"The same way I knew about having a mama."

All eyes were on Victoria. She glanced around nervously before returning her focus to her dad. "Remember when you told me to talk to God about wanting twin cousins?"

"Yes," Josh told her.

"Well, I did. Just like I did when I wanted a mom." She looked at Dana who smiled at her. "God told me I would have a mom, and he told me I'd have twin cousins. And see—it's all true."

The adults around the table stared after Victoria when she followed the other children back to the basement. After a few moments, they all laughed.

Made in the USA
Monee, IL
06 November 2020

46848938R00215